T0107545

Algebra of Hope

RANJIT DIVAKARAN

AuthorHouse™
1663 Liberty Drive
Bloomington, IN 47403
www.authorhouse.com
Phone: 1-800-839-8640

© 2013 Ranjit Divakaran. All rights reserved.

*No part of this book may be reproduced, stored in
a retrieval system, or transmitted by any means
without the written permission of the author.*

Published by AuthorHouse 2/8/2013

ISBN: 978-1-4772-9221-1 (e)
ISBN: 978-1-4772-9600-4 (sc)

Library of Congress Control Number: 2012922721

*Any people depicted in stock imagery provided
by Thinkstock are models, and such images are
being used for illustrative purposes only.
Certain stock imagery © Thinkstock.*

This book is printed on acid-free paper.

*Because of the dynamic nature of the Internet, any
web addresses or links contained in this book may have
changed since publication and may no longer be valid.*

*The views expressed in this work are solely those of the author
and do not necessarily reflect the views of the publisher, and
the publisher hereby disclaims any responsibility for them.*

Life of honor, courage, hugs and kisses.
Proudly treasured, painfully missed.

my father

Chapter 1

It was his first time on a plane: Air India flight, Calicut to Riyadh. Emotions are always mixed, Rakesh realised, and now he felt the pain of parting, the fear of the unknown and the tension of being airborne for the first time. Which one dominated was difficult for him to identify. Maybe they took turns. The only emotion he didn't feel was happiness. Most of the books on success Rakesh had read mentioned that we need to control our minds and never let our minds control us. Neuro-linguistic program gurus said that identifying the causes and intentions of worries will help eliminate them. But here he was in a window seat trying in vain to apply all these tips. The only scene that consistently appeared in his mind was the one in which he kissed his little angel goodbye a couple of hours ago at the airport. She was seventeen days short of her first birthday. Anakitha must have been confused at the shower of kisses and hugs in the departure lounge, a very strange and crowded place. Rakesh wondered why we do this. Will this sort of over-expression of love help dilute the pain, or will it exaggerate it? All he knew was that tears were slowly welling up in his eyes as the aircrew presented the safety instructions.

His lachrymal gland was working. It wanted to show its presence, whilst he did not want it to. He knew every single tiny part of the body had some purpose. To say that this part was an architectural marvel of our creator's would be an understatement, but what was the purpose of irrigating the cheeks when one was in pain? And so the tears spilled over. For some women and children, tears add beauty, but they definitely do not for a middle-aged man. The more he tried to control himself, the more the glands rebelled like revolutionaries of the sixties. He did not want the passenger in the next seat to see this psycho-physiologic effect. Rakesh stole a glance at him through the corner of his flooded eye. He had the look of a spy, as if his purpose was to catch others' emotions. Rakesh wanted to ignore him, but the man met his eye and said, "Hello." *Very untimely*, Rakesh thought. He made an attempt to respond, unsure of the result. The man didn't speak again for the entire four-and-a-half-hour journey, not even to apologise when he spilt Coke on Rakesh's trousers. The air hostess in the front went about her business. As this was Rakesh's first flight, he knew he should attend to the aircrew carefully, but his mind had a different agenda, and he thought only of what and whom he had left behind. The seat belt at his lap appeared symbolic of having lost the freedom to go back, of his imprisonment by his own decision.

The show must go on, as they say in the circus. Here he sat with a heavy heart, but the show in the front went on. But the show was not bad. The air hostess was quite tall and slim, her skin an earthy colour. A mischievous smile crossed her lips at irregular intervals, as if to challenge anyone who would have faintly thought she was not attractive. The only thing Rakesh could hold against her was that when she said, "In the unlikely event of a water landing", his mind heard, "In the likely event of a water crash."

This was a new challenge, added fear, like an icing on the cake of his worries. The picture of *Kanishka*, Air India flight 182, which was bombed and crashed into the sea, killing all on board, came to his mind. That happened some time before TV came to his state. How could he remember that disaster in such minute detail? Maybe some virtual memory fed his imagination. If that hypothesis were true, he was overfed. The mere visualisation of it suffocated him. A few months before, Rakesh had learnt to swim, and remembering this gave him a sense of comfort. *I know how to swim,* he confirmed. 'If you know how to swim, the depth does't matter'.He recollected the quote.Suddenly a twenty meter swimming pool and the Arabian sea appeared the same to him.Positive thinking built on absolute insanity was a newly emerging solution out of distressed compulsion.Rakesh was thankful for all the positive –thinking books he had read.

Next thing he heard was, "Do not inflate the life jacket inside the plane." He had no doubt that he would do exactly the opposite of every instruction at the crucial time and multiply the disaster. Being a surgeon and having attended many training sessions and workshops on managing medical emergencies, Rakesh frequently saw panic in real-life situations.

And now here, with zero experience and very casual attendance to the instructions... No, it just would not work. Best to leave it to God, he felt.

His visual focus again landed on the tall air hostess, who was now showing how to blow a whistle whilst on the sea. Rakesh imagined two hundred other people floating along on the Arabian Sea in colourful life jackets having fun with their red whistles. Meanwhile, he was probably still stuck in the plane for having inflated the jacket before getting out. The woman continued her presentation, and he tuned her out but continued watching. This was one of the rare situations in which he could fix his gaze on a beautiful woman without feeling any sense of guilt or fear or embarrassment, he thought. She went on as if the demonstration were a ritual, a pleasant punishment. Element of fun still lingering on, element of purpose completely evaporated. After a few more minutes, the oxygen mask demonstration over, she concluded with a smile. Rakesh remembered the feeling he had at the end of tenth-grade chemistry class. He never understood organic chemistry, apart from the fact that it was well organised to ruin his school days. But the teacher was a charming young lady.

As the engine roared in the ascent, his thoughts were drowned by prayers. Rakesh wondered how atheists would react in a similar situation. Would they take time out of their disbelief, or would they hold on to it till they had to blow the whistle? Rakesh felt that there were no staunch, complete atheists. He tried to read the in-flight magazine, but his brain disobeyed him. He thought of his earlier tears. *Why is it that I do not have any powers over my own body parts?* he wondered.

When they reached cruising altitude, the air hostess strode along the aisle, reminding Rakesh of a trainee model on a catwalk. When her pace quickened, Rakesh had to will himself not to inflate his own "life jacket". During his first year in medical school, he learnt that each and every activity is controlled by a representative centre in the brain. Watching this woman, he wondered if there was a centre responsible for appreciating feminine beauty. He never read about one in any popular physiology book. Anyway, now was not the time to contemplate any medical breakthrough, both in attitude and altitude.

He looked out the window and saw no trees or valleys moving beneath him. All he could see was a canvas of dull, stationary cotton wool. Even the engine noise had been silenced by its familiarity. He recollected the excitement he and his mates felt as small kids when they spotted a plane. Even they knew that light travelled faster than sound, and the escalating thunder brought all the kids in the vicinity out of their homes to spot the plane. Everyone claimed to be the first to see it, pointing up in every direction. The plane always played hide-and-seek amongst the clouds. All the children stood watching the sky till the vapour trail completely disappeared. They went inside, their happiness abruptly ended, like spectators who, after watching a breathtaking Olympics opening ceremony, are told that the games have been cancelled.

Rakesh attempted to sense any movement. No, the plane felt as though it stood still at six hundred kilometres per hour. He sped at six hundred kilometres per hour away from everything dear to him. *Where am I going, and what for?* Introspection set in. It all started a few weeks before. Rakesh had taught orthopaedics for final-year medical students at Mangalore University, and he received a call from a student friend, Dr Samuel Mathew.

"Sir, would you be interested in taking up a job in a Riyadh hospital? There is an immediate vacancy. They are looking for someone with your education and experience. I know the chief medical officer over there."

Rakesh's antenna for a job in the Middle East, specifically in Saudi Arabia, was very active. He almost involuntarily said, "Yes, if the terms are good."

Samuel said that the chief medical officer would contact him in a couple of days and that he would get more information. At that time, Rakesh was almost one year into his newly opened private practise. He had consultations at his residential clinic and was attached to a leading hospital in the city. He also visited other hospitals in nearby towns for trauma management. Not many specialists in his town stuck exclusively to their specialty, and this gave Rakesh an edge: it encouraged general practitioners and other medical specialists to refer patients to him. His earnings were not too good, but initial indicators were promising. *Why did I give all this up for a job in Riyadh?* He had not had any difficulty making that decision.

Rakesh grew up in an atmosphere that did not fall into the category of rich, or even comfortable middle class. His father, a retired Army officer, had to work long hours to support the family. Even as a small kid Rakesh had sensed the struggle in spite of his parents' efforts to mask it. It surfaced regularly. Moving from one rented house to another was a regular event in his life. Every Vishu, the main festival in north Kerala, his mother said that by the following Vishu the family would have its own house. That never happened. Both his parents came from not-too-wealthy backgrounds and therefore had no financial inheritance. They drained every bit of parenting energy to bring up the kids. Rakesh never had a bicycle whilst he was in the school, although most of his classmates had one. However, his father always provided the best healthy food and taught rich values. His motto was, "Eat well, play well, and pray well". He ensured that these three happened abundantly. Rakesh's mother was a typical homemaker, and her life revolved around her kids and husband. The house would become gloomy and empty if she went out even for few hours. She and Rakesh's father undoubtedly made the best pair of parents anyone could dream of. As years passed and Rakesh grew from the bicycle-less schoolboy to a doctor with a master's in orthopaedic surgery, he learnt that it was the purse that made many decisions for him, and he did not want that to happen anymore. He was aware of this as much as he was aware of himself.

"Would you like to have something to drink, Sir?" A voice interrupted his nostalgia. "Orange or pineapple juice?"

Why had she given him only these two choices when other tall coloured bottles rattled on her trolley? He reluctantly asked if beer was being served.

"Of course, Sir," she said. Her words were very polite, but her body language was not. He asked her which brands of beer were available, though the only one he knew was King Fisher. He nodded when she offered him an option as if that was exactly the one he was looking for. The tall woman with the mischievous smile was serving another row, which was a mild disappointment. As he took a slow sip of the beer, Rakesh slipped back into introspection. The purse made a lot of his decisions, and unpleasant ones at that.

What began as a casual desire for a Saudi job grew intense over the years. It was so strong that he never shared it with anyone for fear of getting talked out of it. So he was not in the least surprised when he said yes to Samuel without thinking. He had done all the thinking long before.

Dr Govardhan rang him within a week. He sounded like he owned the hospital, but he did not. It was a polyclinic with most medical specialties. The orthopaedic clinic was yet to open, but the orthopaedic surgeon who was to serve there had visa problems, so this offer came Rakesh's way. He filtered all the information; the equivalent of fifty thousand rupees a month and a single accommodation is all that registered. Not a brilliant job, but not too bad either. Rakesh heard himself saying, "Yes, okay, yes." And so the job was his. One step closer to achieving his dream!

By now he had had two beers, and they created physiological problems in his bladder. He did not want to move from his seat, partly because the idea of peeing in mid-air was not exciting and partly because the spy beside him had spread out to occupy every inch around his seat. But again a body part seemed to have a brain of its own, and all he could was take orders and rush to the toilet at the tail. Rakesh did not like the idea of the tail. It said to him that it was not part of the main body of the plane, and he thought again of the life jacket and whistle. The slight swaying at the rear gave company to his apprehensions. However, all went well till he flushed the toilet. The noise of the flush had all the elements of the sound of a midair crash. *Why had no one invented a silent flusher?* he thought. His list of potential scientific breakthroughs was lengthening. *Never again will I have a beer on a first flight*, he decided.

When lunch was served, he discovered that the economic manoeuvres of his upper limbs necessary for in-flight eating were a talent that he had yet to develop. This was obviously not the first flight for Rakesh's spy neighbour. He appeared to have a passion for food. Or was it vengeance? Either way, there was lot of water works from his circum oral region. Earplugs and a helmet would be useful additions to the jacket and whistle. Rakesh had never understood why some chewed with such facial acrobatics and energy. The spy's jaw muscles had a personality that stood apart, and he probably would have come close to earning a medal if chewing was an Olympic sport. He emptied his entire tray long before Rakesh touched his main dish. Rakesh was thankful for these distractions. He wanted to sleep for a while, but that was impossible. Now finished with his meal, the chewing champion snored like a trekker with engine trouble. Rakesh envied him.

"Please fasten your seat belts. We shall be landing at King Khaled International Airport in Riyadh in a few minutes." Rakesh had a peculiar feeling. It wasn't excitement, but it had a tinge of happiness, it wasn't fear, although it contained slight apprehension.

"Riyadh," he murmured to himself. The place he wanted to be. To achieve his secretely held ambition, to obtain a fellowship in orthopaedic surgery.Riyadh was the only center apart from Singapore where the Royal College conducted this examination outside of the United Kingdom. Obtaining this fellowship meant the world to Rakesh. It would open up opportunities for higher surgical training in the UK and a much better quality of life. Not many people he knew had obtained this position, and it had an aura of difficulty. All this enhanced its value and his greed to achieve it. And in another few minutes, he would be touching the ground, in Riyadh. This job was only a ticket to the show if the exam was a show.

The tall air hostess stood at the exit door bidding passengers goodbye with a fixed, impersonal smile. Rakesh had not had to use the jacket or whistle. He tried to return her smile, but his facial muscles weren't co-operating, like the labour force of his home state.

As he entered the airport, a sign displayed the outside temperature: 49°C. Riyadh in June is hot, Rakesh knew, but he hadn't known that the air would be this hot. *Walking out there*, Rakesh thought, *would be like getting barbecued*. The airport building was a massive structure, but something that he could not identify seemed to be missing. The streets were empty, he saw through the huge tinted windows. The spy who had sat in the next seat seemed to be very comfortable here, and once outside, he disappeared in an overloaded pickup van.

Rakesh spotted two men holding a placard on which was written, "Welcome, Dr Rakesh". Their doubtful smiles gradually grew until Rakesh approached them and shook their hands. One was Moideen Puthiyaveetil, the manager of the hospital. The other was Purushothaman, the driver. He went by Purushu. The manager fired question after question at Rakesh, leaving him no space to answer. The short pauses that accidentally cropped up were filled by Purushu's attempt at welcoming the new recruit. As they got in the hospital's car, a picture of the globe sprang to Rakesh's mind. The blue between India and the Middle East magnified on his screen, increasing his ache.

First they went to the accommodation, a big villa with a large gate and a large lock and it reminded Rakesh of a prison. This building housed nine doctors, one lab tech, two receptionists, a manager, an accountant, and a cook. Rakesh would share a room with Dr Govardhan, the chief medical officer. This was the best and biggest room. The CMO had influence. Rakesh was given the option of relaxing for the day, but then, he couldn't mentally relax as though a switch has been flipped, so he opted to join the others at the hospital, a four-storey building in an area thickly packed with similar buildings. Years later when he heard the term "concrete jungle", he instantly thought of this area. The sign out front, which read "Farooqia Polyclinic", was massive and lit up. The only one who could miss it would be a completely blind person. That was the first example of the hospital's marketing strategy that he saw.

The entrance lobby was nothing short of a crowded movie house at intermission. Half the crowd, like those competing for popcorn at the concessions stand, was attacking the receptionist, whose presence was made known only by his actions. The ground floor contained only this reception area and a small coffee-making space behind the stairs. Moideen led the others upstairs, talking non-stop. He would not make a good tour guide, Rakesh thought, as he was over-enthusiastic. He was quite well dressed and had an athletic body, although he struggled to conceal a small pot belly. His fixed smile widened occasionally as he greeted other staff. His courtesy questions to Rakesh and the others had a subtle air of authority.

Moideen explained that the first floor housed a general medicine clinic. Rakesh saw a board with the name "Dr Govardhan, Chief Medical Officer" strikingly prominent on it. After the name was a long list of degrees, of which apart from MBBS none seemed familiar. It resembled the political procession in Kerala state. The ones in the front were likely to become ministers, and those behind them were simply there for ornamental value. Most often those at the back did not even have a strong belief in any system; they simply existed there. Moideen's authority appeared to shrink a bit when he gently knocked on Dr Govardhan's door.

"Come in." Rakesh heard the same voice he had heard on the phone a few weeks ago. When Moideen opened the door, Govardhan was holding a knee hammer. Rakesh knew that the instrument did not mean much to him, but it made a great impact on his patients. He stopped everything, completely ignored his patient, and gave Rakesh a hybrid of a handshake and a hug.

"How was your trip?" Govardhan asked in a very

loud voice clearly meant to create an impression more than reflect interest. Rakesh was not comfortable with this intrusion into a patient's privacy, but surprisingly, no one else seemed to take note of it. Patients existed only as a means to an end here. As the conversation progressed, it became even clearer that the patient here was just a commodity. Dr Govardhan demanded full attention. He cracked loud jokes with hidden orders to laugh at the end. Rakesh laughed along with everyone else, but at the distorted drama of patient care, not at the jokes.

Rakesh was overly sensitive to the Jekyll and Hyde behaviour of some people. He was sharp at judging others' genuineness. It bothered him when people said things they did not mean. He felt that the art of communication was a complex affair. It required not just the skill of listening but also of inferring intended meanings and deciphering unsaid meanings. As a young boy, Rakesh had been the anchor of his group friends, taking the lead role of speaking and always lavishly spicing what he said with humour. But then those were the days when he had the freedom to be frank. When others did not say what they meant, it did not sit well with him. Truth had pain in it, and to be truthful required one to endurance of pain, the peculiar type of pain that in its severity yielded pleasure, he believed: the pleasure of saluting the inner self.

Why did people speak falsehoods, be it in what they said, thought, or felt? Rakesh wondered. His ability to see and hear through the falsehoods over time converted Rakesh from a joyful, talkative boy to a nearly silent person. At parties or other social gatherings, Rakesh stuck with his old buddies, for there was comfort, freedom, and openness with them.

New acquaintances tried to impress others and prove themselves, and, he often found, time proved them wrong. Now here was Dr Govardhan, whose volume and misplaced sense of humour failed to conceal his true nature.

"Did you finalise the terms and conditions?" he asked. Rakesh wasn't sure whether that was directed to him or Moideen.

"We shall do that tomorrow. Rakesh must be tired after the journey," the manager answered.

Rakesh wondered what there was to finalise. For him the terms were fixed, and that was why he was here. At this point, Moideen cut short the tour, and Rakesh went back to the villa. The time difference made him sleepy, but Hameed, the cook, would not let him go to bed without having dinner, so he made his way down to the foyer, which also served as the dining room. All the staff, if not at work or sleeping, would sit at this table. To the side of the table was a TV that was never switched off; it was the lifeline of the residents, Rakesh realised.

Hameed brought out two hot paratha and some fried chicken, which was too good. Even though he was sleepy, Rakesh was impressed with Hameed's culinary skills, and even more with his warmth.

Chapter 2

The next morning, according to the plan, Rakesh was to see the manager. Mr Moideen Puthiyaveetil tried to create an aura of authority, and he did not want the previous day's interaction with Dr Govardhan to dilute that authority. He also wanted to be friendly, so he presented to Rakesh the same smile but made it more expansive this time. His office was elite for a hospital manager. The large framed pictures of rulers looked down from the wall. A few patient files and a pack of Dunhills were the only objects on his desk.

"Hello, good morning, how are you?" he greeted Rakesh. "How did you find your accommodation? Did you get a good sleep?"

Rakesh knew by now that a basic principle of verbal communication wasn't followed here: if you ask, listen.

Rakesh smiled and took a seat. Moideen lit a Dunhill and extended one to Rakesh.

"No thanks. I don't smoke." *Smoking in injurious*

to the health and to building new relationships, Rakesh thought.

"You're a doctor, so I do not have to tell you the nature of the work," Moideen went on. "However, it's important that I inform you of certain policies at the beginning."

Rakesh listened attentively to all the policies and made no complaints. Moideen extended a paper to the new doctor to read, approve, and sign. Somewhere close to the bottom Rakesh saw his salary listed as four thousand Saudi riyals per month. Rakesh mentally calculated the exchange rate and arrived at thirty-two thousand rupees.

"Mr Moideen, I was told on the phone that the salary would be fifty thousand Indian rupees."

"Maybe Dr Govardhan made a mistake in his conversion," Moideen responded.

If a CMO makes a conversion mistake to a prospective candidate when presenting the job description and terms on an international phone line, is this not cheating? Rakesh wondered.

The mask-like smile did not leave Moideen's face, but his glow faded. "This is what we offer to all the new doctors, not just to you."

Rakesh was not interested in what others were offered. "I can't sign unless I speak to the CMO," he said.

"That's fine," Moideen said, probably knowing that the ball was very much in the CMO's court.

Rakesh went straight to Govardhan's consulting room, where he was examining an elderly patient with one earpiece of his stethoscope out. Rakesh wasn't sure, but he felt that Govardhan had been expecting him. If the whole episode was an act, the CMO could have earned an Oscar nomination.

"What's the matter?" Govardhan said.

The patient's presence made Rakesh careful to keep his voice low and his annoyance in control. He explained his concern plainly and softy.

Dr Govardhan, completely ignoring his patient, listened to everything and thoughtfully said, "If you're not happy, we can arrange your return ticket."

Rakesh's disappointment became anger. *Why do people in power always cheat? Are their values abraded as they go up the ladder?* Rakesh wondered.

Any decision he made now, even to speak, would be irrational; Rakesh knew it. His first impulse was to poke Govardhan with the handle of the knee hammer, but knew that by doing that he would be throwing away everything. Displays of emotion, particularly anger, never get rewarded. The tortuous journey of life had taught him this and had mellowed him. In drawing class in grade seven, Rakesh had to draw an eggplant from the blackboard. When he took his picture to the teacher, the teacher said he had traced it and called him a cheat. Rakesh threw his drawing book at the teacher in a violent expression to prove his innocence and show his deep disgust for the teacher. After that, he was not allowed to take art classes. Though he liked art, his future did not hang on it like his future hung on this job..

Rakesh headed straight for his room. In the dining room, Hameed, who had been the cook for many years in Jeddah and had come to Riyadh when this branch was founded, was reading the newspaper. He respectfully got up and offered to make tea.

"How do you like the hospital?" Hameed inquired

as he served the tea. Rakesh didn't want to share his concerns.

Rakesh never told his problems to others unless the listener could help to solve them. He didn't follow this principle today. He could not, as his annoyance leaked out. Hameed silently listened. When Rakesh was finished, all Hameed said was, "Perhaps there was someone above watching you? Don't worry; things will straighten out."

Back in Rakesh's room, although everything was in its rightful place, it had suddenly lost the impression of neatness he saw the previous night. Dr Govardhan's corner was disorganised and cluttered. Rakesh sat on his new mattress.

"If you are not happy, we can arrange your return ticket." He dissected that statement with the scalpel of human values. The findings were shameful. In a flash, he saw himself on a return flight and then at the door of his home in Calicut hugging his wife and kid. A cool sense of relief washed over his disturbed psyche. But then he snapped back to reality. Going home was not the right solution, and he did not want to nurture it. Going back was definitely not an option, not for the son of a soldier.

"I'm a slow walker, but I never walk back." He remembered the words of Abraham Lincoln. From a very young age, Rakesh had a fancy for quotations, proverbs, and short poems. He scribbled the ones that interested him in a diary and later realised that all of them represented fragments of his own beliefs. They reinforced those beliefs and reassured him, particularly at times like this.

I'm not going back, he resolved. *I'll stick on and achieve my goal.*

Suddenly the phone rang. It was Govardhan.

"Rakesh, why did you just vanish from my clinic? I was only trying to help you. The salary I mentioned earlier was just a rough estimate."

Did you take your job on a rough estimate? Do they pay you every month on a rough calculation? Do you send money home every month on a rough calculation? Do you prescribe medicines on rough knowledge? A multitude of questions sprouted like mushrooms in Rakesh's already troubled mind.

"Are you with me?" Govardhan's voice resonated over the line. "Here's what I'll do," he continued. "I shall speak to the owner at lunchtime and try my best to help you out."

This was little consolation, and it hardened the notion that this was all part of the play.

The door slowly opened a crack, followed by a gentle knock. It was Hameed. His smile illuminated the room and was contagious. Hameed never began a conversation with the phoney courtesy of a greeting like, "Hello, how are you?" Rakesh, too, felt that asking "How are you?" was an unnecessary social requirement. No one asked this because they wanted to know, and no one answered truthfully. Anything phoney distanced Rakesh. He often kept his greetings to a simple, "Hi." So he welcomed Hameed's direct question: "What are you doing?"

"Nothing much," Rakesh said as he went about organising his wardrobe.

"The owner of the clinic is a very kind and reliable person, unlike some others here." He did not specify who, but Rakesh could fill in the blank. Rakesh explained what Govardhan just told him on the phone.

"Then it's done," Hameed said.

Hameed guffawed. "See? I told you things would straighten out for you. Maybe they will give you some overtime."

"We'll see," Rakesh remarked.

The doorbell rang, followed by noise at the entrance as if lots of people had entered, but it was only Govardhan. He occupied lots of space and attention. Hameed served lunch, which was always a feast. Hameed was more than a cook; he made sure everyone ate well, which was evident in the central obesity of most residents. A loud voice cut through the hallway inviting Rakesh to join the others for lunch.

Rakesh came down and sat with Govardhan.

"I told you I would help you," Govardhan said with his mouth full. "I convinced Hussain to reconsider your salary, and that's done. You don't have to fly back. We are a team here and we help one another. Your concerns are my concerns."

Rakesh despised such platitudes.

"However, to make it workable, Hussain said that you may have to put in some extra hours, which I think is good. Friday is our day off, but what do we bachelors gain by sitting at home? It's better to go to the clinic. Hussain has finalised your schedule and has you working twelve hours a day, including Fridays."

Rakesh liked Hameed's presence there for no reason, and they exchanged glances.

Twelve hours of work with no day off for the next three hundred and sixty-five days would be like going through a long, dark tunnel. He could see the light at the far end only in his mind. Like a miner trapped deep down but faintly aware of the direction of the exit, armed with just one fading lamp, and an unfading belief. He would serve like a humble servant for the reward, no matter the magnitude of the task. Rakesh couldn't remain in a room for a whole hour, and now he had to confine himself to the outpatient clinics for six hours in the morning and six more hours in the evening. He reminded himself that this was his decision. Though not entirely true, the idea gave him a feeling of control.

The next morning, dressed moderately well and wearing a red striped tie, Rakesh reported for his first shift. He had bought a few neckties in Calicut on Dr Govardhan's insistence. He hadn't taken much care in selecting them, instead picking out the least expensive ones and adding to them an old one that had belonged to his father. He wasn't against the tie in principle, but he disliked the feeling of mild strangulation when wearing one. He had harboured different views in earlier days. During the farewell party at the end of medical school, whether to wear a tie for the photo was a divisive issue.

"We never wore ties all through medical school. Why should we suddenly wear them for the farewell snap?" he pointed out. "Our group photograph should reflect, after many years, how we actually looked and lived."

True to his thoughts, the photo reminded him of the divide. Rakesh had worn a tie as part of his school uniform and could easily make the knot. He had had to help many medical school classmates get the knot right for the snap, though he had not worn one. A few others shared Rakesh's view and strong in their unity, didn't wear ties for the photo either. Some had knots like tiny samosas hiding in their collars. Shankaran, Rakesh remembered, wore a tie that dangled close to his knees, a jab at the fashions of the West. Rakesh recollected those wonderful days. Here in the clinic, the tie requirement went over well and everyone wore one properly except the accountant, who always looked like he was struggling for breath.

Judy Eleanor was Rakesh's assistant. She was tall for a Filipino, but otherwise her nationality was well written on her. When she smiled she looked happy. She spoke a lot about exercise and dieting but did the opposite. She was overweight. Like Hameed, Judy had worked with the same company in Jeddah. She was a store of valuable information, but she didn't give it away easily. Her age was difficult to guess like most philipinos. She was punctual and meticulous, and she gave the impression that she loved her work. Rakesh learnt it was a blessing to have her as his assistant. There wasn't much in the hospital that she didn't do or couldn't do.

Rakesh, though an orthopaedic surgeon, would be involved in a bit of general practise as well on this job, and it soon became his workload. His office was on the second floor opposite to the paediatrician's. The paediatrician, Dr Tajudeen, was a tall, handsome guy from Hyderabad. The nephew of a minister in Andhra Pradesh, he was from a very wealthy family and so did not have to be here to earn a better living. He was the only doctor in the clinic who owned a car. Others commuted in the ambulance. He explained to Rakesh that he had come for a break from the overcrowded clinics in Hyderabad and the hassles of income tax. He was offered family status, but, like Rakesh's salary, it wasn't what it appeared to be. Tajudeen pressed Moideen for a family visa, but it hadn't been granted in the last six months. Tajudeen was frank and loud. Though a paediatrician, he had considerable experience in internal medicine, having done one year senior internship and a year as a lecturer in this specialty.

* * *

Chapter 3

Dr Niranjan Sharma walked through reception and into his office, whistling and smiling as if he had reached his holiday destination. That was his style. He always wore a gaudy tie. He appeared happy and made most people whom he met happy too. He cracked jokes, and even if they weren't funny people laughed anyway, sometimes just at his convulsive giggle. He worked at night, midnight to seven in the morning. He was awake all night and slept most of the day – not exactly a life he had once desired. A few patients would trickle in during the first hour and a half of his shift, and after that, the clinics were mostly quiet unless there was a small emergency. Newspapers, a couple of black coffees, and chats with other night staff kept him going to the morning. He wasn't inspired or fulfilled by what he did, but he wasn't unhappy either.

Dr Sharma graduated from Madras Medical College as one of the top students almost eight years before. For some ill-defined reason, he never liked to be addressed as Dr Sharma, though that was his surname. During his school days, he didn't aspire to be a medical man although he was inspired during a class trip in the seventh grade. The class went to a medical science exhibition as part of the curriculum to expose children to the world of medicine. The class had already taken similar trips to nearby factories to nurture interest in engineering in the young minds.

Part of the medical exhibition was a twenty-minute movie on open-heart surgery. As the students sat silently in the dark auditorium, a picture of a large heart sprang up on the huge screen. They watched its regular, rhythmic movement in dreadful amazement. One student fainted. But Niranjan was glued to every fine detail that his eyes could capture. He was fascinated. He started learning about the heart and its role, and he developed his own definition of it: the tangible object that controlled everything intangible.

His parents encouraged him to practise medicine. Around this time he lost an uncle, quite a young guy, to a heart attack. This incident watered the seed sown at the medical exhibition. He completed his medical degree with no particular enthusiasm. He never saw an open-heart surgery during his medical school career, and cardiology postings were confined to the clinics. Cardiothoracic surgery was restricted to MS and MCH candidates, and as he wasn't very persistent, he didn't pursue these degrees.

He lost his father during his internship to myocardial infarction. This fertilised the growing plant of his career, and Niranjan sensed this but never acknowledged it. He worked in a few jobs in his home town before coming to Saudi Arabia for this job. In the six years he had been here, he never thought about the plant of his ambition. Was it despair at seeing it overgrown and without fruit or fear that it had already withered away? He wasn't sure. No one asked him about it, and he never asked himself.

A voice broke the silence in his office. "Hello, Dr Niranjan. What's the news?" It was Khalid, whom everyone called "Khalidbhai" out of respect for his age. He loved to gossip, but not with Niranjan. Niranjan had nicknamed him "the Farooqia Daily". His duties as janitor were only part of his job; supplying news and gossip was his favourite role. He knew about everything that happened at the clinics and everyone's views on the news, and if he was missing any facts, his imagination completed the story. He flourished as a reporter partly because of the secretive nature of the management . Niranjan replied, "What news can I have?"

"Did you know?" Khalid probed.

"Know what?"

"A new doctor joined yesterday. He's from Calicut. I think he's a bone doctor. But be very careful; he is Govardhan's candidate."

Niranjan laughed. Khalidbhai could not grasp the implications of what he said. Khalid left to tell others.

A few hours later, Nurse Richa came in. She often came to him for clarification. Some people called her Richie, but Niranjan sometimes called her *"Poochakutty"*, which meant "kitten". She didn't mind, although she pretended to.

"Dr Niranjan, a new doctor has joined us."

"Did you see him?" Niranjan inquired.

"Briefly, when he came out of Govardhan's clinic."

"Is he handsome?" Niranjan asked mischievously.

"Don't worry; you will not have any competitors as long as you wear such stupid ties."

Niranjan laughed loudly. Occasionally the people on the floor below could hear his laugh. "Did he say hello to you?"

"I told you, I haven't met him."

They continued chatting for quite some time although Richa gave the impression she was about to leave through it all. Their communication had only one purpose: to keep her there for a while. Niranjan liked Richa in a peculiar way. Her husband came from the same village as Niranjan's mother, And Richa visited Niranjan's mother during her vacations and brought back snacks and savouries his mum had made. When Richa's pay cheque was delayed or if there was some urgent need, Niranjan helped her to send money home. They had a very jovial and respectful bond. Others thought otherwise, but they never bothered to correct anyone.

Rakesh normally returned to his room close to midnight, just as Niranjan was leaving for his night shift. They chatted for a few minutes at the dining table along with Hameed and his special dinner. Rakesh reflected on the day's work, but with time, the conversation drifted beyond the hospital corridors. Rather than complain about management or the difficulties of expat life, they talked of their hopes and aspirations. Their conversations soon became routine and helped Rakesh to unwind. Hameed also casually chipped in almost daily. Most of the doctors treated Hameed only as a cook, but these two were different, and Hameed was excited to be considered an equal amongst doctors.

"I am feeling bored, like I'm stagnating, with nothing to look forward to. The monotony—" started Niranjan.

"That is bird in a cage syndrome," interrupted Rakesh.

"What do you mean, bird in a cage?" Niranjan responded.

Niranjan listened to whatever Rakesh said with the respect a disciple would give a guru. They had a very close bond. Their conversations were an oasis in an intellectual desert for Niranjan. Rakesh had read a lot of self-improvement books and had taken part in many seminars. However, he never shared this knowledge unless he felt the listener was genuinely interested, and he was more inclined to listen than to talk.

The most important part of communication was listening, and he listened almost to a fault. Whenever he felt even faintly that others did not appear keen to listen, he would not waste his energy speaking. He never spoke for the sake of it. Rakesh also developed a special interest in watching other people talk. He often observed that in others' conversations, everyone was talking but no one was listening. The person who talked loudest silenced others. Conversations were similar to traffic jams: everyone wanted to go first but everyone got stuck. If everyone respected others and offered others priority, the conversational congestion could be minimised. Rakesh made it a practise to be courteous on the road and to drive defensively. This made him a slow driver. When he practised similar principles in conversations, he was mostly silent. He only opened up to those in whom he saw a part of himself. Niranjan was one of them. During their regular dinners,

Rakesh continued, "All are born with wings, but not all can fly."

Niranjan shifted his chair closer to Rakesh and leaned towards him, listening attentively.

"Birds are meant to fly, but the ones in the cages can't fly."

"But who is in the cage?" Niranjan asked.

"Most of us," Rakesh replied. "The cage is safe and comfortable. The bird inside doesn't have to hunt for food; its owner brings it regularly."

"That is fantastic," Niranjan commented and broke into thunderous laughter.

He often laughed wildly at his own jokes, or even at no joke, but no one took offence, as he had a warm heart. Even Rakesh did not mind his interruptions, for he knew that he was listening intently.

"Sometimes the bird gets special feed, sometimes water. Occasionally the owner forgets to feed it for a day or two, and then all the bird can do is chirp."

"That's sad," Niranjan said. He was starting to identify with the metaphor.

"But the bird is safe; other animals or larger birds can't attack it."

Though Niranjan sensed the meaning of the metaphor, he wanted to hear it from Rakesh. "Who is in this cage?" he asked.

"Well, most of us."

"What is this cage?"

"The place or system in which we are stuck."

"You mean Farooqia Hospital?"

"I can't tell you that; it differs from person to person."

Niranjan knew that the feed was the pay cheque. It was unclear whether his cage offered him safety, as there was little job security here.

Niranjan thought of his ambition to become a cardiac surgeon. With that qualification he would be paid much more than what he was earning now, and life would be a lot more fulfilling. He focussed only on the pay cheque now.

"Sometimes the feed can be really good," Niranjan pointed out.

Rakesh agreed, knowing very well what Niranjan spoke of. He responded, "Yes, there are golden cages, and maybe bigger ones, too. Over time, a year or, for some, a few years, the cage is no longer an external entity; it becomes the fabric of life. We don't see it or feel it because it becomes a part of us.

"The painful fact," he continued, "is that when that happens, the bird's wings can no longer function, and it loses its ability to fly."

In medical terms, he called this "disuse atrophy", a process by which an organ or tissue becomes functionless over time when not used.

"All are born with wings, but not all can fly," Rakesh repeated. When we are young, we are encouraged to dream big and follow our dreams. But if you look around, the facts are obvious. Very few really chase their dreams all the way to their ends. Very few fly to their passions."

"But that is because the cage is closed," Niranjan said to invite further insight.

Rakesh liked that comment and continued, "Opportunities come up all the time, but we can only see them if they are what our minds crave."

Niranjan remembered the words of his radiology

professor: "Your eyes will only see what your mind already knows."

Though not exactly, this saying seemed to apply in this case. Opportunities are not marked with a sign or a label. Niranjan now understood what Rakesh was saying.

"We are the birds inside this cage, given feed every month. But how do I escape?" Niranjan paused. "I think it is time for me to go on duty, but we should continue this conversation tomorrow before I break out of the cage."

"Breaking out of the cage is easy. The challenge is to fly. See you tomorrow," Rakesh said.

* * *

Throughout his shift, Niranjan reflected on the discussion and very much looked forward to their next talk.

"But what's the guarantee that you succeed if you get out of the cage?" Niranjan jumped straight into the conversation where they had left off the previous night.

Rakesh smiled. "Well, that's normal thinking, the badge of an ordinary person. This badge will always prevent him from attaching the word 'extra' to 'ordinary'."

"But what if our plans fail? Don't you think we should have a plan B in case plan A doesn't work out?" Niranjan inquired.

"Not if life depends on plan A," Rakesh said firmly.

"But what's the guarantee plan A will work?" Niranjan now seemed confused.

"There's no such thing as a guarantee in life. Maybe there is when you buy a TV or a washing machine, but not in life's *purposeful* journey," Rakesh responded.

"But without surety, how can we—?"

Rakesh held up his hand to cut Niranjan off. He told a true story to clarify the point.

His father had told him this story a long time ago, but it was etched deep into his memory. Rakesh's father had been in the thick of the Second World War. The bedtime stories he told his kids were always about his experiences, mostly in the War. He spiced the stories up, but their messages were always profound. Lying on either side of their father, Rakesh and his little sister would listen with much more excitement than they would feel watching a war movie on TV. Those days Rakesh felt that his father was the bravest man on the planet. Over the years, this feeling only got stronger. This story, about courage and confidence, displayed the hollowness of a guarantee.

Sometime in 1944, somewhere in the Congo, the Army was moving through the forest and had to cross a narrow river. The whole battalion, which included sixteen trucks and four Patton tanks, had to cross. The leaders were unsure of how to do this, but not for long. Subaidar Randhir Singh stepped forward and addressed the commanding officer.

"Sir, I have an engineering background. Give me all the men and forty-eight hours. I shall build a bridge." Orders were given, and work commenced. That was the beauty of the Army: decision-making and implementation worked in unison. Randhir Singh and his men cut down trees and hanging roots in shifts. The rain shower that rolled in did not hamper their progress. By the third day, the manual marvel of a bridge was ready. Randhir Singh had designed it with support beams every three metres, as he knew the tanks were heavier than overcrowded buses. He reported to the commanding officer.

"Sir, the bridge is ready. We can move."

The officer smiled in approval but asked, "What's the guarantee your bridge won't collapse?"

Randhir replied with firmness equal to the officer's. "No guarantee, Sir, but when the first tank crosses, I shall remain in a raft under the bridge ." He meant it. All crossed safely.

Niranjan sat motionless. The essence of the story sank in, unsure if he was over or under the bridge.

"Now stop all those war stories," Hameed interrupted. "It's time for dinner. Today it's aloo paratha." He arranged the dishes on the dining table. Aloo paratha was the one dish Rakesh's mother made, and as far as he was concerned, no one else made it properly. Not even good restaurants came close. Aloo paratha came to stand for his mother's cooking, like the cigarette trade name "Scissors" which came to mean any cigarettes. As Rakesh studied at Trivandrum Medical School, he often travelled overnight, and his mother always packed him a dinner of aloo paratha for the train ride. He had once told his friends that he could travel without a ticket but not without his packed dinner. His mother made the dish with a lot of love, which restaurants could never duplicate. The plantain-leaf wrapping preserved the aroma till Rakesh impatiently opened it at Shornur Railway Station. Rakesh once wrote a short piece about this dish for the newspaper:

> Countries have united, countries have divided; wars have been won and wars have been lost; science has progressed beyond the thinkable; sports records have been broken; values have been violated…
>
> But the paratha my mother makes has never changed.
>
> It remains the same in colour, in flavour, in consistency, in aroma, in value, in satisfaction, in love, in bond, in care, in duty, in everything that describes a mother's love. It is probably the only thing that will remain unchanged.

So when Hameed mentioned aloo paratha, Rakesh knew it had to be named something else.

Chapter 4

Sister Shoshamma, the head nurse, enjoyed the self-imposed role of a guide to new staff. Be they doctors or nurses, she shared her experience with all new recruits. Her presentations were designed to scare them, and it worked effectively with most.

"Those who come to Saudi Arabia or to any Persian Gulf country once did so with an objective, even if it wasn't very well defined. They had hopes, dreams, and vague timelines," Sister Shoshamma explained to Rakesh.

"Are you talking about everyone who came here or a particular group?" Rakesh asked.

"Mainly labourers or other non-professionals. Dr Rakesh, you may not be aware that there are thousands of people who have been away from home for two or three years, maybe more."

"Why is that so?"

"Well, they can't afford to go home. A visit home would drain whatever they have earned. And so they prefer to send home money and stay here. Their physical presence is not needed in many homes, but the cash that comes every month is," Sister Shoshamma remarked with a deep sigh.

Rakesh thought about Hameed. Such a wonderful person. He had never seen his four-year-old son.

Shoshamma continued, "Once here, most people get entangled in the rat race and, sadly, most don't even know that their plans have got all messed up. They work only to stand in line at the money-exchange centre every month."

Rakesh had seen the Al Kooheji Money Centre near the hospital at the end of the previous month. With ten counters and a huge hall, it was still swollen with crowds of people of all nationalities, but mostly south Indians. The colour of dirt and mud, the smell of sweat and blood, the sound of abuses and insults, it was the picture of a man's struggle for his loved ones. A few Saudi riyals and the bank account number of his family back home in the pocket, he waits in the endless queue.

Shoshamma continued, "Many people see their monthly remittance as their identity." She compared them to curry leaves: Once curry leaves lose their aroma, they're no longer wanted. Only a lucky few men were able to return for an annual visit to rekindle their marital bond. Many wives back home learnt to live without their husbands. Many children grew up without a father figure. The person slowly became irrelevant, only what he did so long as he did. Like a train for the passengers on the platform, the identity of the driver was irrelevant as long as the train arrived. He was important only as long as he sent money home. This idea disturbed Rakesh.

James, Dr Govardhan's patient, had walked in with

a slip for augmentin injection. He was an old friend of Sister Shoshamma's and chippd in, "Gulf life is for people with a high degree of self-discipline and self-love. Most people acquire the first one in time, but they don't acquire the second and they slowly wither away."

"Very true," Shoshamma said. James had come to Saudi Arabia almost twenty years before as a bachelor for a driver's job in Jubail. The salary was small, but it had been good enough over the years to support his parents, to marry off his only sister, and to put his younger brother through polytechnic. He worked with such dedication that he was blind to the additions to his own years. He changed jobs and places and now worked in a supermarket in Riyadh. He had lost his youth and had never found a female companion. Each strand of his personal ambition, of his dreams and hopes, had got tangled into a ball. He couldn't untangle it, but he couldn't throw it either, for somewhere in that tangle was his life.

His injection administered, James left the lab. "James is staying on here as he doesn't know where else to go," Shoshamma said.

"What about his parents?" asked Rakesh?

"Well, they moved with his brother after he completed his ITI, married a girl from his college, and built his own house in Trichur. James even sent money for the construction of his brother's house, sometimes in a rush to meet deadlines."

"How about his sister?"

"She married a lab technician working in Salalah, and both are doing well there. Most of James's friends here are trying to talk him into a marriage. James is not sure if he should or wants to go through with it. His age failed his looks, and his looks failed his thoughts."

Rakesh saw the curry leaves now.

"If you talk long enough with James you will see his sense of pride in what he did for the family," Shoshamma said, "although he's unsure if those on the receiving end ever felt the same. The transition of their pride to regret was too smudged.

"There are thousands of Jameses here. They gave the best of their lives for the financial security of their families, societies, and country, but becoming irrelevant is the tragedy of many an expat's life."

Rakesh moved to leave, and Shoshamma called after him, "Don't forget to love yourself or else you'll be one more James."

✳ ✳ ✳

"Dr Niranjan, Hussain is coming tomorrow," Hameed said with earnest excitement at dinner that night.

"Let him come. What difference does it make to us?" Niranjan remarked. He had never held the owner, the manager, or anyone at the hospital in more esteem than anyone else, and he made this known.

Hameed turned to Rakesh. "You haven't met him yet, so you should meet him tomorrow." Rakesh decided he would.

"Whenever he comes he pays us extra," Hameed added innocently.

Rakesh, though he settled into the job and the long hours, still felt he had been cheated, and that feeling formed the foundation on which everything related to this job was built. Now he thought it was time to address his concerns with the owner himself.

"Dear Rakesh, don't be silly," Niranjan said. "Nothing happens without Hussain's knowledge. He controls everything behind the curtain of his esteemed isolation. The orchestra you see every day is only an extension of him. He's one of the new breed of owners who hide behind the barricade of managers."

"But why hide?" Rakesh responded.

"Well, this strategy allows him to maintain his likeable image, or so he thinks. Don't bother speaking to him about your salary and overtime. He'll just say that he'll look into it, and that'll never happen. You'll just end up feeling bitter. Take this from me: just get on with it." Niranjan was firm.

The news of Hussain's visit rippled through the hospital corridors. The source wasn't known. The nurses spoke about it as if everyone except the individual who talked about it would be happy.

Everyone knew when he came, but nobody saw him. "This is the third-rate drama they get caught up in," Niranjan remarked.

Towards the end of the night, news trickled down that Hussain had invited all the staff for dinner at the Blue Lagoon restaurant. The source of this news was again unknown, and only Dr Govardhan was interested in going. Govardhan acted as if Hussain had come to Riyadh for management guidance, which he always willingly gave. Govardhan invited Rakesh to join them for dinner like a leading architect bringing along an upcoming junior to meet an elite client. It was only a display.

Hussain didn't look like what many at the hospital expected. Not too tall, he was moderately built. He put a good amount of effort into his attire, but it did not do him any justice. His face was powdered and creamed.

His cheeks had a glow not regularly seen around the hospital. His hair was jet black and messy, as though he had run away halfway through his appointment with the hairdresser. He wore an odd tie that hung proudly from his neck and secured haphazardly with a jewelled aeroplane tie clip. The broad horizontal stripes on his trousers completed the look of a neo-Impressionism if he were an art object. As if the artist forgot the purpose, but got hallucinated by the product. Respect and regard coming only from the signature. Here the signature was the knowledge that he owned this hospital in Riyadh and many others across Saudi Arabia. He spoke little and laughed lots. Govardhan did most of the talking during dinner, laughing about routine things as if it was all news. He and Hussain took turns laughing, occasionally laughing together. If Rakesh had been a stranger at the next table, he would have mistaken this for a rehearsal of a cheap TV comedy show. Hussain sustained his guffaws much longer than he should have. Was he hiding his poor conversation skills or preventing Rakesh from bringing up sensitive topics? Rakesh didn't know, but he had made up his mind not to discuss his concerns. He believed Niranjan when he said that this was not a civilised system of discussion. The only system Hussain cared about the one in his hospital: patients walked in daily by the hundreds, paid consultation fees, got lots of lab tests done, paid more, and left to come back again later. This system was a well-oiled machine, and it never creaked.

Rakesh felt lonely during dinner. It was like long overdue exercise: Its completion was the only expected happiness. He suddenly and intensely longed for his wife's presence. Instead he was seated between two comedians united in conversation without content, jokes without humour.

"Are you happy?" Hussain asked Rakesh.

There are times when sensibility overshadows reality, and Rakesh sensibly answered, "Very much."

"He is more than happy. How many doctors would have got overtime right from day one? Very lucky. He is settling in well," Govardhan answered for Rakesh. He only wanted to put an end to the topic. Rakesh wondered whether he and Hussain shared a common guilt.

By the time Rakesh reached home it was quite late, and Niranjan had already left for duty. Hameed was wide awake, as always. He never let anyone go to bed without having dinner. He was good at persuasion, and his culinary skills did most of the talking.

"How did you find Hussain? Is he not a good guy? What did he tell you? Did he inquire about your family? Did he ask about me? Is he coming to our villa tomorrow?"

Hameed was excited, and Rakesh wasn't sure why. Rakesh replied with a smiling, "I have not gone on a date with Demi Moore."

Hameed didn't know who Demi Moore was, but he knew that Hussain had failed to impress Rakesh. Hameed could never understand why every single doctor except Govardhan disliked Hussain right from the very first meeting.

* * *

Rakesh quickly blended into the system as if he had been there for ages. He did his job well and was quite popular amongst his colleagues. He often bent an ear to their concerns. Somehow many felt he could be trusted and confided in him. Most of what they said stayed with him, as if locking their concerns within him was the solution to their problems. Days and weeks and months rolled on like a cartwheel, with resistance at first and then smoothly. Three months went by, and Rakesh occasionally felt homesick, but less frequently all the time. He spoke to his family every ten days. International phone calls weren't easy to make, and no one had cell phones. He had to stand at a roadside phone booth. When he exhausted his coins, the conversation suffered premature and abrupt death. Moideen offered the phone facilities in his office, but no one used them except for emergencies. On the way to the phone booth with a plastic cover filled with coins, Rakesh felt distinctly different than he did on the way back. Ache replaced enthusiasm as if the phone booth took away not just his coins but also his energy and happiness.

Rakesh's family celebrated his daughter's first birthday. He wasn't sure if anyone but his wife missed him. She sent him copies of all the snaps of the occasion. He looked at them every day, then every hour then any time and mostly all the time.The snaps gave him a painful sort of comfort. Whether this was more painful or comforting Rakesh didn't know. He displayed one of the snaps on his desk. It eased his loneliness and energised him during his long hours at the clinic.Colleagues and patients glanced at the photo from time to time. They didn't comment but could read what was written on it, a language that had no alphabet or grammer, but palpabale by the silence that ensued. A language known by those who lived far from those for whom they lived. Gradually the picture became a symbol of hope as if it was the light at the end of the tunnel. It even cast its light on the fellowship exam.For Rakesh, this picture was his inspiration and it solidified his aspiration.

The military hospital in Riyadh was the centre for all overseas medical exams, Rakesh learnt from Govardhan. As he had been in Saudi for four months, the time had come to register for the exam, but he could only go there during his break between one and four in the afternoon. As the military hospital closed to visitors at two o'clock, he had to rush. When he arrived, he found that the military hospital complex was really complex, and the signs weren't much help. With a bit of English, a bit of Arabic, and a lot of sign language, he finally made it to the second floor of the administrative block, which housed the examination department. A Sudanese woman sat at reception. Her desk was a huge heap of stuff; either she was poorly organised or she was overloaded. Though it was nearing closing time, she appeared in no rush and provided all the information Rakesh needed.

"The next exam will be held during the last week of May. On the first day you will have the multiple-choice portion followed by the essays in the afternoon. On the following day is the clinical examination, and after a day's gap, the final viva voce. The exact dates, times, and fees will be announced six months prior to the exams."

Rakesh had to wait two more months for that. The woman took down his address and said she would post further details as they came.

As he leisurely walked around the hospital on the way back, the innumerable white coats that went past amused him in a pleasantly unpleasant way. He wanted to be part of a well-established hospital. It was not size that attracted him but a good flow of trauma patients. After medical school in Trivandrum, Rakesh did his internship at Calicut Medical College. He didn't have a clear plan for the future. After twelfth grade, his marks effortlessly streamed him into the medical school and rolled him out five and a half years later. His two-month posting in the orthopaedic department during his internship completely changed his outlook.

Calicut Medical College catered to the large population of five districts. Disregard to traffic rules, seat belt–less driving, Formula 1 attitudes on the highways, potholes and caves all worked in perfect harmony to deliver patients to the orthopaedic department in abundance. Accidents transformed lives in a flash, changing priorities without warning. Rakesh saw a huge crowd of such patients every day in the orthopaedic outpatient clinic. Some came on stretchers, some in wheelchairs, some limping, and some carried by bystanders. Being a part of the system to aid them back to normal life was instantly gratifying. The boundaries of duty, nature, or timing did not confine Rakesh. He willingly wheeled patients if porters weren't available. He had completed his postings in general medicine, gynaecology, and paediatrics, but never before had he felt like this. Somewhere in his unchartered intellect orthopaedics struck a chord. He spent hours in the operating theatre with the senior staff and many more hours in the plastering room. If someone had closely observed him, it would have been difficult for that person to figure out whether Rakesh represented the hospital or belonged to the patient's side.

If you want to be a farmer, as the saying goes, be prepared to get your hands dirty. Rakesh found passion in this dirt, and he got it all over him. He identified that this was his calling. As he walked back, he envied the consultants at the military complex. He wanted to get back to orthopaedics work and away from the general practise he did now. He wanted to advance his career, And he dreamt of anchoring an efficient unit that treated trauma patients.

Rakesh returned home with the pleasant awareness that he had re-visualised his goal and the steep uphill challenge that lay ahead. The receptionist had disclosed the pass percentage on the previous year's exam: only twenty per cent. Rakesh had about eight months to organise and prepare. Twelve-hour shifts at the hospital and a few hours of sleep didn't leave much time. He knew he couldn't push it any further. He devoted the following two weeks to collecting books and study materials and chalking out a plan. This was system he had learnt from his father. He knew that any big task becomes achievable if properly organised and divided.

At college Rakesh had not been the type who opened books on a daily basis. He enjoyed college and hostel life and had loads of fun, and studies weren't an ingredient of his fun. He always postponed studying until he could postpone it no more. But once he began, it was like a switch had been flipped. He cut off everything and focused intently on his books, and in the end, his grades weren't too bad. He never failed a single university exam. His friends had joked that he was the only guy who saw the sunset and sunrise in one sitting. And that had been true on the eve of a physiology exam.

He never followed other students' strategies; he didn't have to. And no one followed Rakesh; that would be disastrous. He had never been any teacher's pet, for he never attempted to be one. His presence was vibrant in the college corridors, hostel lobby, and sports ground but dim in the classroom. During one of his final-year exams, on the eve of medicine clinic, he had to play a cricket match. This was the annual tournament, and he played for a local club. He wasn't a great player by any standards, but he excelled in generating team spirit. He glued and led the team. He could have opted out of this particular match, but he chose otherwise. He played the whole day, revised the whole night, and cleared the exam. When he brought home the certificate of his medical degree, he also brought along five years of rich memories of student life. But here at Farooqia Hospital, the playground, the rules, and the stakes were different. The exams were the only thing on his mind. It had been a fantasy, but not anymore. It was the rope on which he would swing across this valley to the mountain of his dreams. The rope was thin and short as told by Mrs Wafa, the Sudanese lady at the military hospital.

❖ ❖ ❖

Chapter 5

Hi. I heard you didn't turn up for lunch today. What's up?" Niranjan asked Rakesh at dinner time. A skipped meal was always news, for no one did it. If anyone attempted, Hameed wouldn't allow it.

"Well, I had something to take care of outside the hospital," Rakesh answered.

"You don't seem to be revealing much."

"There's nothing much to reveal. I went to the military medical complex."

"Are you trying for a job there?" Niranjan asked.

Hameed set down the dishes of hot bread and his special chicken 66, named so because everyone felt it was better than the chicken 65 served in restaurants, and, curious to hear what Rakesh would say, turned his attention to the conversation. Though Rakesh never revealed much, everyone sensed that he wasn't very happy in his current position, so a job change seemed logical to Hameed.

"No, not at all," Rakesh reassured Niranjan. "I went to inquire about the FRCS exams."

"Are you planning to sit them?" Niranjan asked.

"I'm thinking about it," Rakesh said carefully. He didn't want to reveal the intensity of his desire.

"Those exams are very tough, man. I know many doctors who regularly take them and ritually waste the exam fee. This includes our great chief medical officer."

"Have you ever taken them?" Rakesh asked.

"With this night shift?" Niranjan laughed. "You must be joking. They're meant for those working in academic settings with decent working hours. Not like ours. And last year, only eight candidates from Saudi passed."

"You know a lot about them," Rakesh said.

"Yes, an old classmate of mine, Sridhar, who works in the Buraidah Ministry of Health, sat them last year and told me about them."

"Did he pass?"

"Well, I told you, the exams are not for everyone."

"Did he really prepare well?"

"Who wouldn't with such a high exam fee of six hundred dollars?"

Rakesh listened attentively as if the information Niranjan gave him would come up on the exam. Then Niranjan left for work. Rakesh went to his room after the heavy meal with heavy thoughts. What he had learnt about the exams from the receptionist and Niranjan chained his thoughts. The energy and discipline that he would need to break the chain, Rakesh realised, would be enormous. He spoke to himself softly in the privacy of his room.

"If eight candidates can pass, I can." He stopped and corrected himself. "No. if anyone can, I can." This gave him the enthusiasm he was looking for. He knew motivation and the power to overcome demotivating factors outside himself came only from within.

Rakesh took out a notebook. As he began scribbling, Hameed knocked and peeked into his room.

"Are you sure that you're not looking for another job?" Hameed said. "Please don't. You will find happiness here."

"Ah! Hameed, I never said I was unhappy. How can anyone be unhappy with the kind of food you serve?" Rakesh commented lightly. Hameed disappeared as if he had got what he came for.

❖ ❖ ❖

Without knocking, Moideen walked into Rakesh's office. "Hello, Sir. How's it going? I haven't seen you for a while. Patients have said they're very happy with you."

Moideen never knocked before entering. It was a show of authority, Rakesh thought. *Authority without confidence is like a heavy suitcase without a handle. It can't be properly moved*, thought Rakesh.

"Ah, yes," Rakesh responded. "I am getting on well."

"I can see a lot of books here," Moideen said, looking around. "That's good. It's very important in your profession to always update yourself. The more you know, the better you can help your patients. Is it not so?"

"You know as well as I do."

This was common sense, and when it came from

Moideen, the statement was hollow. Rakesh, even as a small kid, could see through such statements. This used to make him angry, but not anymore. At least not evidently.

"Do you get time to read much with such a busy clinic?" Moideen asked.

"Not a lot, but I read whenever I get the chance."

Moideen had something on his mind; Rakesh could feel it. It had to be something weighty that would have more impact if withheld until after small talk.

"How do you find the other staff? How do you feel other doctors are performing?"

"I'm not sure I should comment on others, but they're all friendly and helpful," Rakesh said in his ordinary diplomatic way.

"What do you think of Govardhan?" Moideen probed.

"I think that question should be better answered by his patients," Rakesh responded.

Moideen interpreted this as a joke and laughed.

"Okay, Dr Rakesh, carry on. I'll see you later." Moideen swiftly left, as if he had suddenly remembered an important task. Rakesh could not figure out the purpose of his visit. All he could grasp was that Moideen had come there with a hidden purpose but the right moment to reveal it hadn't come up.

Later that evening, a fragile voice greeted Rakesh as he walked out of the pathology lab. "Hello. Good evening, Doctor."

"Very good evening, Poochakutty," Rakesh responded to Nurse Richa.

She gave him a look as though she didn't know how to respond, for she didn't know how she should feel about being called this name. Silence would be regarded as weakness, which was not appropriate. A smile would give him the freedom to address her in that manner regularly. It was like a heavy, candy-coated weight had fallen on her unawares, leaving her defenceless. She hesitated a moment and then quickly walked away. Only Niranjan was allowed to call her Poochakutty openly.

One morning as Rakesh walked into the office, Judy handed him an envelope from the military hospital. With enthusiasm, he tore it open, tearing off the corner of the letter inside. It was from the military hospital. Enclosed were the exam prospectus and application form. Rakesh couldn't conceal his excitement.

"What's that?" Judy asked.

Rakesh didn't hear her. Even the empty application form made him euphoric. It was like the salad before the main meal. *The meal will come next*, he thought. But in this case, his meal could end with the salad. He remembered all those who only had the salad but paid for the entire meal year after year, including the CMO.

"Now, what is it?" Judy repeated.

"It's information about the exam," Rakesh said, snapped out of his reverie.

"When is it exactly?"

Rakesh pulled out the schedule, and they read it together.

Judy marked it in the office calendar, implying that it was significant to her as well. Rakesh saw himself as a lone warrior facing a fast-approaching enemy.

In his inner shrine, a voice echoed. *You will defeat everyone one by one.* He knew it wasn't as simple as that. He vacillated between reason and unreason, possible and impossible, past evidence and present belief, fantasy and reality. Ultimately, he concentrated on his victory. Suddenly he no longer felt he was a lone warrior. Judy was his assistant commander in chief.

The news of the exam date was like a bus that arrived after a long wait. Its sight reflecting the destination.

* * *

Rakesh glanced at the expat page in the newspaper as he regularly did. He was the only staff member, who subscribed to an English paper, but he shared it with the other staff, and everyone read it purposefully, as if doing so was part of their job description. A headline announced the new chapter of an association of Indian doctors serving in Saudi Arabia. The article explained that the association had been in operation for quite some years and had chapters in many countries. Rakesh saw associations like this one only as a platform for socialising over sumptuous food. The fact that they broke the monotony of work in the clinics ensured a moderate attendance. This association's regular dinners, normally sponsored by a medical or pharmaceutical company, were its main attraction. Busy practitioners always arrived late, just in time for the dinner. The dinners always included speeches on insignificant topics by significant personalities. This chapter's inaugural meeting would include a speech by Dr Kamal titled *Medical Service at a Crossroads*, the article explained.

Dr Kamal had been Rakesh's teacher at Trivandrum. He was one of the very few in his profession who practised simply because he loved to serve. His ideal of a medical man was the doctor who came to Kamal's village when he was a child. This doctor made house calls at any time, day or night, at any distance. The chance to serve was all that mattered. Everyone in the village loved him even more than they respected him. He also operated a small clinic where people visited for treatment or for a chat. He was always approachable and warm. A lack of patients or an overcrowded clinic never upset or irritated him.

When he made house calls, sometimes the village boys guided him and carried his bag. To walk alongside the doctor was a privilege, the simple pleasure of simple human beings. Kamal saw a lot of truth here. He was never in a hurry, and he treated patients as though his day had more than twenty-four hours. He followed up with the sick as needed. He derived pleasure from watching the progress of his patients and from being a part of that progress. Consultation fees did not exist, instead a flexible token of gratitude did. This man was Kamal's hero and role model.

During one of Rakesh's classes, Kamal vividly recounted a time when this doctor was called to see a man in the neighbourhood with severe chest pain. The village doctor, realising the critical nature of the case, advised that the man be sent to the nearest medical college, which was about a hundred kilometres away. He not only arranged for a cab, but he accompanied the patient to the college and took care of the admission formalities. Kamal explained to his students that they could never put a price on their service, and if they do, it became a sale, and a doctor could not sell medical service. This inspired Kamal as a kid and motivated him, Kamal Sridhar, son of a railway porter, to become Dr Sridhar.

Kamal developed an interest in internal medicine and obtained his MD. He took up a job as a tutor in internal medicine. In his lectures, he invariably touched on ethics. He couldn't teach medicine without speaking about ethics. This was an essential part of the profession. His classes were interesting and humorous. He peppered his lectures with sarcasm when referring to unfair and corrupt medical practises. His students admired him immensely, and for many, he personified medical values. He said only what he meant, and he practised what he taught. He stood out in a world where speech and deed were increasingly distinct.

His relationships with his colleagues were varied and peculiar. The faith his patients had in him made some of his colleagues uncomfortable. Postgraduate students enthusiastically sought him out for academic discussions, which angered some senior staff. Kamal never demanded superiority but received it by virtue of his knowledge. He never imposed his authority but had it by virtue of his principles. Most colleagues publicly respected him but privately disliked, despised, or even envied him. A few adored him.

Professional associations and organisations sought him out to deliver lectures or chair seminars and secured a place for him in the limelight. However, the spotlight didn't blind him. He saw himself as a crusader, a person with a mission. The ship of medical service, he said, was slowly sinking. Tiny holes created by unethical practises were causing it to take on water. He believed that he could warn those boarding the ship and inspire them to seal the holes. Audiences listened to what he said, nodded in approval, and applauded in appreciation. To respect Kamal was to acknowledge his values publicly. Who did what in their private lives didn't matter. How they appeared before the world was all that was important.

Over time, Kamal realised the futility of these talks. They served only to drive away the guilt for the guilty, to shelter them under an umbrella of ethics that made them feel secure in their wrongdoing. Kamal slowly cut back on his speaking engagements and turned to writing. Some of his research articles were published in an international journal of medical ethics. Rakesh remembered one article that was published in the student magazine:

Ours field experiences leaps of advancement in diagnostic and therapeutic knowledge. A million thanks to all those women and men who lived and died for their passion and gave us miraculous inventions and great discoveries. We the medical practitioners only operate the tools they invented. All we have done is learn how to use them, and sometimes we wholeheartedly accept the credit that others deserve. When we hold up a CT scan, we read what we see; we see what we learnt from Roentgen, Houndsfield, Gray, and other legends and we deliver treatment. The general public gives us disproportionate respect that we sometimes don't deserve at all. With respect comes responsibility. When we recognise this responsibility and practise with humility, we can attach the tag "noble" to our profession. Humility is not weakness but strength. Bow down to your patients in service like water flowing to the lowest point.

Enjoy the satisfaction of the healing that our tools deliver. Pass up gratitude and accolades.

Kamal's lecture added immense significance to this meeting for Rakesh. The article noted that it was to be held in the Dr Abdurrahman Auditorium on the university campus in Riyadh. He knew it would be inspiring and recharging, but it clashed with his duty hours.

* * *

Niranjan had reached the multipurpose hall ten minutes earlier. *How could a room serve as a badminton court, a basketball court, and now a medical lecture hall?* he thought. He looked up at the four seats on the dais and then turned to watch people trickle in. They sat in scattered groups and slowly filled the gaps between groups. Niranjan was happy to see a large number of Indian doctors in Saudi Arabia. He settled down with a few acquaintances. After the welcome speech, Dr Ibrahim got up to introduce the guest speaker. To anyone who had attended Trivandrum Medical College, Dr Kamal needed no introduction.

"It is a blessing for Dr Kamal to be with us today," Dr Ibrahim began. "He is the assistant professor in internal medicine at Trivandrum Medical College. He has devoted his career to teaching medicine and to re-establishing its fundamental values, which are showing signs of wear. He has always included ethics as a part of his curriculum. He has many national and international publications to his credit. Most of all, he's the most loved personality on the college campus, and we have become immensely rich by being his students." Trivandrum alumni forcefully applauded, and others in the audience followed, not knowing when to stop. The applause lasted for a long while.

Dr Kamal never dressed up for any occasion, and this was no different. He wore his normal dark trousers and light shirt one size too large. He greeted the crowd by joining his hands in the traditional namaste; he also gave the traditional Arabic greeting to acknowledge the land where he stood. Niranjan waited with impatient pleasure for him to begin his lecture.

When the applause finally died down, Kamal began, "How many of you sitting here joined the medical profession to serve humanity? How many of you became doctors solely for the glamour and money? How many of you consider money to be the by-product of your service? How many of you consider service the by-product of your earnings?"

It took courage to open the speech with such a frank question, thought Niranjan. But Dr Kamal just said what was on his mind as casually as he would ask a passerby for the time. He paused out of the habit of a teacher to invite responses. But he was met with silence.

After waiting a good length of time, he continued, "You all know your answers. That is the essence of today's lecture, *Medical Service at a Crossroads*.

"However, the profession is not in any way at a crossroads. That is a misnomer. A crossroads is a junction. When you approach one, you may be unsure in which direction to proceed. But we are not unsure, are we?" Again his question was met with silence. "We chose our way long ago, the day we stepped into that first class in medical school. You may hear in meetings and seminars that time have changed. True, times have changed. Science has leaped forwards faster than we could have comprehended. The medical field has made a magical ascent with great inventions and discoveries. The desire to reduce pain has led us to new and effective treatments. It seems everything in our field is new, but, dear friends, there is one thing that is not new. It's called values. There are no new values, and there are no old values. There are only values."

Niranjan hung on his every word; he never heard anything like this before. Medical school taught only about diseases of the body; values were never discussed, as if students would acquire them spontaneously or did not desire them. The first did not happen; the second was partly true.

"Let's look into the aetiology of today's malady. An artist who paints does so with devotion to his purpose. He doesn't have anything to prove or disprove in the process. He creates his art for himself and would go to any extent to carry out this purpose. Never once could deceit or impurity sneak in. An artist owes his allegiance more to what he does than to an end product, and this inevitably leads to a worthy outcome. He is simply what he does, not what others think of what he does. His passion is his identity.

"This beautiful truth," Kamal continued, "applies to any deed of passion, be it painting, music, sculpting, drama, or engineering. Now the question is: are we passionate about what we do? Those who do not ask themselves this will have difficulty uncovering the truth, and it is important to do so. Any profession performed without passion is worthless, and its product is bound to be rubbish. Left in that state, it stinks."

Niranjan sensed the stink suddenly in that auditorium, as if it followed him and the other doctors from the hospitals where they worked. He knew that, in their mental privacy, some in the audience would blame others, and others would search their souls.

Kamal went on, "Having the degree designations decorate our names doesn't make us doctors. These qualifications only tell you what to do. It's how you do it that concerns us today. Now let's get some facts straight. Do we owe anything to society or does society owe us?" Niranjan liked the question.

"We owe society," Dr Kamal said, raising his voice in purposeful vehemence.

"We owe everyone in society. We are showered with respect out of proportion to what we do and that we do not deserve. The fact is that we are in debt. By serving others, we repay it."

Niranjan's thoughts distracted him from the rest of the speech. When it was over, Niranjan approached Kamal and arranged an appointment for Rakesh to meet him at his hotel on the following day.

Niranjan now had a lot to think about. He had a passion for cardiology, but he felt like a boy who lost a kite because he wasn't holding the string tightly enough. Now that it was gone, he longed for it.

Chapter 6

It was December, and the weather turned cold. The intensity shook Rakesh as the heat on his arrival in the summer had. The wind shot arrows of cold deep into his body. He wore a heavy sweater with a tall turtleneck and still felt cold. Standing at the window, he aimlessly looked at the street below. Overcrowded shops serviced automobiles. Cars and trucks that needed attention added to the traffic chaos. Everything except the engine could be replaced there; anything could be changed for comfort or beauty. With stained overalls and greasy hands the mechanics laboured. These men, mostly Indians and Pakistanis, added luxury to these carriages. Rakesh wondered whether they made these improvements to their own lives or whether theirs were just skeletal carts with engines, the bare minimum to move. Some shops had flickering lights. The activity and colourful lights reminded Rakesh of a celebration, but he knew it only looked so. Like the unsure happiness of expats, it was only a display. Each labourer down there was toiling in the piercing cold on the pavement to build a cathedral for their dear ones who, miles away, were in the comfort of their homes secure with their monthly checks. What lay beneath the thin mask of happiness on these men's faces was evident to anyone who spoke to them with compassion. Rakesh had seen this in very many patients that visited him.

Across the lanes of another street, he saw a high-rise building growing. Hundreds of workers were scattered all over it, and from here, they looked like ants swarming a bottle of honey. At the building's nearest corner, Rakesh could make out some men bending wires. He saw their dirty, ill-fitting sweaters, their balaclavas under their hard hats, and their greasy gloves. They were working on the core of vertical concrete beams. *As kids, did they dream of doing this?* Rakesh wondered. Today they did this not out by choice but by necessity created by choices they had made along life's journey. The graph of their lives, slashed with dashed hopes and failed goals, finally evened into one horizontal line like a flat line on an ECG monitor, marking the adventureless quest for survival. Living had stopped but life continued. This pattern was common to thousands and thousands of expat labourers in the Middle East. They were stuck of doing what they were told to. Thinking was a luxury they could not afford. Happiness was a guest which visited them once a month and stayed only as long as the queue in the money-exchange centre. This pattern of life was glued to them like concrete stuck to their heavy gloves. It was possible but difficult to remove, and many feared removing it. They feared everything; even a cough or a cold worried them. Mild back pain upset them. They feared these were warning signs of more sinister conditions.

Rakesh looked at the other tall buildings in the neighbourhood. He tried to call to mind the men who had worked on them as if he knew them. Did the owners of these buildings or those who lived there know that it more than just concrete, tile, and pipes mixed, placed, and fixed? It was built in perfect harmony by thousands whose lives probably had no harmony. Rakesh didn't know why his thoughts had gone into this direction. The phone rang. It was Govardhan.

"Hello. Can I see you sometime today? Probably late evening. Nothing important, but we need to talk," Govardhan said.

Rakesh didn't find a free time that coincided with a free moment for Govardhan until 11.20 p.m. When Rakesh arrived at his office, Govardhan sat watching TV news. He was the only one on staff who had a TV in his office, evidence of his close relationship with the owner.

"Hi, Rakesh," Govardhan said, turning off the set. "It is getting so difficult to meet you these days. The American president is easier to reach." He punctuated this statement with his usual loud laugh.

Rakesh synthesised a reluctant smile. "I'm always around."

"Whenever I try to meet you, I'm told you have patients. The income from your clinic must be really high."

"I don't know," Rakesh responded with irritation. "Is it?"

"You should know that, Rakesh."

"I don't really keep track of that."

"You should." Now Govardhan was getting irritated.

"What for?"

"Come on, Rakesh, that's your barometer of success that you can use to impress the management."

"No one told me that when I started here," Rakesh said with a sarcastic smile.

"Come on. Every doctor should know this."

"My only barometer is the quality of my service."

"That is a wonderful policy," Govardhan conceded, sensing the conversation taking a cold twist. "The reason I wanted to see you is because you are like my brother, and it disturbs me when I hear accusations about you."

"Accusations?" Rakesh said plainly with an amused smile.

"Well, you don't have to take them seriously, but I thought you should be aware of them."

"Aware of what?" Rakesh's smile broadened.

Govardhan looked annoyed. It was clear he wanted to see a troubled expression on Rakesh's face so he could erase it. Rakesh denied him that pleasure unintentionally.

"Look, Rakesh, we are all away from our homes and families for a specific purpose, and that purpose comes from the pay cheque that management gives us."

"Management doesn't give it to us; we earn it," Rakesh corrected him.

"In a way, you are right."

"I am right in every way."

"Regardless, we should respect management's view. At the end of the day, this is their establishment."

Rakesh was consciously aware that Govardhan had not spilt the beans about the accusations yet. Instead he was weaving a conversational web around and around the issue. Rakesh sensed that Govardhan had difficulty relaying the message and was looking for the right time. For Rakesh to ask about it out of impatience, out of puzzled guilt, but Rakesh wouldn't give that to him.

"Management should be happy with us," Govardhan pressed.

"That's true."

"So we should try to keep them happy."

"That will be the natural by-product of our service," Rakesh responded.

"Most often it is, but not always." A look in Govardhan's eyes told Rakesh that he sensed the time to deliver his message was approaching.

"That's interesting," commented Rakesh, taking the edge away.

Govardhan looked uncomfortable now. He was losing his dominance. He finally came out with it: "Look, Rakesh, I have had complaints that you are ignoring patients when you are at the books."

He went on to explain that Moideen, the manager, wasn't excited about Rakesh's attempt at the exam. The staff, Moideen felt, were hired from their home country to serve the hospital. Nothing more, nothing less. Preparation for an exam did not tally with this concept. It was clear to Rakesh that in his imagination, he saw Rakesh focussing on studies and so he must be ignoring patients. That would make patients unhappy, and the clinic's income would steadily decline. He wanted to nip the problem in the bud. Moideen had had this bullet in his gun when he met with Rakesh a few days earlier. He failed to pull the trigger then, and concentrated instead on niceties. Now he had given the gun to Govardhan.

"Dr Govardhan, how often do you refer patients to the government hospital?" Rakesh asked.

"Not regularly. It depends on the situation."

Rakesh controlling the conversation was the last thing Govardhan would have wanted. Rakesh knew he didn't have to say much to control the discussion. Govardhan's displeasure grew with each passing minute. It was nearing midnight when Govardhan took back control.

"Rakesh, studying is fine, but it can't be done on hospital time."

"Is that it? Don't worry; I'll take care of it." Saying this, Rakesh left.

Govardhan felt miserably silly, like he had missed a winning goal shot from close range with no goalkeeper or defender. His vague dislike for Rakesh was getting less vague. But Govardhan has his ways of winning.

* * *

Rakesh managed to leave his shift a bit early to join Dr Kamal at his hotel for lunch. The hotel was about twenty minutes' drive from the clinic, and he went down to catch a cab. He let a couple go by and finally hailed one with an Indian driver. The cab driver was short and sat propped up on a big cushion. He spoke more with his body than with his mouth.

"Yes, Sir. Where to?"

"Hotel Black Pearl."

"The fee will be twenty-five riyals," the driver said.

"Okay." Rakesh settled in the front seat and fastened his seat belt as the driver changed gears and rolled on. The driver wore an undisciplined beard like an untrimmed coniferous hedge. Its salt-and-pepper colour spoke of his years in the desert land.

"What is your name?" Rakesh asked.

"Karam Dev. People call me Devji."

"Where are you from?"

"Uttar Pradesh."

"And how long have you been here?"

Devji laughed. "I don't know. Maybe eighteen years? No, it is around twenty. No, I think it's almost twenty-two years now. It doesn't matter to me anyway. A day is marked when I hit the bed. A year is marked when it's time to renew my ID card. Nothing much happens in between." Devji tried to whistle an old Mohammed Rafi song. It seemed to be an act of happiness which was not happy.

"What about your family?"

"I haven't met my family for the last five years. My father used to work in Saabs land, but he is too old now. Mother still goes to a wheat farm for a part-time job. She doesn't have to with the money I send, but she feels empty without it."

"Are you married?"

He glanced at Rakesh, clapped his hands, and giggled loudly. "Brilliant question."

Rakesh was worried, as Devji's hands were off the wheel.

"You think I look like an eligible bachelor?"

Rakesh didn't understand the meaning of that question and was unsure if he had been too nosy.

"Marriages are meant for engineers and people like you. No one wants us old and cold drivers. Not girls, not even my parents. Many years ago I worked as a company driver in a factory in Buraidah and went home every year for vacation. Those days life had hope and meaning. My homecoming was loaded with excitement and gifts. One of those days I did meet a girl from my village. I liked her. Her parents liked me. But she didn't like my height. That was the only time I thought about marriage.

"The only time.... Slowly annual vacations lost their charm. It had become an empty ritual. My parents never inquired about my life or attempted to find me a girl. So I only went home every three or four years, and now I think it's almost five years since I was last there."

"Do you still talk to your parents?"

"Well, I send money regularly, and when that's delayed by two weeks, I get a letter, maybe to check if I'm alive."

"I'm sorry, Devji. I didn't mean to remind you of your pains."

Devji let out the same loud giggle. Rakesh knew it was nothing but an audible expression of the pain.

At a stoplight, Devji pulled out a passport snap from his wallet. "This is me when I first came here."

The photo was worn, with wrinkles and tears at the edges. The picture did not in any way resemble the bearded guy sitting next to Rakesh. The photo showed the vibrancy of youth in full fury. Devji waited for Rakesh to say something.

"Have a clean shave and you will look the same," Rakesh finally said.

Devji laughed violently and underscored it with

another clap. His laughter was contagious, and Rakesh joined him, and reason washed away. Devji continued till his eyes were watering. Afterwards they sat in silence till they reached the hotel. Devji stopped a little away from the entrance, and it was evident that he wanted to speak.

"Now, Dr Saab, tell me something about you. We are almost to your destination. Sorry if I bored you. Dr Saab, this is my phone number. If you want to go anywhere, ring me the previous day after midnight."

"Yes, I will." Rakesh paid the fair and handed him five riyals extra, but he refused. Rakesh could see a moist glow in Devji's eyes as he said goodbye.

"Dr Saab, always listen to your heart, or else…"

And he rolled on.

Rakesh went into the hotel, spoke to the person at the desk, and took a seat at the coffee shop in the lobby. Just as he opened a travel magazine, Dr Kamal arrived. Rakesh was surprised at the vitality in his face. It was as if he had completely deceived the passage of time. Too much stressful work can accelerate the ageing process, yet here stood a man who was proof of the reverse. They shook hands, squeezing with both hands. Neither man spoke for a few minutes. They only exchanged acknowledging smiles, each looking at something unseen and back at each other. That something was probably hidden in their joint memory of their days at the medical college. One had been a teacher, the other a student, but the ideals they shared closed whatever distance existed between them.

"Rakesh, I'm happy to see you after a long time. How is it for you here?" Dr Kamal said.

"It's not what I wanted in life, but it provides me

a launching pad. I'm not happy in my current job but happy I got it. I only need to hold on till May."

"Oh yes. Niranjan did mention your exams."

"He also said your speech was great as usual. I heard you took some privately managed hospitals to task."

"Well, not precisely, but what my audience infers is always beyond me. Tell me about your news."

"Sir, I don't feel I should bother you with the details of my position. It's not something to rejoice in. It's the system."

"Rakesh, it's never the system, it's the people in the system," Dr Kamal reassured him.

"I am supposed to be a team player, part of a symphony, or something like that, but I am not. I don't like the music it generates. It's not music. But I have to be there. It's a pain and a pleasure. A pain because the management's philosophy contradicts everything I believe about medical practise. A pleasure, as it is fun to see all of the unseen and undiscussed parts that sum up what this hospital is about."

"Now, Rakesh, you should realise that in any fight, if your weapon is integrity, you will be the one who has mental harmony. It's like what artists say about colours. When the hue of your character is strong, it influences the canvas; if it's weak, the surrounding colours will drown yours out. Most people have weak characters; they're devoid of any individuality. They don't live, they survive. They don't radiate their values; instead they imbibe others' lack of values. You don't have to fight the system or the people who run it. Simply remain uninfluenced. If you are a musical note, stand apart from the chorus. Allow yourself to be supported only by the invisible strand of unyielding integrity. Then, even the discord in the symphony becomes soothing. It may not be to the conductor, but it will be to those you serve, your patients."

Rakesh loved to listen to Kamal's unique way of expressing his views on life.

"The words *ethics* and *values* are sometimes like pictures of beautiful women in ads," Kamal went on. "They're designed only to attract. Beyond that, they don't exist."

Rakesh very much agreed with this comparison and said that it described what was happening in his hospital.

As always, Rakesh realised, Kamal got straight to the heart of the issue. They never had to slog through layer upon layer of polite nothings to get there. Speaking directly was not rude here but the way they spoke most comfortably. They spoke as if they met every day and picked up where they had left off the previous day, only it had been years since they had last seen each other. Kamal's presence had a strangely positive power, Rakesh felt. It was as if he walked inside a huge bubble of energy that those close to him could feel.

"Your friend Johnson is here," said Kamal.

"The dentist?"

"Yes, Johnson from the Rhythm group."

"Where is he?"

"He was at my talk. I can't recollect the name of his hospital, but I have his number."

"Oh, that's fantastic. I haven't seen or heard him for a while."

"Your friend Niranjan met me after Johnson left or I would have connected you straight away."

"I'm so excited to have Johnson around."

"I heard something about him."

"He is simply too human. An extinct attribute of humanity today," Rakesh mused.

"Why do you say that? Especially now?" inquired Kamal.

"I was told he delivers food to many prisoners here."

"Really? I'm not surprised by that."

Johnson was Rakesh's contemporary at university, but he was in the dental school. Johnson was rebellious. He never joined a mainstream college political group. Instead, he and a few like-minded friends formed their own organisation called Rhythm to expose anything that didn't synchronise with virtuous social rhythm. Rhythm had many intimate friends and enemies. Both provided a sense of accomplishment in equal measures. Their membership was small but strongly committed. Every semester they conducted a debate on current issues concerning the medical profession. These debates became popular partly because of the vibrant topics and partly because it was often chaired by popular literary figures. Rakesh participated during his third year. The topic was "Why are doctors arrogant?" The views he expressed earned him Johnson's friendship. They soon realised more similarities in what they believed, and their bond grew.

"Arrogance is the twin brother of ignorance," Rakesh said in his speech. "Arrogance is weakness used to distance others and to mask ignorance. Some teachers are rude to students and some doctors are to patients. They create a barrier through which questions, doubts, and concerns can't reach them. With it, they guard their authority. How many of you sitting here have ever gone up to a big head to ask a question? That proves my point." Rakesh concluded his speech there.

Teachers were not allowed at Rhythm meetings. This kept the discussion frank and open. However, ripples extended to every faculty on the campus. Arrogance was not perceived as authority, but a shameful mask of ignorance.This accusational tag to some extend helped eliminate such a human attribute. For the first time, Rhythm not only exposed a problem but also found a solution.

"Johnson is still the same," commented Kamal as Rakesh came back from the past.

* * *

Chapter 7

Rakesh walked into Moideen's office, as he had been summoned. It was unusual to see Govardhan there. Govardhan rarely went to someone else's office or clinic, distancing himself to magnify his superiority. Rakesh was unsure of the purpose of this meeting. He sat opposite Moideen with an amused smile still on his face. Moideen and Govardhan exchanged whispers.

"How's your clinic?" Moideen said, turning to Rakesh.

"As usual. Doing well, I suppose."

"I hate to discuss this with you, but the protocol demands it," Govardhan said. "I tried to avoid this a few weeks ago, if you recall."

Rakesh couldn't remember the meeting exactly, but he was sure that he'd hear the message soon enough. Moideen dispensed with his usual smile, puffed himself up, and fiddled with the cigarette lighter on the desk.

"Dr Rakesh, you have a great future ahead of you," Moideen said. That sounded hollow coming from an ex-police constable who had never gone to college and who by a bizarre twist of fate had become a hospital manager, Rakesh thought. "You shouldn't ruin your future."

"Well, I don't think I am," Rakesh replied.

"That's exactly your problem, the way you think. You have been employed to serve the patients. You work for the hospital for the twelve hours you're on duty. Those twelve hours do not belong to you."

Rakesh patiently listened, waiting for him to deliver the final punch. Govardhan screwed up his face in an attempt to look deeply concerned. "I have a responsibility towards you, as I brought you here, and I want you to get the best treatment."

People in power do not say what they mean. The greater the power, the greater the deception, Rakesh thought.

"We had some complaints that you tend to delay seeing patients and that you sometimes even ignore them when you are preparing for exams," Govardhan continued.

Rakesh remained silent. His face was blank, showing no shock or fear, as those across the table likely expected. He was calm. They were expecting an answer, a denial, a justification. He said nothing. He just sat and stared at Moideen and Govardhan. It was like one circuit that misfired in a planned and rehearsed electric programme, the only one possibility that was not anticipated. He could see uncertainty in their eyes. Govardhan and Moideen likely desired many reactions, but not this calmness.

Rakesh knew that Govardhan was a cheat the day he landed in Saudi Arabia. This episode simply proved it. Beyond that, Rakesh didn't see any implications to this discussion. It was like watching a roadside brawl but not getting involved. Moideen and Govardhan were on one side and the truth was on the other side.

Cheating was not acceptable to Rakesh. It used to make him hysterical even if he wasn't a victim of it. In school, if he sensed a foul play during a game, he couldn't keep his mouth shut. This made him his classmates' punching bag more than once, but even their assaults didn't silence him.

Once in grade four, a group of boys was playing with matchbox pictures, a children's version of playing cards with pictures on them. The game was a blend of bluff and flash. The aim of the game was to win the most pictures by guessing. The game took up most of recess time. Once, Lother lost a round and had to pay Gilbert sixty pictures. Rakesh had seen Lother add blank papers cut to same size as the cards to the pile of remaining pictures. He gave the pile, including the blanks, to Gilbert. Gilbert shoved them into his bag, excited in his victory. Rakesh screamed and told everyone what he had seen. Next thing he knew, Lother was hitting Rakesh in the face with a closed fist and an open palm. He pulled Rakesh's shirt, tearing a few button holes and his tie. Blood dripped from Rakesh's nose.

Rakesh shouted, "You are a cheat and a liar!" Lother delivered a few more blows. Other boys circled around to watch the fight, entertained and surprised. They were surprised because no one stood up to or spoke against Lother. He was big and strong, and his size and strength had earned him a notorious reputation.

Rakesh lay in a heap.

"You're father is a cheat too!" Rakesh yelled. Lother continued his assault. Pain and anger grew in

Rakesh. First the pain diluted the anger, and then the anger diluted the pain. He firmly resolved not to give in to the physical superiority of those morally inferior to him.

Lother's anger was peaking, but he grew tired and fed up, and he walked away. Rakesh, bloody and bruised, called after him, "Lother, it's not your fault. You were born to rotten animals. That is why you act like one."

Lother saw that Rakesh had infinite resolve and unwavering determination. Gilbert had already left, but that didn't matter to Rakesh, for he was not standing up for Gilbert, he was only standing up against Lother. Lother tasted humiliation for the first time, for he had never been defeated in a fight. Rakesh's mental power had overcome Lother's brute strength. Only after all the other students had gone back to their respective classes at the bell did Rakesh notice the extent of the injuries and felt their pain.

But this new accusation did not induce the anger in him. Instead he felt sympathy. He had learnt to refine his reaction, and his smile clearly worried his accusers. He did not fight, for there was no enemy to fight, and that multiplied the insult to Moideen and Govardhan. But Rakesh didn't mean to insult anyone. He simply knew that the accusations were untrue. They only deserved ridicule.

"Doc, what do you say to this?" Moideen said.

"I have no comments to make," Rakesh said calmly.

"What do you mean?"

"I mean exactly what I said."

"Don't you think you should take responsibility for your actions?" Moideen said.

"Well, I do," Rakesh responded.

"I don't want to prolong this meeting, so I'll just tell you: don't misuse hospital facilities and your time at the clinic for your personal goals," Dr Govardhan said.

Moideen echoed Govardhan's point with a nod.

"I haven't done that, and I don't intend to."

"But the reports tell a different story," Govardhan said.

"I don't base my work on others' reports and views."

"Dr Rakesh, sometimes in life you have to," Moideen chipped in.

"Yes, I agree, I will listen only to the views of those who are morally qualified to voice them."

Moideen looked shocked. He clearly couldn't fathom what that statement conveyed, but he interpreted sarcasm in Rakesh's words. Rakesh hadn't intended that. Govardhan looked as though he had been directly insulted.

"Look, Rakesh, I too read to keep up-to-date, but I never disturb the system in any measure when I do so. If we get anymore such complaints, we may be forced to take action," Govardhan said firmly.

Rakesh maintained his peculiar smile as he listened to this, and then he said, "I am afraid you will not be able to do that if you base your actions on facts."

"Don't see us as the enemies," Moideen said. "We are only trying to warn and protect you. When this information gets to Hussain, we can't predict the consequences."

"Thank you for your concern, but you don't have to worry about me. I think I can handle myself," Rakesh responded.

"Okay, let's wind up. Rakesh, I hope the message is very clear," Moideen said finally.

"It was very clear on the first day I came here," replied Rakesh. Govardhan knew what he meant. Rakesh was annoyed. He did not understand their motive. It left an unpleasant taste in his mouth which he knew would linger for quite some time.

Rakesh thought back to his first job in Mavoor in Calicut district soon after his internship. He had received the job offer through a medical representative. It was for an immediate appointment as a duty medical officer in a fifty-bed private hospital. The medical director, Dr Soorya, was also the owner. No one knew which university he had received his medical training from, and he hadn't touched a medical book since graduating. He was a shrewd businessman who built this establishment and ran it successfully. He had bought it for peanuts from an ageing doctor and changed the way things were done. He talked and walked as though he was well updated academically, but he tactfully avoided treating patients who had cases more serious than the common cold. A physician and a surgeon, the functional pillars of Devamatha Hospital, assisted him. Rakesh met Dr Soorya for the interview, and they discussing the conditions and terms of employment, or, more precisely, Dr Soorya told Rakesh what they were. Dr Soorya had a puzzling look. He had a huge pot belly that implied prosperity and baldness that did not convey authority.

"We perform here like a family. There are no individuals here, only a team. We expect you to be well integrated into it."

Rakesh didn't bother to untangle what that meant and was not even sure whether there was anything to untangle. He joined the staff two days later. On his third working day, he received a memo with a list of drugs available in the hospital store which should be given preference whilst writing prescriptions. Rakesh saw this memo as nothing abnormal or against his principles, particularly because the policy wasn't enforced. Because it said that these drugs should only be "given preference", he wrongly thought that he still had the freedom to prescribe what he chose.

The amoxicillin dispensed at the hospital store came from a disreputable no-name company, so Rakesh preferred to prescribe alternatives. On his sixth day on the job at noon, Dr Soorya walked into Rakesh's clinic.

"Have you not read the memo regarding drugs?" Dr Soorya yelled.

Rakesh was shocked by the sudden intrusion and his boss's volume. Rakesh looked down at his tie, which now looked more like a noose.

"Yes," Rakesh responded quietly.

"Well, then, stick to it," Dr Soorya shouted.

"Dr Soorya, the amoxicillin here, I don't think—"

"You don't have to think; we do the thinking for you," Soorya interrupted. "You just work as a part of the system. Is that clear?"

Soorya looked like a wrestler in the final round. His eyes bulged and his forehead glowed with perspiration. When Rakesh didn't answer, he said even more loudly, "Are you following what I just said?"

"Well, I'm not sure," Rakesh responded.

"You better be sure." He turned and slammed the door behind him. Soon afterwards, two nurses entered, giggling quietly. They seemed to have overheard.

"This is a regular scene here," one of them said. "He sometimes behaves like the ringmaster in a circus. Just take it in your stride," she said.

Though Rakesh had said he wasn't sure, he was very sure. At five o'clock that the evening after seeing his last patient, he went to his quarters packed his bag, and took the bus to Calicut. Next morning when he hadn't arrived after ten, there was a commotion. The patients grew impatient. At about eleven, a telegram arrived addressed to Dr Soorya:

Dear Sir,

You may please appoint someone who can surrender his ability to think.

Thank you,
Dr Rakesh

The job at Devamatha Hospital had been only a job, but here at Farooqia, it was the tunnel to his dream.

Chapter 8

It was just another busy day, and as usual, Rakesh was engaged in medical acrobatics. He sensed an increase in patients recently. Jabber, the receptionist, had mentioned that some patients, even those who did not have orthopaedic complaints, had specifically asked for him,. The waiting area outside his office was rarely empty. He developed speedy patient management, and Judy efficiently helped him in that. Management watched the activity in Rakesh's office with secret satisfaction, but they wished he ordered more tests. They also did not approve of his UK examination plans and preparations. Until recently, Dr Govardhan had been the leader both in the number of patients he treated and in the revenue he generated. He most often cooked up some story to give the figures away at the dinner table. He complained about the long, tiring day and the number of patients he saw to reaffirm his role as leader in the hospital's success. The commission he pocketed from unnecessary tests was commonly known. But recently, there had been a decline in Govardhan's patients. He angrily rang Jabber.

"Why do you send my old patients to Rakesh?" Govardhan yelled over the phone.

Jabber answered with suppressed cheer, "I never do that unless a patient specifically requests to be seen by Rakesh."

Govardhan wasn't happy about this. He never accepted defeat.

"Doc, your next patient is an elderly man," Judy said this with a smile that meant something Rakesh couldn't decipher.

"What's so funny about it?" he asked

"Do you know Cyril?"

"I don't think so."

Judy approached him and whispered in his ear with a tinge of triumph, "Cyril and his whole family have been Dr Govardhan's patients the whole time I've been here, and now he has specifically asked Jabber to see you."

"I see."

"That would upset Govardhan," Judy said, still smiling.

"I don't think we should bother about that."

Judy's smile widened when Rakesh said "we".

"Well, I'm just informing you." Judy let Cyril enter.

"Hello, Doctor. How are you? I am Cyril." He settled in the patient's chair.

"I wanted to get your advice about my daughter. For about six months, she's been treated by your colleague, Dr Govardhan, and I feel a second opinion is appropriate. Her condition started as an ache in the right knee. Dr Govardhan has prescribed different medications and done different tests, but her condition didn't change much, and in the past few days, the pain has gotten worse and her movement has been restricted. Can I bring her to you?"

"Yes, that's not a problem," Rakesh said, "but I would prefer to discuss the case with Dr Govardhan first."

"Well, I prefer that she not see him, if you don't mind."

"Okay," Rakesh relented. "Bring her in tomorrow at six o'clock. In the meantime, I'll review her file and radiographs. Has she already had X-rays?"

"Yes. She had one when she first came in and another two months later. Govardhan said they were all normal, but the condition isn't improving."

Rakesh wrote him an appointment slip to give to Judy, and Judy put it in the diary.

"Your next patient is Cyril," Judy reminded Rakesh the next day with the excitement of having got a front seat to watch a favourite play. This consultation was the first sign of triumph of virtue over vice, of efficiency over inefficiency, of excellence over mediocrity, of everything good over everything bad. She couldn't hide her joy.

"Am I developing a sense of possessiveness?" she asked herself. This puzzling question popped up in her joyous confusion. *This is not a thought that should be nurtured*, she told herself, *for a multitude of reasons*.

"Can I call him in?" she asked Rakesh.

"Okay, I'm ready," he responded. She left his office, and in a few minutes, Cyril entered with a young woman.

"Good morning, Doctor," Cyril said. "This is my daughter, Cynthia."

"Hello. How are you, Cynthia?" Rakesh greeted here.

She responded with a shy smile.

"I would like you to give me the whole story from the beginning."

Cynthia looked younger than seventeen, which was the age on her chart. Her face looked sad but brightened when she smiled. Cynthia and her father narrated the history of her case, starting with the sudden pain she felt at school during physical education class. Rakesh asked questions to fill in the missing links in the story.

"Govardhan treated her," continued Cyril, "with different medications, and although they offered temporary relief, nothing helped in the end."

Rakesh examined Cynthia's knee and other joints. "I don't think there is anything seriously wrong, but I need to take some pictures."

"But Dr Govardhan has already taken two sets of X-rays," Cyril complained.

"Well, I'm sorry, but I could not trace the films, so we need to take a new one. I'll see you again once they're ready."

As they left the office, Rakesh rang the cash counter and requested that they not charge for Cynthia's radiograph. When Rakesh told Judy of this, her face showed her gratification. She and Rakesh said nothing further, and she called the next patient.

❖ ❖ ❖

The injection room and the lab were two adjoining parts of the same corner room on the first floor, and each had its own entrance. Most treatment procedures, such as dressings, drainage of abscesses, and local excisions happened in the injection room. Nurses also gathered there to chat. The lab was always busy, and occasionally its activities overflowed into the injection room. The nurses' lunchtime was noon to one o'clock, but work didn't stop, and the nurses had no dedicated place to eat.

"Where do I have lunch?" Neerja said to no one in particular as she entered the injection room.

"When the crowd of patients subsides, we have it in here," replied Sister Shoshamma.

"You mean you dine in the same room that you handle infected blood and sputum?" Neerja replied.

"That corner is clean," Shoshamma said, pointing to the far end of the countertop. "It's okay for all of us."

"Shoshamma, it's not okay for me," Neerja said.

Shoshamma and the two other nurses in the room froze, their eyes widening in surprise, their mouths agape. No one addressed Shoshamma by her first name, and no one expressed disapproval at their improvised canteen. Everyone called Shoshamma Sister Shoshamma or Mrs Abraham or simply Sister, but never Shoshamma alone. Neerja looked confused. Rita, the lab technician, broke the silence.

"We've always had lunch here, and we're comfortable doing so."

"But are there no other rooms?" Neerja pressed.

The other nurses' displeasure at the frankness of this new recruit on her very first day was evident. Shoshamma composed herself and said in her most authoritative voice, "Look, Neerja, you are new and you do not yet know how we do things here. It's advisable that you act as part of the team and follow the system."

Shoshamma, being the most senior both in age and position, served as guardian of the nurses under her. She had allies and enemies amongst the nursing staff. She often implied that she was very close to Moideen and Hussain and had influence with them, but that was not entirely true. She never supported or brought up any issue that would even faintly be against the management's interest.

"Earning our monthly salaries should be our only objective," she had often said to her colleagues. "If you encounter any obstacle, challenge, or even insult, ignore it." This was her philosophy. Accommodating Neerja's request for a separate place to eat was not permissible, and Neerja had been insubordinate to even make such a request.

"We can provide more space for you," Shoshamma said to pacify her.

"Sorry, I can't eat here," Neerja said firmly. "I will speak to the manager." She took her lunchbox and left. No one had done this before. Nurses never went to Moideen or to anyone to complain. They silently accepted any orders and rules. Changes in shifts, shuffling of clinic assignments, extensions of duty hours, even the requirements or withholding of overtime – they accepted everything in stride. The entire staff, doctors included, accepted such changes with outward enthusiasm, even if they were internally reluctant. The result was the mindless obedience. Anyone who acted otherwise didn't last long. Rational or rebellious thoughts found an outlet only in whispers and gossip amongst very close friends. Neerja's request showed disloyalty and arrogance to the others. For Neerja this was an uncomplicated issue that had to be addressed. When she returned at one o'clock, the silence in the clinic was palpable. No one inquired after the outcome, assuming she would be embarrassed.

The next day at noon when she took out her lunchbox, she announced, "If anyone wants to join me for lunch, I'm having it in the conference room."

"The conference room?" everyone said in a wave of astonished murmurs. Shoshamma tried to appear casual, but her expression deceived her.

"How did you manage that?" Preetha asked.

"There was nothing much to manage," Neerja replied confidently. "I asked the manager for a private and clean place to eat, and he offered the conference room."

Neerja couldn't figure out why everyone was so shocked. Nothing much puzzled her.Either she knew it or she didn't.There was nothing much in between. She was the only child of a confused father, and she thoroughly enjoyed school but not books. She hung around with boys more than girls and was mischievously playful. Some of her companions called her Neeraj, which she liked and even wished were her name. Her teachers disapproved of her preference for boyish activities, such as climbing trees, playing football, and playing kabaddi. Once she was suspended from school for three days for having stolen coconuts from trees on campus along with a group of boys in her class. The boys were suspended for only two days, and she objected to the double standard. One her third day of suspension, she went to class. Her teacher reported her unauthorised entry into school, and the principal came to class. He told her to go home. When Neerja asked why, the principal replied, "Because you are a girl."

Neerja asked him, "How many days would you suspend our teacher if she stole coconuts?" The whole class, and even the teacher, laughed. Eventually the principal was laughing too. She never knew if he took shelter in that commotion. She didn't even know what the joke was.

She loved watching work at construction sites. She could sit endlessly and stare at the labourers piling, drilling, and pouring concrete. The obedience of Earth to the power of man and machine delighted her. The effortless bending of huge steel rods by the power of the human brain fascinated her. Her parents thought she would become an engineer, but she never overcame her dislike for books. At the compulsion of her missionary father, she trained in nursing. Her four years in nursing school transformed her from a tomboy into a beautiful young lady, thanks to the growth spurt that carved a splendid job.

* * *

Chapter 9

By the middle of March, the weather showed signs of early summer. Rakesh had rushed to a nearby mall to pick up a birthday gift for his brother to be sent with a friend flying to India that night, and he arrived for his evening shift a bit late. As he crossed the lobby and passed reception, he saw people standing around an elderly man who was visibly in severe pain, groaning loudly and intensely and grasping another man's arm to his chest. The people's muddy boots and dirty clothes indicated that they had come straight from a construction site.

"What's this?" Rakesh asked Jabber, the receptionist.

"We have called for the ambulance."

"Has anyone here seen him?"

Jabber whispered loudly, "Moideen told us to call an ambulance to get him to the central hospital as quickly as possible."

"Does Moideen know what's happening here?" Rakesh said, raising his voice.

Jabber got up and approached Rakesh. "It was Dr Govardhan who made the decision to send him to the central hospital. It is very risky situation, so Dr Govardhan advised that we should get him elsewhere before anything happens. Moideen then told me to arrange for the ambulance."

Jabber's tone belied his displeasure at the order. His position didn't permit him to disobey orders, but his conscience told him otherwise. Rakesh darted into the human circle that had grown as he spoke to Jabber. He fired a few questions at the man who now was sweating and said his pain was worsening.

"Jabber, get him into the observation room," ordered Rakesh.

"But what about the CMO's order?"

"Damn that spineless man. Do as I say," he commanded. The order was purposeful and clear and delivered with sufficient volume to quash any resistance. "Get one nurse right now and also page Dr Tajudeen."

Jabber was taken aback for a moment but quickly altered his disposition. An adrenaline rush propelled him to carry out Rakesh's order. He was urged on by Rakesh's recognition of him not only as a receptionist but also as a human being. He announced over the PA system, "Code blue, code blue in observation. Nurse Richa to attend."

If violating protocol was like cutting down trees, then that overhead announcement was the last tree Jabber felled. He had now disobeyed the CMO, acted against the decision of the manager, and taken orders from someone who had a rift in his relationship with management.

As the patient was wheeled to observation, Rakesh

took a quick history: his name was Ramdas, fifty-nine years old, a crane operator in Saudi for seventeen years, hypertensive, not on medication, a heavy smoker, complaining of chest pain at the job site a few minutes prior. This was his first episode. His family was back in Tirunelveli.

Dr Govardhan was the main policymaker, he had told Hussain with emphasis at a formal meeting in his first few years at the hospital.

"The reputation of a hospital hangs by a thread: all the goodwill that we build through collective commitment and hard work can be tarnished by one stroke. This can come from a single casualty. We don't have the facilities or infrastructure to manage medical emergencies, particularly life-threatening ones. Death has no designated location. In government hospitals, it is accepted as the inevitable sequelae of certain illnesses. In private hospitals, it is always caused by avoidable negligence. Such a black mark on a hospital's reputation can never be completely erased. In a field as fiercely competitive as ours, that would be the best possible weapon our competitors could use against us. So don't touch any emergency patients. Send them packing straight away."

This argument made complete sense to the management, and it then became the hospital's policy. Between this sense and policy Govardhan craftfully buried his incomptetence.

"Only one bystander. All others out, please," ordered Richa who was already in observation when the others arrived. Neerja joined them without being called. She quickly blended into the scene. Richa was a bit slow to meet demands, but Neerja's speed and precision complemented Richa's shortcomings.

"Give him glyceryl trinitrate spray," Rakesh said.

"No spray available," responded Neerja.

"Okay, give him sublingual tabs, then, and put him on oxygen, five litres. Where is Tajudeen?"

"It's his day off," Neerja said, "but Jabber contacted him."

Moideen joined the crowd outside the room. Rakesh didn't acknowledge him and Jabber purposefully avoided him. Moideen was stranded outside like a schoolkid whose parents had been called in to discuss his poor report card with his teacher.

"The ambulance is here. What do we do?" Jabber said to Rakesh with the sharpness of a loyal subordinate.

"Tell them we are stabilising the patient. I want Tajudeen's opinion regarding transfer."

"Okay," Jabber said, and sped out to the ambulance and told them to stand by. Soon after, the phone rang at reception. "Doc, Tajudeen's on the phone," Jabber called out.

Rakesh picked up the phone and gave Tajudeen a brief summary.

"Keep him on observation," Tajudeen said. "Do an ECG, and I'll be there in less than an hour."

"Can I send the ambulance away?"

"If he's stable, yes."

As an expression of calm slowly returned to Ramdas's face, Neerja removed his dirty boots, a task that most of the nurses would have left for those who accompanied the patient. Happiness in that room was an emotion pasted only on one face and that was Neerja. To smile when someone was in pain may have been inappropriate, but it provided comfort to everyone in the room. Rakesh ran further tests and determined that the GTN and oxygen were doing the job.

The next day, the incident over, Rakesh tried to study but couldn't read a line. He had never felt this way before. He felt helpless. The management's ineptitude frustrated him. Fortunately there were no patients waiting to be seen. He put his head down on the opened Guyton's *Textbook of Medical Physiology* on his desk. Judy came in and silently sat on the corner of the desk, aware of his pain. Jabber hadn't come on duty that evening, and he was not in his apartment. He hadn't mentioned any travel plans or requested leave from any of his colleagues, including Shankar, with whom he shared his room. He had been on duty till ten the previous night, but at four in the afternoon today, he was missing. What had happened was obvious, but that he should disappear without a trace was mystifying. The only person who would know where he was was Moideen, but he had taken a week's leave to Jeddah. Govardhan would probably know, too, but it was certain he would not give that information out. This was a victory for Govardhan and a frightening lesson for those who acted according to their own decisions, a warning to those who disregarded authority. Rakesh knew that any encounter with Govardhan at this point, even a courteous one, would make him blow his top, and it was not yet time. He felt terrible for Jabber, as he had stood by him to save a patient. In any other hospital Jabber would have been lauded for his exemplary work beyond his specified role, but here he was punished. *If anyone should be punished, it should be me and not Jabber. He only did as he was instructed*, thought Rakesh.

"Why don't you call Jeddah?" Judy said, blinking back tears. Judy had called Jeddah a few times already but got the same answer each time: "Moideen is not here."

As news of Jabber's disappearance made its way around, the gloom spread. Most of the employees were aware by now of what had happened. Khalidbhai had spread the story of what Rakesh and Jabber did, spicing it up with his own imagination, sensationalising their anti-management act. Most of the nursing and paramedical staff received this news with silent envy and suppressed appreciation. . For many it was like watching 'Enter the Dragon'. A sudden sense of victory; of the strong against the nasty – a victory to which they too belonged, or wished to belong, or could not belong. for some it was like reading a leaders struggle for freedom; an elated sense of comradeship – of being a part of that struggle, of a voice that was louder than the vice; only that it wasn't their voice – their thoughts were never voiced. It was always only thoughts. But now Jabber's disappearance further silenced the silent and suppressed them further.

In the lab, Shoshamma said, "See? I told you all many, many times: stick to doing what you're told. Be obedient to the one who pays you or you'll suffer Jabber's fate."

"But where is he?" said Neerja, the only one who was still brave enough to be loud.

"Ask Dr Govardhan," Shoshamma replied sarcastically.

Neerja ignored the sarcasm and decided to meet with Govardhan.

❖ ❖ ❖

It was not freshness or restlessness but an ill-defined sense of nearing an accomplishment that clouded Rakesh's thoughts as the clock ticked five in the morning. He went closer to the window and watched the slow birth of the day. An orange hue rose in the darkness far beyond the horizon of buildings. Rakesh had always been a night owl. The serene calmness of the night stimulated his creativity and ability to learn. He remembered Hotel California, the tea and omelette place right across from the medical college hostel in Trivandrum.No one knew why it was called hotel California, not even the owner. It was owned and run by a man who looked elderly but whose agility kept him young. A black coffee and an omelette from this restaurant were a staple for those who studied into the wee hours of the night. Rakesh was a regular there, usually going in between two and three in the morning close to the exam days. He rewarded himself with a red-chilli omelette when he completed a chapter or a topic. In his youth the hostel would be silently dark except for a few patches of light from the rooms of other nocturnals. The road slept except for the odd truck that passed. An occasional line from a Boney M or Carpenters song quietly flowed from one of the rooms, highlighting the depth of the night and the solitude of Rakesh's endeavour.

When he went to Hotel California in his early twenties, Rakesh believed that hard work was the only requirement for success, but now after twelve years, as he prepared for the fellowship exams on the fifth floor of an apartment building in Riyadh, sacrificing almost seventy per cent of his sleep after twelve hours of work, he wasn't sure if this was still true.

Now the orange light dissolved the darkness. The new day would mean different things to each person. Rakesh wondered about those who would be seeing their last day today, unaware as they woke up that they would never see another sunrise. He thought of those who were terminally ill and were happy to have one more day with their loved ones. He thought of those who would get married that day and wondered how many of them would be fulfilled in their matrimony. He thought of those who would make a mark in the world with their genius and of those who would be killed on the roads by reckless drivers. He thought of those parents who would lose their kids. He thought of those who would discover today that they had a dreaded disease and whose lives would never be the same again. The sun sent its bright and innocent rays to all of them, equally unaware of what was in store for them. *The only genuinely inexhaustible fuel is hope*, Rakesh thought. Now the sun cast regular geometric shadows of the buildings. How unlike the irregular shadows he saw in his home town, where the rays filtered through the treetops. Was dawn intrinsically beautiful, or was it beautiful because it was filled with the hope of the day? He wasn't sure as he sank into bed.

Chapter 10

At eleven in the morning on a Wednesday almost a month after Jabber disappeared, Moideen walked into Rakesh's room without knocking. Rakesh was examining a patient and had his back to the door. Although he hadn't seen who came in, he was sure who it was. Without turning his head, he gestured with his hand for the intruder to leave. Judy, who was also in the office, whispered to Rakesh, "It's the boss."

Rakesh was annoyed at the breach of his patient's privacy, a concept which the ex-policeman had never understood.

"Oh, Moideen, it's you. I don't mind you barging into my office, but not when I am with a patient."

Moideen coloured. No one spoke to him like that, not even the sub-inspector or circle inspector had when he was at Malapurum Police Station. Judy's presence compounded the humiliation. Moideen was quick to let out a chuckle, implying nothing had happened.

"It's just that there's a guy outside with a broken jaw," Moideen said. "He fell whilst having a shower."

Rakesh tried to convey controlled displeasure to Moideen. This was the wrong person giving him a medical history at the wrong time. It was clear the next statement from Rakesh wouldn't be quite so polite, so Moideen left, telling Judy that the file was in his office.

When Rakesh had finished with the patient and paperwork, he asked Judy, "What was Moideen saying?"

"A patient who has a broken jaw in a fall is waiting outside."

"But why's Moideen so keen?"

"Maybe it's someone he knows or a regular patient at the hospital, or maybe… I don't know."

"Anyway, bring him in."

A few minutes later, the patient came in and greeted Rakesh with folded hands. He looked like someone who struggled with a meagre salary, and an irregular one at that. He wore a long kurta that probably hadn't seen water for weeks. He mumbled in a mixture of English and Urdu and stank unbearably. As soon as he sat, Moideen appeared out of nowhere.

"Dr Rakesh, I can help you with translation," Moideen said.

"Okay," Rakesh responded.

"His name is Taher. He fell whilst having a shower in the bathroom a week back and now he is unable to eat or close his mouth properly. We need to help him; he can't pay," Moideen summed up.

This man didn't look like someone who had had a shower in the last week or even the last month. Moideen gave Rakesh further details of his history.

"But why did he not come here the day of the accident?" Rakesh asked.

Moideen replied, without asking Taher, "You know how these people live and work. They have no access to medical care. And anyway, the pain got worse today."

Rakesh continued with the examination. "I think Taher has sustained a fracture of the right angle of the lower jaw," he said. "It's infected and compounded into the mouth. We need some pictures to start with."

Rakesh wrote up his findings: "Step defect at lower border of right mandible. Disturbed occlusion of the teeth, limited range of motion. Paraesthesia of the right lower lip and chin."

Rakesh then told Judy that he needed to be treated by a maxillofacial surgeon, but there wasn't one available here. Taher wouldn't be able to afford treatment if her were referred to another private hospital, and government hospitals treated expats only in emergencies. A bathroom trauma suffered a week back wouldn't fall into that category. His radiograph confirmed the fracture. As Taher also had a fever from the infection, he needed IV antibiotics.

"Call Moideen back in," Rakesh said.

Moideen walked in as though he had been hiding behind the door and listening.

"Taher needs to be treated by maxillofacial surgeon," Rakesh explained to him.

"No, you should help him," Moideen said, clearly disturbed.

"Giving the right advice is all the help I can give."

"Well, he can't afford any other hospital, and I want him to get the treatment here. That's the only way we can help him," Moideen countered.

"I wish I could, but this is not in my area of expertise." Rakesh stood firm.

"What are you saying, Doc? You are the bone surgeon, and the jaw is a bone."

"That's right, but facial bones, particularly jaws, need specialised treatment, as they also involve the teeth."

"Then we can get our dentist to do that," Moideen concluded.

"Okay, we can try that if the dentist is willing, but I very much doubt he will be."

Moideen rang Dr Jaleel, the dentist, who joined them in Rakesh's office a few minutes later.

"Hello, Rakesh," Jaleel said. "I don't see you very often these days. How are your exam preparations going?"

"Not exactly as expected, but I'm trying my best," Rakesh responded.

"Rakesh, I tell you, it's a challenge to study and work; even more so in a place like this." As Jaleel said the last sentence, he smiled at Moideen.

Jaleel went ahead with the examination. "I don't think we should fiddle with this man's jaw," he concluded. "It's already messed up."

"Look, Dr Jaleel, ours is a service profession. Sometimes we need to modify our routine to help those who need our service. What will happen if you leave Taher's jaw untreated?" inquired Moideen.

"Oh, it would be nasty. It's already infected. He would end up getting osteomyelitis, a bone infection, and you can see that he's malnourished."

"Now that's my point," Moideen said, as if his hypothesis of a rare medical condition had been proved.

"We need to help him and prevent those complications. He cannot and will not go to another hospital."

Jaleel quickly looked at the radiographs and said, "He has to be seen by a specialist. I can talk to Manu."

"Who is Manu?" Moideen asked impatiently.

"He is a maxillofacial surgeon at the specialist hospital in Riyadh. He was my senior at Calicut Medical College. I'm sure he'll be able to waive some of the charges."

"Then get in touch with him," Rakesh said. He had heard of Manu but had never met him. Moideen provided his contact information, and Judy rang him up on speaker phone.

When he answered, Jaleel got on the line. "Hi, Manu, this is Jaleel from Farooqia."

"Hello. It's been a long time."

"Yes, I know. That's the quality of our life. Listen, I need some help," Jaleel said, not wasting any more time. He explained the patient's situation.

"The registration fee here is a hundred riyals, but I can get thirty per cent discount. I need to see the patient to decide the treatment plan, but from what I gather, he'll need fixation, maybe an inter-maxillary fixation. That would cost about a thousand riyals, but I can get a thirty per cent discount for that as well."

"Okay, Manu, give me your direct number. I shall discuss this with my team and get back to you. I think we should meet one of these days."

"We sure should," Manu said. He gave his direct phone number and then rang off.

All theses figured appeared astronomical. "Can we ask Dr Manu to treat him in our hospital? We could then pay him here," Moideen said, breaking the brief silence.

"You know the legal side of things much more than any of us. If you're prepared to pay, why don't you just refer him to the specialist hospital?" asked Rakesh.

"Well, that fee is too high," said Moideen.

"I'm not comfortable requesting that of Manu. Good luck to you all," Jaleel said. And with that, he went back to his office.

Moideen rarely had a problem for which he couldn't find a solution, but this was one of them. Rakesh suddenly thought of the patients for whom he had paid bus fare when he was at Calicut Medical College, of those whom he wheeled out of the theatre, of those to whom he had given money so they could buy medicine. And now this Taher needed help. That gave Rakesh a new resolve. He was puzzled by Moideen's sudden bout off humanitarian concern.

"Moideen, let him take his IV antibiotics and come back in the evening. Let me see how we can sort this out," Rakesh said.

Moideen got up with a grateful smile. "You are a star," he said, and he left the office. Such comments often sounded deceitful, and for Rakesh, they always did the opposite of what they were intended to do.

Rakesh rang Jaleel that evening after the rush. "I need to meet with you once you're finished," he said.

"Come down in ten minutes," Jaleel responded.

Jaleel was sipping a black coffee as Rakesh went in.

"Rakesh, this fractured mandible seems to be bothering you."

"Well, yes it is, Jaleel. I'm here with an unusual

request. It isn't entirely proper, but it's quite ethical. I want you to speak to Manu again and get him to do the fixation in our hospital. The whole procedure will be unofficial; the records all show that he's my patient. I don't want to debate the right and wrong of it. It's simply the only way to help that guy."

"So the ball is in my court," commented Jaleel.

"I wouldn't mind making the request myself," said Rakesh, "but a request from you would carry more weight. We can fix a time that suits him."

"I've known Manu for a quite a long time. He's a skilled surgeon with strong values but no halo. I'll make the request, but I won't persuade him."

"Okay. I'll leave the matter with you. Once in a while we all need reminders."

"What do you mean, reminders?"

"Competitive commercialisation of the medical profession has made finances the only measure of accomplishment. The number of patients examined each day has become the only barometer of practitioners' efficacy. Management has artfully sprayed this philosophy onto the psyches of the hospital staff. To them, genuine concern for patients should not exist except within the limits set by managers, not medical practitioners. Patient care beyond that would be anti-management."

Jaleel sat in silence, listening to Rakesh's every word, a language he had not heard within the walls of Farooqia Hospital.

"It is so difficult to get a discount for a deserving patient," Rakesh went on, "but it's not so difficult to accept a dozen more patients than a doctor has time for. They talk of service with care, but that's just marketing. They are interested only in turnover at the cash desk. Fortunately, the bulk of patients who came here are uneducated and have weak critical thinking skills or expressive abilities."

"But the hospital needs to make money, doesn't it?" Jaleel said.

"Earning money and looting are two different entities," Rakesh said.

Jaleel smiled.

Rakesh continued, "What do you call the investigations that are done that are not clinically indicated?"

"I know what you mean," said Jaleel.

"Everyone knows about it except the patient who has to pay the absolutely unnecessary bill."

"But dont these patients feel satisfied when they have radiographs and blood work done?"

"They do, but that's an illusion that we're guilty of creating. Well, Jaleel, I'm no policymaker. It's just the whole idea of the medical profession as a business is steadily undermining our values. Patients like Taher are reminders of our values. I know that reminders aren't always welcome, for they only show us the ugly. They expose the illusion that makes facts foggy. I feel Taher ought to be treated."

"I fully understand your concerns, but I don't understand Moideen's motivation."

"Nor do I, but that's irrelevant. Our aims are the same though our reasons may vary. Taher will be back late this evening. Give me an update after you speak to that maxillofacial surgeon."

Chapter 11

"Quite an impressive application form," Rakesh said as he scraped the sides of the ice cream cup. Niranjan loved ice cream. He treated everyone to assorted ice creams most Thursday nights.

"Impressive application form? That's a bizarre compliment," commented Niranjan.

"You know what? It didn't ask you for your religion. That's impressive."

Niranjan took a spoonful from his second cup of strawberry, and now with a the pink mush, he responded, "So what? Why should that be impressive?"

"Asking someone's religion is a way to categorise them."

"Rakesh, don't you feel proud of your religion?"

"Being proud of one's religion is a manifestation of a social pathology. I'm happy about mine but not proud of it," Rakesh continued. "Pride is an emotion attached to an accomplishment. You aim for something, work towards it, and feel something when you accomplish it.

You feel joy, satisfaction, self-appreciation. That's what pride is all about. It has to be earned through effort and desereved by the result. The religion to which we belong is not an achievement; it's just an occurrence of birth, an event on which we have no influence."

Dr Tajudeen, who had joined them for dinner, chipped in, "But what's so wrong about asking about one's religion?"

"If someone inquires about the religion, there has to be a reason, and that reason is always distasteful," replied Rakesh.

Tajudeen, half smiling, added, "But that's a part of our identity."

"That's the whole point. We often think of our religion as our identity, a label for our character, and this is a fantasy. The answer to this question categorises people. A person's true ability and character take a back seat to baseless generalisations of people based on religious attributes.

"Have you ever seen a patient ask the religion of a doctor? No, but the reverse happens. Would a student ask the religion of a teacher? Would an employee ask the religion of an employer? Would a job applicant ask the religion of the interviewer? Why is it that this question is only asked by a person in a position of authority? It's because the reverse is always considered offensive."

Dr Tajudeen's smile evaporated to a thoughtful look. Hameed, who had been listening from the kitchen, joined them with a smile.

"I can see your point," said Niranjan. "But I fail to understand why you're annoyed if someone wants to know what your religion is."

"It's not the question that's annoying; it's the

purpose behind it that's repulsive. A person can and should be judged only by the calibre of his or her deeds. Is anyone ever bothered about the religion of a newspaper boy? No; all that matters is if he delivers the paper on time each day. Did you want to know the religion or the caste of your banker, postman, photographer, bus driver, and pilot? No. It's what they do that counts. .Even a fanatic would not bother the religion or faith of a blood donor when critically ill; only the compatibility of blood group would matter. So what is the relevance of this information? When someone has nothing to lose, they ask this question to assert their own flawed superiority."

"Anyway, let's leave religion aside," Tajudeen said. "The purpose of my visit is to invite you all to my place for lunch this coming Friday."

Hameed couldn't condone plans that would permit them to eat else where. However, he was the first to respond. "What's the occasion?"

"Just a lot of simple reasons. I moved to a new apartment, my family finally joined me last week, and I think we should all meet once in a while outside the hospital walls."

"I'll be there," said Niranjan. Niranjan looked forward to such social gatherings, as they existed as windows to the world outside his night shift. The last event he had attended was Dr Kamal's speech.

"What time?" Rakesh inquired.

"Any time between noon and two o'clock is fine."

"So we will miss Hameed's Friday biryani," said Rakesh.

"Who likes my biryani?" responded Hameed with

a giggle that had a twinge of mock humility. He was clearly fishing for compliments.

"I have arranged a cook. Though his food may not come close to Hameed's, I hope it will be okay?"

Hameed blushed and shook his head in negation, but he loved such comments. Rakesh often found Hameed to be an amusing blend of simplicity, humility, and sincerity.

"Who all are going?" Niranjan was nosy.

"I don't know, but I'm inviting all the staff at Farooqia."

"That will be one big crowd," Niranjan said.

"But with their shifts," added Tajudeen, "they will have to come in batches."

"Did you invite Hussain?" inquired Hameed.

"He is in Jeddah, and I never felt that he was a part of the team," said Tajudeen. There was no joke in what he had said, but Niranjan laughed so loudly that he surprised everyone. Niranjan simply wanted to publicly show his appreciation for that statement.

"Okay, guys, see you," Tajudeen said.

"Thanks," said Rakesh as Tajudeen took to his long strides out. When he reached the door, he whispered to Hameed, "I just want to give these guys a break from your torture." Before Hameed could react, he was gone.

❊ ❊ ❊

"I have good news for you," Rakesh heard Jaleel call out behind him. By now, Rakesh was used to people, even doctors, barging in without knocking.

"Oh, come in," Rakesh said. He and Judy were at

work removing the plaster cast from a young boy's ankle. Jaleel came closer to watch them.

"Manu agrees with the plan. He'll see Taher tonight after he gets off work at about ten. If needed, he'll do the fixation tomorrow morning before regular clinical hours."

"That's fantastic," Rakesh said. "Get Moideen to sort out the formalities."

"Well, Manu has two conditions."

"Whatever they are, we have to oblige. What are they?"

"First, he doesn't want anyone to be in the office during the procedure except the assistant and myself, not even the manager. Second, he doesn't want the headache of a fee. He said no outright."

"Okay," Rakesh agreed. "Thanks. Bye, now!"

Jaleel left. As he shut the door behind, Judy was quick to speak. "Doc, Moideen requested Taher's radiograph and took it to Dr Govardhan's office."

"That's okay," Rakesh said.

"I could be wrong, but my sixth sense is telling me that something is not okay."

"Judy, I have no inclination to speculate about why he did that."

"When is your preparatory course?" Judy said, changing the subject.

"I don't know the exact date, but it should be any day now."

"How many days does it last?"

"In the UK, it's two weeks, but I'm not sure how long it is here."

"Do you think you'll be able to attend?"

"We'll see," Rakesh said, returning to his work.

✳ ✳ ✳

"We still have three more consultations and one review to get through," That was Judy said to Rosemary, over the phone. "You go ahead. I'll join you later."

"You can go now," Rakesh said when she hung up. "I can manage myself."

"Are you not coming to the party?"

"I know I should," Rakesh said. "I might be able to get there at two this afternoon."

"That's too late, Doc," Judy said, disappointed.

"But that will help me reduce the time spent there"

"Doc, you should take a break and relax for a day."

"I wish I could afford that luxury, but I need to prepare for exams."

"I'm sure you'll do well on them anyway."

"How are you so sure?"

"I had a dream that you passed the exams and left the very next day without even saying goodbye to me."

"I hope that's true."

"You mean you would just disappear like that?" Judy was taken aback.

"I mean the firat part of your dream."

Rakesh knew it wasn't a dream, only thought. The first part strongly desired and the remaining, unavoidable sequelae which she feared.

Most expats had to create their own happiness being away from home. For Judy's came from being a part of Rakesh's clinic. Though she had been in Saudi Arabia for a while, the orthopaedic clinic had rekindled her passion for nursing. Waking up in the morning was not just the end of sleep like for many, instead was the beginning of another enthusiastic day. This position had redefined her commitment to the patients and dignified her loyalty to management again.A balanced blend of this, she knew was Rakesh ideal image of an assistant

She strived to reach that ideal in her deeds and words. Before Rakesh had arrived, she was just another member of the hospital staff, but now was the most sought-after assistant, a reputation she had earned as a by-product of working to live up to Rakesh's standards. She had never realised that she was only living up to her own standards.

He staked a lot on her organisational skills not only in the clinic but also in his exam preparations. In her free time she photocopied preparation materials. She enjoyed her role as his secretary role and the envy it attracted from the other nurses. Deep within her, she knew that Rakesh wouldn't serve this hospital one extra day after passing the exam. She knew of the difficulties that lay in his path and his patient attempts to overcome them. She had seen the pain and helplessness that lavishly painted his few months here, but he never let it affect him. She adored his unwavering persistence in the pursuit of his dream.

She could not recall when or comprehend why his dreams had become hers too. She once got a pathology textbook for him from a friend in the UK when she learnt that it was important for the exams but unavailable in Riyadh. To see this gift on his desk one evening made him boundlessly happy, but it sparked a peculiar confusion in Rakesh. Once, on seeing her photocopy an entire book, the accountant joked about how expensive photocopier ink was. She told him to take the cost out of her salary. When that didn't happen, she bought a toner cartridge and left it on the accountant's desk and pasted a note that read "From Judy" to it. For her, this wasn't just an exam, it was a war between one man with integrity fighting with nothing but his conviction against many others without integrity. A victory would make his academic dreams come true. But in the end, she would be left with a void, and she dreaded that.

At one thirty, Rakesh rushed to Tajudeen's apartment. This party was an unavoidable time drain, but he went because he didn't want to displease Tajudeen. The heap of footwear outside the front door indicated the crowd inside. He opened the door and greeted Feroz, Tajudeen's brother-in-law, who worked in banking. He had brought Tajudeen to Riyadh.

"Hi, Dr Rakesh," Feroz said. "Please come in."

"You already know my name?" Rakesh said.

"Why should that surprise you? According to my brother, you're the only one in the hospital with… with…" As he searched for the right word, Preetha, the lab technician, came up to them.

"So, you decided to come?" Preetha said.

"Where did you get that impression that I wouldn't?" Rakesh responded.

"Your secretary said these days, you don't have time even for a shower," Preetha said with accusatory humour and a tinge of envy.

"I never knew she was so perceptive," Rakesh said. He walked further into the hall. A party here was rare, so many people had turned out in colourful clothes and glittering ornaments. This was a welcome break from the hospital uniform and abaya. Favourite dresses and silky saris had been paroled from their imprisonment in the wardrobe.

At the far end, Niranjan was immersed in telling jokes and laughing, leaving few pauses for responses. Nurse Richa was amongst those listening. Recognising Rakesh, Niranjan called out, "Here comes the man!", much louder than was necessary. Heads turned towards him, embarrassing him.

The apartment was well furnished and richly decorated. The hall was an L shape, with the extension serving as the dining room. Moideen was seated there along with Dr Jaleel and an unfamiliar man wearing a suit. The reason for Niranjan's volume was now obvious. Sister Shoshamma broke from a gathering of women to greet Rakesh. She had attempted to match the younger women's style with moderate success.

Rakesh was not one for parties, not anymore. In medical school and shortly after, he actively enjoyed social gatherings and contributed to the fun. The genuineness of such gatherings slowly faded after that, especially in official and professional gatherings. An element of pretence became an integral part: The loud warm greetings amongst colleagues who weren't warm:delegates who spoke of principles they never followed:doctors who spoke of patient concerns that did not concern them:public personalities who who upheld ethics publicly in words and shamelessly mutilated them in private deeds. Rakesh felt he no longer fit in, and he despised having to play his part. He often didn't know what to talk about. Discussions of hospital events and patients were too sensitive. He also disliked discussing current events, as people's opinions were exclusively fed to them by the media and filtered through their communal and political backgrounds. Moreover, his mind was occupied by topics and strategies for his exam revision. He had biochemistry on his mind that day, a particularly difficult subject. Chemistry had been a horror for him in school, and biochemistry was its obese brother.

"The world is making progress because of lazy people," a short balding man in the midst of an attentive crowd said. He seemed to be drowning in the crowd; only his bald patch was visible above the circle of people. Back home in India he had been an English professor but now worked as a salesman in a hypermarket.

"That is unbelievable," someone in the crowd said.

"Good. Most truths are unbelievable," the balding man said. "Years ago, when the only mode of transportation was walking, the lazy man was not comfortable, so he invented carts and then cars. Years ago we used stones to grind grain, then lazy men invented mixers and blenders. Years ago we had to boil meat for hours; an impatient man invented the pressure cooker. Every invention addressed people's laziness, and that's the curse of our time." Rakesh gradually blend into the group. Rakesh felt this was a good discussion to pass the time before the food was served.

"Hello, Rakesh," a happy voice called out from an adjoining room. It still baffled many people when addressed him without the title "doctor", although Rakesh had always encouraged his colleagues to address him by his first name. He did this not out of humility, as many people misinterpreted it, but to show equality. He often argued that if a doctor could call an assistant, nurse, lab tech, receptionist, or driver by his or her first name, then that person should have the liberty to address him in this way also. But Neerja was the only subordinate who did so.

"Hello, Neerja," Rakesh said as she approached him. "You look great." It was unusual for Rakesh to comment on someone's looks. He was usually conservative when complementing people, especially women, but the words escaped his mouth before he could consciously suppress them. She had made no attempt to dress up for the occasion. The only ornament she wore was a small dangling bracelet on her long, slender, otherwise bare arm. Her blue jeans and short-sleeved turquoise T-shirt were conspicuously casual. "HI" was printed in black on the back of the shirt, reflect her friendliness to everyone. Most of the other women wore varying shades of rouge, mascara, and lipstick in the right places but in the wrong quantities, as if the expiry dates were soon approaching. Neerja's wore none. The simplicity of her dress gave her an earthy appeal.

"When are you throwing a party?" Neerja asked.

"If I pass the exams, I'll treat you to dinner at any place you choose," Rakesh answered.

"Is that a promise?"

"One hundred and two percent."

"How about the Hyatt?"

"Done. That is, if I pass."

The Hyatt Regency was on the way to the hospital. A banner out front advertising a barbecue buffet on Fridays had often caught her attention.

"Don't use the word *if*," she said. "It assumes you might fail. No ifs, ands, or buts. You might check out how much the buffet costs."

"It doesn't matter if it costs an entire month's salary if I—"

"There's another *if*. You know what? It stands for *inviting failure*. The more you use that word, the more you subconsciously prepare to fail, and that can have a strong effect on the outcome of the exam."

That statement was like a morning breeze to Rakesh. He was delighted to hear that someone was thinking beyond daily chores.

"If you desire something intensely and strive for it vigorously, then your dream will follow like an obedient pet," Neerja added. "Our vice principal said something like that on our graduation day."

Rakesh watched her as she went on. The brisk movement of her hands matched the radiant expression in her eyes, and her bracelet reflected nameless shades in varying tones. *It's rare to hear inspirational words outside of a book or seminar*, Rakesh thought.

"Tell me, what is it you dream of?" Rakesh asked.

Neerja laughed for a long while. People around them glanced at her out of the corners of their eyes.

"I really don't know. Maybe I don't have a dream," she finally said.

"Why did you go into nursing?"

"I had to do something to earn a living. Nursing for me is just a means to a happy life. I have no passion or dislike for it. It doesn't take much skill to deliver a jab or plaster a broken bone or whatever."

"How do you like it here?" Rakesh said to keep her going. He enjoyed watching her talk.

"This place is full of surprises. The surprises started right from the first day. The most puzzling thing I've observed is that all the staff behave like robots. Why is that?"

"That's funny," Rakesh said. "Yes, it is puzzling."

"I have yet to see an assistant or a nurse speak or act without fear, Neerja explained. "They lower their volume even in normal conversation if Moideen walks by. Why do they do that?"

Rakesh understood what Neerja was saying.

"They speak in whispers at work," Neerja continued, "but they act differently in their apartments. Why do they behave like that at work? They don't say anything to Moideen or any of the doctors except 'yes Sir, no Sir, okay Sir.' Shoshamma's always nagging us about what she calls 'practical philosophy'. I've had an argument with her almost daily, but you know what? I've started enjoying the job. I like all of the nurses, but they're not free. Something outside them dictates their behaviour. Why do they all shy away from everything and everyone? I feel sorry for them. It's like they left their self-esteem in India."

"I fully agree with you." Rakesh was impressed that Neerja had made this analysis in such a short time and that she expressed it so casually. Uninhibited, intelligent conversation was rare these days, at least amongst the staff at Farooqia.

"What else has surprised you?" Rakesh prompted

"Look at this party. All the men are gathered over there and all the women are in the adjacent room. Why do they do the exact opposite of what they desire? Who are they trying to impress? Or what are they trying in vain to express?"

Rakesh looked around. She was right. Even Nurse Richa had moved over to the ladies' wing of the hall.

"How do you know that that's not what they desire?" he asked.

"Come on, Rakesh, don't be stupid. They're not from Mars."

Tajudeen's wife, a dutiful hostess, interrupted them and took Neerja away as if she was meant to be elsewhere.

Rakesh suddenly realised the time and remembered that he should be studying his biochemistry. He had been here for almost an hour, but there had been no announcement for food. The bald man was still going strong, and the crowd around him, now all men, had swelled. Moideen and the other man at the table occasionally laughed loudly.

Rakesh hadn't seen Govardhan, but he was engaged in conversation at the table as though he had come in a while ago. Tajudeen called Rakesh over to the table, and Moideen introduced the man in the suit.

"This is Dr Abdullah Shewaqee, our medical director. In fact, he's the director of all the hospitals in the Farooqia group."

"Pleased to meet you," Shewaqee said. "I've heard a lot about you." Rakesh shook his huge hand. If he were a surgeon, he would require size 10 gloves.

"Actually," Rakesh said, "I'm ashamed to admit that I wasn't aware that we had a medical director and that I had to learn at a venue like."

"I understand," Shewaqee said. "I mostly do administrative work in Jeddah. Moideen tells me a lots good things about you and your patients."

"Oh really?" Rakesh smiled.

"How is that man, that... what's his name?" Shewaqee looked at Govardhan and then at Moideen for the answer. "That guy with chest pain."

"Oh yes. Ramdas," Moideen said as if he had difficulty recollecting the incident and the patient.

This is the wrong place and the wrong time to discuss such a sensitive topic, thought Rakesh, but he replied, "He is doing fine under the care of Dr Tajudeen."

"But, Doc, don't you think it was risky to admit him?" Shewaqee asked.

Rakesh knew that was a polite beginning to an impolite discussion.

"Wouldn't it be more appropriate if we discussed this in the hospital?" Rakesh said, getting quite impatient to get back to his apartment.

"Are you uncomfortable speaking about that episode?" Shewaqee inquired.

"I don't think this is the time or place for that. But if you insist, then I won't be the one who's uneasy talking about it."

"But Dr Rakesh, I am not in any way referring to your treatment skills. This is about a policy matter."

"What policy?" Rakesh responded, his reluctance to talk melting away.

Moideen smiled in an attempt to keep the discussion cordial. Govardhan was hostilely silent.

"We have certain policies which we all should follow," Shewaqee answered.

"What policies are you referring to specifically?" Rakesh pressed.

"Well, you should know that by now."

"Dr Shewaqee, you brought this up, so you have the responsibility to be clear and precise. I'm sorry, but I don't grasp what you're trying to convey."

"I appreciate your frankness," Shewaqee said. He paused, as if searching for the right words. "Here at Farooqia, all of us, including yourself, have put in a lot of effort to make the hospital a very popular and reliable treatment centre. All we need is your full co-operation."

"Yes, Sir, you will always have that," said Rakesh. He could sense Shewaqee's difficulty in getting at the real issue. "As you said that you are primarily concerned with policy matters, can I ask you a question?"

"Of course, my dear friend," Shewaqee answered.

"And can I get a truthful answer?" Rakesh added.

"If I know it," Shewaqee said. He directed a puzzled half smile at Govardhan.

"What happened to Jabber?"

The Moideen's synthetic smile disappeared from his face like a bright patch of sky obscured by a moving cloud. Govardhan maintained his sullen expression. Shewaqee cleared his throat and said, "Jabber's job should not concern you."

"That does not answer my question.'"

Shewaqee was now trapped. He had to choose between his personal values and his duty to the hospital. He started, "Actually, Jabber—"

Moideen interrupted, "Jabber had an emergency at home, and we had to arrange his exit."

Rakesh smile sarcastically. "Moideen, I always wanted to believe you were an honest man, but this—"

"Dr Rakesh," Moideen cut in, "let me get one point straight. Jabber was only a receptionist. Why should he concern you?"

"Do you really want to know why? Are you prepared to hear the truth?" Rakesh asked, knowing he left room only for one answer.

"I think we should know what's on your

mind," Shewaqee said, forcing himself back into the discussion.

"I'll explain provided you permit me to speak without interruption," Rakesh said.

Moideen and Govardhan exchanged glances. Both looked uneasy.

"Please, go ahead," said Shewaqee.

"To management, Jabber was just the receptionist. That was his title, and it defined his role. But to us, he was a colleague, part of the family – a member of the team. Sticking strictly within the boundaries of a job description degrades an employee and makes him apathetic. A person who fails to use his own skills erodes his competence over time. Matches are not won by those who restrict themselves to playing a single position but by those whose passion allows them to go much further. Job descriptions are only guidelines aimed to prevent under-performance. You must have heard of goalkeepers who have scored winning goals. They were driven to do so by passion, passion for the success of the team. In doing so, they didn't compromise their performance in their defined role but instead performed at much higher level. They cared more about their teams' fame than their own names. Empowering our colleagues to work hard towards a common objective is immensely gratifying. Believe me, these objectives are not achieved within the confines of a single office or by those who only give orders and make unilateral decisions. Jabber was a situational leader. The paging system was disused, and many in the hospital had forgotten what code blue was. Jabber's timely announcement got the treatment rolling efficiently and probably saved Ramdas's life.

"When I gave Jabber orders, he paused a while

before taking action. What he thought is anybody's guess, but we all know he was intelligent enough to know the consequences of ignoring you guys. Yet he decided to obey my orders. He did so not out of arrogance but out of integrity."

"But, Dr Rakesh," Shewaqee said, "wasn't it wrong to disobey instructions from the chief of the hospital and act on his own?"

"He was not acting on his own," Rakesh corrected him. "I ordered him to do what he did. And I am responsible for what happened. Sir, what is right and what is wrong is relative. If Ramdas was your brother, what do you think would have been right? Can you for a moment visualise that? Any of you would have been eternally indebted to Jabber for what he did. Instead, you kicked him out."

"He was not kicked out!" Moideen said, flustered. "He had an emergency at home, and so—"

"Shh," Shewaqee interrupted.

"In a football match," Rakesh continued, "the world applauds and remembers those who score goals. The unsung heroes are those who made assists, feeding the ball to the right person at the right place at the right time. That was what Jabber did.

"Every single person brings to his or her workplace inherent skills, talents, attitudes, and energy that is not required for the job. These extras tip the scales, making the difference between an ordinary teacher and a great one, an ordinary player and a great one, an ordinary manager and a great one. Circumstances have a prominent role in supporting those attributes – or in weakening them. I am not sure what message were you trying to convey to other staff members by terminating Jabber. That they should work with fear or with honour? That they should perform as robots or as humans? Do we uphold compassion, the primary principle of the medical profession, or do we dump that in the trashcan in an attempt to safeguard the hospital's reputation?"

"Where is Jabber now?" Everyone looked up to see Neerja. Rakesh hadn't realised how many people had crowded around. Even the balding philosopher was standing there. He also hadn't realised how loudly he was speaking until Neerja's question silenced the room.

"Jabber is in Trivandrum. I spoke to him yesterday," said Rakesh. Moideen's expression changed from uneasiness to worry.

"How did you manage to get his contact information?" Moideen asked.

* * *

Chapter 12

Fancy cars, Jeeps, and other four-wheel drives sped past. Rakesh's eyes were on the road this Saturday morning. Most of the drivers kept to their lanes, separated by the broken white lines. He felt this reflected the social living in Riyadh. People stuck to their own lives, their thoughts and activities revolving exclusively around their jobs. Beyond work, life hardly existed. In most apartment buildings, next-door neighbours were total strangers, sometimes never seeing each other at all. Rakesh had never seen the people who lived on his floor. The only signs of occupancy were the shoe stands at each door. People considered time and space to be exclusive personal property. Taking up someone else's amounted to trespassing. The social fabric normally was a composite of smaller units interacting to give it its vibrancy and colour. The absence of social interaction made the fabric of Saudi Arabia gloomy.

Rakesh visualised his home town on a Monday morning. To call the roads chaotic would be an understatement. They were filled with overcrowded city buses with overconfident drivers, autorickshaws bulging with school bags and schoolkids, two-wheelers with two and half riders. Pedestrians almost needed providential approval to reach home in one piece. *Does this picture not also reflect the pulse of society?* Rakesh wondered. At home, time and space didn't have personal boundaries. In the jumble was the warmth and comfort of human closeness. An unannounced visit from a friend or family member was never an intrusion, a birthday party or wedding reception never a bother. Interactivity and interdependency formed the core of life. Gazing at the traffic below, Rakesh felt that such a meticulously methodical life was devoid of charms. It was nothing but a monotonous routine followed with mechanical efficiency. An occasional surprise, if there was one, was mostly unhappy ones. He hadn't realized that he had stood there watching for almost thirty minutes until he felt a tap on his shoulder.

"You seem to be very thoughtful," Dr Tajudeen said when Rakesh turned around.

"Hello," Rakesh said. "Thanks for lunch. It was really good."

"It was my pleasure, Rakesh. You did a good job opening up to management. They were my guests, so I had to intervene, but you expressed what everyone working here feels. But believe me, that was not the end of it. Govardhan will devise a new strategy to pull you down. I have no clue how he'll do it, but he will. He knows how important your exams are, and I think he'll hit you there. Just be extra cautious."

"Thanks for your concern. I've known about him

from the first day I met him. I've put up with lots of rubbish for good reason."

"That's exactly my point," Tajudeen said. "You are so close to your goal. Don't throw it away now."

✣ ✣ ✣

Khalidbhai hovered after he served Govardhan and Moideen their tea, his ears attentive as he pretended to tidy up and clean. He was attempting to hear some news signals from their conversation. All he wanted was the nucleus; he'd devise the rest of the story, as he always did.

"If you have finished, you may go," Moideen said. Khalid had no option but to follow the order.

Govardhan sat upright in a show of authority. Moideen smiled in an attempt to erase the tinge of guilt at submitting to him.

Govardhan, annoyed, had urgently called this meeting. Its general purpose was clear, and Moideen would soon find out the details. He was sure to make Moideen feel guilty for having under-performed as a manager. Both of them knew that attempts to impose authority through brutality didn't work with some employees, and although Govardhan and Moideen were equally at fault for the problem, the blame lay only with Moideen. He knew that too well. Now he was into his second cigarette and they still hadn't uttered a word about the simmering issue.

Khalidbhai popped in again to take back the empty teacups. When he shut the door behind him, Govardhan said flatly, "Pack him off to Jeddah and bring the orthopaedic surgeon over from there."

Moideen maintained a blank expression, showing neither surprise nor relief, approval nor disapproval.

"Did you hear me?" Govardhan prompted.

"Yes, I did."

"Then do it."

"I don't think we should do that," Moideen managed to say.

"What you think does not concern me. I am concerned only about what's best for this institution," Govardhan said, playing his trump card straight away.

"I have seen that you have no authority over that man," Moideen explained. "You have not been able to discipline him like other staff. Haven't you seen him growing horns? It's too late. Do you want him to wreck everything?"

Rakesh had become a nagging headache, but Moideen hadn't anticipated such a drastic decision. Moideen couldn't transfer a staff member to another institution on his own. He needed Husain's approval. But Govardhan had strong influence over Hussain.

"He has only a few more months before his one-year contract is up," Moideen said. "After that we can transfer him."

"That short time is all he needs. We will all regret it if we allow him to stay. He is too outspoken against the management. Did you not hear him at Tajudeen's party? If he can use such strong language in our presence and the presence of the medical director, what must he be saying behind our backs? My dear manager, negative opinions spread fast. What are you talking about, a few months? A day and a half is too much."

"I wouldn't," Moideen said carefully, "put Rakesh

into the category that would work against the establishment."

"Oh? That's what smartness is. No one can decipher his intentions – it's all wrapped up in his overblown sense of patient care. There are things you are not aware of."

Moideen raised his eyebrows in astonishment. "Like what?"

"Well, he is on some secret mission to finding out where, what, and why radiographs are being done in this hospital. I have no clue what he's aiming at. Are you aware that we are not strictly following the Ministry of Health regulations for radiation protection? What if his aim is to find evidence to support this and complain? Do you know the repercussions?"

Moideen sat motionless, as if the new information froze him into realisation. His face remained blank, but his glance oscillated between Govardhan and a faraway point.

"He is not team player, but since I had a role in getting him here, I just kept silent. But now I can see that things are going beyond acceptable limits, and that can be malignant for our firm. He has a charm that he has been using to poison other employees. Have you seen that new girl frequenting his office? Have you the faintest idea what transpires between them?"

"Which girl?"

"That stupid, outspoken one."

"Neerja?"

"Yes. That's the one."

"She is efficient."

"Efficient, my foot. Simply because she is attractive, you all fall for her tricks. You should be more professional."

Moideen couldn't help recalling Govardhan's request a few weeks back to post Neerja with him for orientation and training.

"Shall we will discuss this with Hussain, or should we wait and see what happens? By terminating Jabber, we've already conveyed our policy," Moideen said, seeking some comfort in his position.

"That's exactly what Rakesh is using against us. Did he not tell you to your face that sacking Jabber was wicked? Did you not permit him to say that in front of the whole hospital? By failing to cut him off, you did."

"Why am I being blamed? Shewaqee also let him talk, and you were silent yourself."

"I simply don't want another similar episode."

"What episode are you referring to?"

"Accepting critically ill patients."

"I think this is a purely medical issue and that it would be better for you to speak to him about it."

"Discussions are only effective with sane people. The solution here is to send him away." Govardhan took a breath to collect himself.

"Now, look, Moideen," he continued. "Medicine is an intricate field. Our aim is for the system to operate efficiently and bring in revenue. Anything that gets in the way of that goal should be removed. What if the next emergency patient drops dead in reception? Have you ever wondered what the consequences would be? All our competitors are envious of our success. They just need us to make one mistake before they run us out of business, and then you'll be back to your police job, if they still have room for you."

Moideen, frightened by this message, ignored the sarcasm of Govardhan's last remark.

"To determine which patients to treat here and which ones to refer requires common sense and a love of the institution. That man has neither quality."

Moideen let this sink in for a moment, and then he inquired, "When is the medial negligence committee meeting? Maybe that would be the ideal platform to give him what's coming to him."

* * *

Rakesh sat lazily at his desk staring at his wristwatch as if its function amused him. It had been a gift from one of his aunts on obtaining his MS. His eyes followed the second hand as it glided smoothly over the face, undisturbed by anything. *This man-made device,* he thought, *will always remind me that time never waits. That's a fact that is so well known yet frequently unacknowledged.* He watched it go round and round and visualised it ticking off the minutes, the hours, the days, the weeks, and then, in two months and seven days, the decisive day would arrive.

He wished he could be like the watch and perform consistently, ignoring every unimportant errand he had to do. But he knew too well they were all unavoidable. The watch needed electricity to perform, and that came from the small battery within it. His energy to perform came from his brain, but unlike the battery, it served more than one purpose. It processed a multitude of thoughts and feelings. Most of these thoughts simply stole the time. The only spans of time over which he had complete control was midnight to nine in the morning and one to four in the afternoon, but other tasks chipped away at those times too, and he had increasing difficulty staying focussed.

Distractions came from all around him all the time. The Taher issue, the Jabber issue, the Cyril issue, and the painful letters from home. The Titan watch looked up at him with superiority as it ticked eleven o'clock. Khalidbhai entered with two letters. One was from the Royal College of Surgeons in Edinburgh, which excited him, and one was from the medical director of Farooqia Hospital, which puzzled him. Like a kid who has nothing better to do, he spent time deciding which to open first. Finally he tore open the one from Edinburgh.

"Judy, my prep course starts two weeks from today," he called out.

"Oh, that's good," she replied with enthusiasm that vanished swiftly. "Do you think you can attend?"

"Of course I will."

and Judy felt that Rakesh's focus on the exam was too intense and that it distracted him from certain realities.

"Doc, I hope you're able to attend, but do you remember Dr Gafoor?"

"I haven't met him, but I've heard about him," Rakesh responded. "Isn't he the ENT surgeon who left a couple of years ago?"

"Exactly."

"What about him?"

"He was an ardent cricket fan, and he watched as many games as he could on TV. Cricket fever gripped him whenever India played One Day Internationals. Once, when India was to play Pakistan in the Sharjah Cup final, he planned to go to the match. He bought a ticket through a friend in Sharjah and booked a flight, but Moideen didn't permit him to go. Everyone else felt his enthusiasm when India played, and now they all felt his disappointment. I think management considered this a message to everyone that no leave except annual leave would be permitted – not even sick leave."

Rakesh sat in thoughtful silence for a moment then said, "I think that's probably because Dr Gafoor sought permission."

"You mean you would just vanish?" Judy was surprised. "I'm sure you wouldn't do that."

"When you seek permission you offer the other person a choice. When you provide information you don't".

Rakesh saved the other letter until after he saw his next few patients.

When he opened it, he saw "Medical Negligence" printed boldly at the top of the page. He read:

> There has been a complaint from a patient named Taher Mohammed that he has lost sensation in his right lower lip following the treatment of a mandible fracture.
>
> I understand that you were responsible for his treatment. The patient is planning to pursue a legal course to claim compensation. You are hence requested to be present for an inquiry at the conference hall at 9.00 p.m. on 30 April.

It was signed by Dr Shewaqee, the medical director.

Rakesh's mind flashed back to a chess game he played as a schoolboy. He had learnt to play the game a year earlier and now sat across Balagobal in the finals of a tournament for a local chess club. Balagobal was two years his senior. Although he looked like a rugby player, he was the undisputed king of chess amongst students in that area. A small crowd of enthusiasts had gathered to watch, and Rakesh was winning. When the outcome became more certain, Balagobal smashed the board and shouted, "You are cheating!"

His thoughts of Balagobal took him to his drawing teacher at school, and then to Dr Soorya at Devmatha hospital and now to Dr Govardhan. All these people's actions were fuelled by frustration which in turn was fuelled by an inability to achieve. Rational thought was alien to them. The only way they could respond to others' success was with resentment. They tried only to destroy this success with power, either physical or positional. This malignancy was invisible to the mediocre beings. Those who pursued dreams invariably met these sorts of people as their success attracted attention. As their success grew, so did others' resentment. Those envious people hid behind officialdom, legality, humanitarian values, anything honourable and agreeable on the surface. Only the targets of this resentment could see through the facade. Rakesh was the target. Dr Shewaqee's signature was part of the facade.

"Shall I call the next patient?"

Rakesh was relieved to hear Judy's voice. He nodded, and Cyril and his daughter, Cynthia, walked in. Since Rakesh had given her a steroid injection few weeks before, she had slowly but steadily improved.

"Nice to see you," Rakesh greeted them.

"Thank you, Doctor. Cynthia is a lot better now. She's been able to attend PE again," Cyril said.

Rakesh examined Cynthia's knee and asked her to make some movements.

"Good. Schedule another visit for a month's time. Take it slow. Don't rush back to normal activity."

As they turned to leave, Cyril grabbed Rakesh's hand with both of his and gave it a squeeze. *Sometimes words aren't needed to express relief and joy*, Rakesh thought.

When Rakesh escorted them out of his office, he saw a smile on Judy's face. It wasn't clear if it was growing or shrinking. It was like the expression of an artist admiring her work from a distance. *That hand squeeze from Cyril was timely*, Rakesh thought. The gesture reminded him of the pleasure of his profession. That gratification was compensation enough for this job. It took away the despair caused by the letter about Taher's case, at least for now.

✻ ✻ ✻

Niranjan sat at the dining table gazing at the smoke rings from his cigarette. He was halfway ready for duty in a long-sleeved cream shirt and a purple floral tie, but he still wore his lungi. He looked clownish, and that was probably the only reason he had delayed changing into his trousers. He held Rakesh's memo in his hands. He wanted to confront Dr Govardhan when he came in for dinner, much to Rakesh's dislike. Most people in the hospital had heard parts of the Taher story by now.

"Do you know who's responsible for this?" Niranjan asked Hameed.

"Dr Shewaqee, our director. I never thought he could be so wicked," replied Hameed innocently.

Niranjan convulsed as if that was the best joke ever told. The new receptionist couldn't help joining Niranjan and Hameed. The noise of their conversation brought Rakesh out of his room. When he appeared, Niranjan had tears streaming down his cheeks.

Govardhan walked in too. "Share the joke with me," he said.

"Hameed says Shewaqee must be wicked to have issued this memo," said Niranjan between chuckles.

"Yes, for sure," Govardhan said.

"Wicked, I agree, but that is not like Shewaqee," said Niranjan. He erupted into another bout of laughter. Now Hameed was reluctant to speak, as he watching Govardhan carefully. After a moment without reaction, Govardhan then joined Niranjan with a perturbed smile. That was probably the best reaction he could come up with. Silence would have made him look guilty. Hameed looked at Rakesh, who looked uninterested. There had been an uncomfortable silence between Govardhan and Rakesh after the incident about Jabber's exit at Tajudeen's party.

"Don't you think you should be the one to have signed this memo, being the CMO?" Niranjan asked Govardhan innocently. "Dr Shewaqee doesn't even know what happened."

"I do not want to get into administrative matters," Govardhan said firmly. "Hussain pressured me to be the CMO. That's all. I prefer to stay out of all this."

"But this is not an administrative issue. Moreover, Shewaqee is a radiologist." insisted Niranjan.

Rakesh wanted to leave but felt it wasn't appropriate whilst Niranjan was defending him, and his silent presence seemed to have a buffering effect.

"What is this inquiry all about?" Niranjan inquired.

"I don't think it should be a cause for any concern," Govardhan said. "It may be just a formality."

"Whatever the case, one thing is certain: the man behind this is a spineless bastard who should be thrown out of this profession." The fact that Shewaqee had signed the memo gave Niranjan the freedom to speak so plainly, but everyone knew who was responsible. Govardhan for an instant felt it would have been much better had he signed it himself; then the abuses would be less harsh, or at least not as direct.

"What are you looking at?" Govardhan snapped at Hameed. "I'm starving." Govardhan then stormed off to his room. He locked the door, picked up the phone, and rang Moideen.

"Didn't I tell you to wait to issue the memo until two days before the hearing? Now look what's happening. It's me who's the target. Either you listen to me completely or leave me out of it, and don't come running to me when the hospital's image is stained. Didn't I tell you a million times that this is to clip his wings and not to make a sensation out of it?"

Invoking the hospital's image always worked with Moideen. Years ago when Hussain,the owner had pulled Moideen out of the police force and offered him the manager's post, Husain demanded only one thing of him: that he preserve the hospital's name and fame at any cost.

Chapter 13

Neerja rarely sat idle in the lab. If she was free, she visited her colleagues in other departments. She carried with her joyous energy which was welcome everywhere she visited. Shoshamma had even stopped chastising her for roaming around.

"If I can walk in and out of clinics and offices for patient-related work, what's the harm in doing that for other reasons?" Neerja had said in her defence.

Shoshamma reminded her, "You may if you have some purpose that is acceptable, and not otherwise."

Whenever Shoshamma persisted, Neerja would say with playful sarcasm, "My dear Mother Shoshamma, if my meeting and chatting with colleagues is improper, then I am happy to face the consequences."

Shoshamma had to give up, for she never won an arguments with Neerja. It was not that Neerja had any special verbal skills, but she flatly spoke the truth, expressing what everyone said only in the privacy of their minds. Though Neerja had visited employees throughout the hospital, over time, she restricted her wanderings to the radiology department, Rakesh's office, Tajudeen's clinic, and, once in a while, to reception.

It was 14 April, and Neerja brought cake for everyone. Today was her parents' twenty-fifth wedding anniversary. Normally such a job was delegated to Khalidbhai or the driver, but Neerja preferred to do this herself. Purushu, the driver had helped her pick up the cake from the nearest bakery. Neerja excused herself from the lab and carried the huge tray of cake. Shoshamma stared at the tray as if it were the object of sin.

"Don't salivate; I will definitely come back with your share," Neerja said.

Shoshamma now shifted her gaze of disgust from the tray to Neerja's jubilant face. She couldn't conceal her embarrassment and contempt. But only Shoshamma knew that beneath these feelings was envy of someone who enjoyed life so fearlessly.

Neerja started off towards reception, and she distributed pieces to a few patients seated in the lobby. It was an unusual delight to see a tall, charming lady walk around with a tray of cake in the hospital. She then went to Govardhan's office. He was percussing someone's chest behind a partially closed curtain.

Without turning around, he said, "Leave my share on my desk."

"Okay, boss, but one glance away won't harm your patient," she said with a chuckle, and she walked out. After completing the rounds of the ground and first floors, she walked into Rakesh's office and sat down for a brief moment of rest. This was the only office where she knew she wouldn't be met by courteous insults. She would sit in any empty chair, including Rakesh's.

This had once created some turbulence when Moideen walked in to find Neerja in Rakesh's place. Moideen's earlobes turned pink, which most employees knew was a sign of concealed anger. Without uttering a word, Moideen retreated and rang up Rakesh from his office. Neerja was still there, and she listened to Rakesh's side of the conversation, making comical faces to distract him.

"Relax, Mr Moideen, relax. Try to calm down.... I don't want you to worry about such irrelevant matters." Rakesh's tone was composed, and he spoke slowly. "Well, Moideen, do you think it's the chair that's important?... Respect, oh yes, respect. If I sat at your desk, do you honestly think that would damage the respect you receive? Respect is earned through a person's deeds and attitudes, not by where they park their bums."

Neerja burst out laughing.

"If Hussain wouldn't approve of it, he better guard his chair. Leave my office to my ways.... Now, if you're seriously concerned about me, please don't interfere into simple personal matters. To me, that amounts to disrespect. Let me ask you, honestly, whose respect are you concerned about?... Moideen, I don't have the slightest affinity for such issues. The more we discuss it, the less human we become. I have no concern with anyone else's chairs, even if they would prefer to glue their bottoms to them.... My seat is only a place to sit.... Let's leave it at that." Rakesh's tone had steadily become more firm, and he told Neerja that Moideen hung up on him. Khalidbhai had overheard the conversation, and he dutifully spread it to the gossips.

"What's the cake for?" Rakesh asked.

"You suffer from amnesia. Probably age related," Neerja joked. "Didn't I tell you about my parents' anniversary?"

"That was true? I thought it was your way of conveying your age."

"Shut up and take a piece."

"One small piece of cake? Is that how I should be celebrating the silver jubilee of two great people who had to bear the torture of bringing you up? I think as a tribute to their struggle we should go to the Hyatt."

Judy took three pieces from the tray.

"I'll see you at the Hyatt on twenty-ninth May." Neerja smiled and strode out. Rakesh turned the page of his calendar and stared at 29 May, the day he'd receive the results of his exams. He wasn't sure what emotion he would feel then. Regardless, it would be intense. Rakesh made a silent prayer, which had become a habit he engaged in more frequently as the exams approached, and cleared his mind.

Neerja made her way to the X-ray tech's office and gave Preetha a big corner piece of cake. Preetha had been Neerja's roommate in the first month. She was a friendly but timid girl, and Neerja knew she loved anything sweet. As they talked, a patient walked in with a request for a chest X-ray.It was from Dr.Govardhan. Preetha went on with her work, and Neerja sat at the desk. Her eyes followed Preetha's slow economical movements. She wondered why some people performed everything slowly, even routine tasks that should have become swift and effortless. Preetha walked as if her steps hurt the ground. She slowly positioned the patient, focussed the central beam, and instructed him to hold his breath. She went behind the lead barrier and prepared to shoot.

Neerja shouted out, "You didn't keep the cassette!"

"Yes I did," Preetha replied.

"No you didn't!"

"Oh, just let me do my job," Preetha said, silencing Neerja.

The X-ray taken, Preetha scribbled a bill for fifty riyals and handed it to the patient.

"Do I come back to collect the picture?" the patient asked, his eyes on Neerja.

"No. The doctor will review the picture sometime this evening, and you can see him tomorrow to discuss it."

The patient left but Neerja didn't. She waited to see if Preetha would remove the cassette. Nothing happened for quite some time, so she asked, "Why aren't you washing the film?"

"I know what to do and when to do it," retorted Preetha, who seemed to be more uncomfortable than annoyed.

"Okay, okay, but Preetha, I want to see that film." Neerja knew Preetha didn't have to answer to her, but Neerja also wasn't easily fooled.

"What was that patient's name?" Neerja asked.

"Why are you so keen?"

"I'm just curious to see invisible things," Neerja asked innocently.

"His name is Anwarkutty; he is thirty-six years old. You can see his file in Dr Govardhan's office this evening."

"Are you sure that's who he is?"

* * *

On Fridays the morning shift was generally light. Most people went to bed late on Thursdays and woke on Friday near noon. But Rakesh valued Friday mornings to catch up with his revision, which invariably ran behind schedule. This gave Judy some leisure time in which should could organise the clinic and clear her backlog of paperwork. She brought a small stereo, a luxury she allowed herself to use only on Fridays.

On this Friday, Rakesh was going through the anatomy multiple choice section. Anatomy was a subject he had once hated but had developed a liking for recently. Dislike was often a consequence of a lack of understanding, Rakesh had found. He thought back to his dissection, remembering the repulsive odour of formalin and the students' disgusting disregard for the cadavers. When the tutors entered the lab, the students went silent. When the tutors asked for demonstrations, they asked only the four to five students who had somehow managed to become their favourites. The rest circled around to watch.

Looking back, Rakesh thought it would have been sensible to spend a few sessions in the lab prior to dissection to salute the people whose bodies they'd be dissecting. This would remind the beginners to be respectful to these cadavers. This should have been a place where students conducted themselves with dignity; instead it was a venue for vulgar jokes and distasteful pranks.

During one session, a boy challenged a girl named Susan to chew the little finger of the allotted body. Her reward was to be chicken biryani. When other students heard about the deal, they kicked up some hype, and she finally did it. She chopped off the tip of the finger with her scalpel and bit it. Susan became instantly popular. The news rippled through campus. Many students looked up to her courage, but Rakesh felt she had stooped too low.

Once, Rakesh asked her, "Would you have done the same thing for a million rupees if that was your father's body?"

She replied, "Rakesh, don't be so silly. It's not my father or my grandfather."

Rakesh shot back, "Well, he was someone's father, and he was probably more honourable than you."

He came back to his anatomy book feeling a pang of guilt. He moved on to the self-assessment questions, which enhanced his confidence, and he swiftly turned the pages until his attention was drawn to a familiar tune.

"Judy, put that louder," he called.

"Do you know this song?"

"It was one of my favourite songs as a kid."

He joined Judy in singing:

It was not your face – tara tum tum
It was not your voice – tara tum tum
It's something in your ways – tara tum tum

He knew only the chorus, but he whistled through the rest as Judy sang.

"Who sang this?" Rakesh asked.

"Jeff Orangegate."

"Yeah, yeah. I remember Orangegate. We used to play his songs sometime in third or fourth grade." Rakesh loved the tune and the simple lyrics, although he didn't know their meaning back then. He hadn't heard the song since school. *The storage system of human memory is quite impressive*, Rakesh thought.

"Judy, don't you think the words are so true? It's never the beauty of one's face or the melody of one's voice that attracts us; it's something beyond that."

Rakesh didn't understand why Judy blushed, but she did.

She replied, "Maybe."

"No, it is. Have we not seen many ravishingly beautiful women divorced? Have we not heard of many gifted singers who've failed in relationships?"

"Maybe."

"In any human relationship, the bond comes not from what's seen, not from what's heard, but from what's felt."

"Maybe."

"What do you mean, maybe?"

"I mean maybe you should get back to that book in front of you."

"Maybe I should. Do you know any more of Orangegate's songs?"

* * *

Embryology was not one of Rakesh's favourite topics, and he had much to memorise. He was certain that a few MCQs will come from this subject.So he was revising. This was the branch of biology that dealt with the formation and development of the human structure, the fantastic process of how various organs and structures gradually took shape, a harmonious co-ordination of differential growth, both in space and time. A small defect in the sequence could lead to developmental defects such as a cleft lip, so knowledge of organogenesis was significant for doctors to diagnose a defect and thereby institute treatment measures. He wondered if there was a similar science to the formation of human relationships that had discovered a step-by-step sequence. If that were so, it would have been a lot easier to diagnose the cause of a dysfunctional relationship and repair it. Unfortunately that wasn't the case – everyone had a provisional diagnosis of a problem, which was mostly accusations, but no one could make a final diagnosis, for there were no investigations or lab tests to support one. Or maybe a few people could make such a diagnosis on introspection.

Rakesh's door opened, and Hameed said, "Phone for you."

"Who is it?"

"I didn't ask," replied Hameed apologetically with a slight childish smile. Hameed never inquired who the caller was when he answered the phone. He felt it was beyond his role as a cook to do that. Most calls to the residence were from the staff inquiring what was for lunch or dinner. Every time Hameed was on the phone, his delight was obvious, as if the marvel of Alexander Graham Bell's ingenuity continued to amuse him. Rakesh lazily dragged himself to the phone.

"Hello?"

"You think you can hide in Riyadh and that I wouldn't find you?" a familiar voice said over the line.

"Oh, it's you, Johnson."

"I knew you were here, but only learnt of your workplace this morning."

"Kamal told me you were here, but I just kept

postponing contacting you. You know how things are here in Riyadh."

"Cut all that crap. Come to my place tonight."

"I can't. Maybe this weekend."

"Don't speak like those others with the typical Gulf syndrome putting on that stupid act of being busy all the time. I'll come and pick you after you finish."

Arguing with Johnson was pointless, so Rakesh responded, "Okay. Come around eleven-thirty tonight. Do you know where my place is?"

"What the hell are you doing working that late? I will be there."

As Rakesh put down the phone, happy memories of his medical school days flooded back to him. Tonight he wouldn't be able to study, so Rakesh spent his entire break time with embryology.

Johnson was a stickler for punctuality and arrived at reception at eleven-twenty. They got in his Crown Victoria, the big old American car very much like those in the English movies of the early seventies. The colour of the car made it a look like it was ten years old, and the engine noise added another ten years, but he drove it like someone who just wheeled out an S-Class Mercedes from the showroom. Johnson believed in enjoying every day – postponing fun was not for him. He found joy in everything he did in a way unique to him.

Rakesh looked at him and said, "Your hairline is receding."

"Hey, the only thing that should not recede is the joy of living." Johnson shot him a serious look that faded into a you-know-what-I-mean smile.

"This car is like a boat. It feels like it's floating or gliding over the road," commented Rakesh.

"That's the beauty of American cars," Johnson said. "Particularly the old ones." He seemed to be thoroughly enjoying his car and the long, wide roads.

"How long have you been here?"

"In Saudi, it's two years, but this is my third job. A few weeks ago I heard you were somewhere in Riyadh, but then Pradeep, a mate of your dentist, told me of your place. But what are you doing sitting there till almost midnight?"

"I'll tell you the whole lot once we get to your place."

"How are you getting on with your exam prep?"

"So, you are well updated."

"Come on, it's a small world, and Riyadh is even smaller."

"How come you've had three jobs in such a short time?" Rakesh asked. "That's a bit unusual in Saudi."

"Rakesh, unusual, abnormal, and difficult exist everywhere. If you want to live happily, you define your own life."

Rakesh realised that Johnson hasn't changed one bit since college. He had always been flexible in situations but rigid in principles.

"The first job was a joke," Johnson explained. "It was a small but busy clinic. An Egyptian dentist and I split the work. He worked mornings, and I was supposed to work evenings, or so they called it. But the shift was four in the afternoon to midnight. When negotiating the terms of the position, we agreed on eight-hour shifts. Which eight hours was not discussed, and I didn't ask. A calculated omission on their side and ignorance on my side."

"And what did you do?" Rakesh was curious, as he thought of his own share of challenges related to the terms of his employment.

"I expressed my unwillingness to give up my entire evening in the clinics; management said they'd make some modifications. I patiently continued, but after a month, I sensed their lack of genuineness in their willingness to change my shift time, so I resigned. I stayed on till they hired a replacement. Then I went home with a month and a half of Gulf experience."

"And then what happened?"

"Well, there are always jobs. Within two months, I got an offer from another hospital, this time in Jizan. It was a good establishment that housed most specialties and had friendly colleagues. But then again it was the working hours. I started out with an acceptable shift, from nine to one and four to eight. But as the practise improved, management wanted me to work until ten. That was the beginning of the end. I was prepared to start early, but I definitely did not want to stay beyond eight at night. Management was rigid, and so was I."

The road now narrowed to a single lane bordered by fewer buildings and more pedestrians. And then a few kilometres up, they turned into a deserted area on a road that looked as though it had been abandoned halfway through metalling. A security guard, who seemed more concerned with saluting Johnson than doing his job, opened a gate. Rakesh knew that Johnson must have won the guard over with big tips for small errands. The loyalty was palpable. Ahead of them lay a row of villas, each with a small garden. It looked like a resort. Rakesh had never seen anything like it in Saudi. All he had known were cramped apartment buildings on narrow streets. This was sheer luxury in comparison. Johnson parked the car and cut the engine; the sudden silence was like a power failure in the midst of a war movie. Rakesh followed Johnson inside and settled in the living room facing the veranda.

"All the greenery is very stimulating," he remarked.

"I have something even more stimulating for you," Johnson said. "Give me a few minutes."

Rakesh gazed around. *Wherever you live, whatever job you do, it's up to you to make life purposeful.* Johnson had said this long ago, and Rakesh thought of that simple motto then. All doctors in private hospitals in Riyadh drew roughly the same salary. Most huddled into poorly furnished apartments or even shared rooms, but here was a man living independently in his own villa. Most doctors relied on the hospital ambulance for transportation, but here was a man with his own car. Most doctors silently accepted senselessly long working hours, but here was a man who threw away two jobs until he found the one he was comfortable with. This wasn't about money but attitude.

"Remove that dangling bit from your neck; loosen up and relax," Johnson said. "This is a special juice made from dates. You will love it." He poured out a clear liquid that didn't look like it came from dates. Rakesh took a sip. It tasted like dates.

"It's my own special recipe. The boys here love it."

In the stillness and purity of the night, they stretched and relaxed. Rakesh subconsciously felt the burden of his long hours, the stress of exams, and the rift with management all gradually receding as he sipped the date juice. His memory darted from event to event, from his college days to his hostel days to his vacation days. It was like the route map of an international airline: innumerable intersecting lines of different lengths and curves all originating from one point, the best point in Rakesh's life, undergraduate medical school.

"I'll leave you to rest for a while. Let me organise something to eat," Johnson said, getting up. Johnson was an excellent cook who liked to experiment. If he did something, he excelled in it, and if he didn't enjoy doing something, he paid someone else to do it.

"Do you want something to change into?" he called from the depth of the kitchen. "I can give you a thope if you'd like."

"No, it's okay. I'll be leaving after a while."

"Nobody leaves my place after dinner. This is no restaurant. I'll drop you back at work or your flat in the morning."

That left no room for discussion.

"Try the thope. I'll tell you, there is nothing as comfortable as that."

After a shower, Rakesh slid into the thope. It felt peculiarly loose, with nothing binding anywhere. Rakesh felt uneasy in the freedom, and the full-length mirror almost laughed at him.

"Now tell me," Johnson said after Rakesh returned to the sitting room. "Why are you slogging this late like a slave? You have been here for how long?"

"Another two months will complete a year." Rakesh gave him the story of his coming here and the months that followed, highlighting the events that deserved it. Johnson sat intently like a lawyer listening to his client, nodding and occasionally interrupting to ask questions.

"Interesting story. I think you made a costly mistake on your first day. When Govardhan said he would arrange your return ticket, you should have flat-out said yes. Believe me, they cannot and will not do that. Instead they would have yielded to your demands. Unfortunately, you acted like thousands of others who work here, treating your employer as your provider. That is wrong. We are the providers."

"Johnson, you do have a point, but I did not want to make any move that would even faintly disturb my prospects for the fellowship. In the process, I took a lot of dirt."

"Hmmm. See, look at it this way: the employee-employer relationship is like a game of chess or of cards. Whoever is in the strong position dictates the game; the opponent follows. Believe me, the employer is always weak in private polyclinics. But he projects the opposite, and most workers fall for that act. The employer is dependent on you to run the show, to keep the patients happy and to keep the revenue flowing in. He has nothing without you. Even the salary he pays you is what you generate for him. Very few managers really believe in the win-win policy. They may talk about it in meetings and in mission statements, but you can decipher the reality from their deeds. If we do not enforce our own priorities, who will? Many employees fail to enforce their preferences or even express them for the fear of being misread as disloyal. This fear is the hallmark of the weak, of those who are unsure of their own worth and ignorant of their strengths. You know what happened a few months back? The management of my present hospital tried to pull a fast one on me.

When the director was on leave, the acting director issued a memo increasing my hours. I am still not sure if this was a play or if the guy was stupid."

"How did you react?"

"I didn't react."

"And what happened?"

"When I continued with my regular schedule, he phoned me to inquire what was going on, and I flatly told him I would accept no unilateral decisions. And the chapter was closed. Rakesh, it's all a matter of making your priorities very clear. From that clarity stems strength. The irony of it all was that two months ago, my contract was up for renewal, and this guy said he was going to increase my salary, and he requested my comments. Do you know what I said? Salary hike or no, the quality and quantity of my service would be the same. He won't offer me that carrot anymore. At least now we know each other very well." He paused for a moment.

"Rakesh, you did undergraduation and post graduation from one of the best universities. Some of our teachers were giants in their respective fields. We had very rich clinical experience. Above all, you did well on the university exams. Your credentials are packed with so much strength. Do you recall those exams? The sleepless nights? The sadistic examiners? And then the celebration when the results were out? Was it all for you to one day slog like a donkey at the whim of someone who had never even seen a university building? Come on, Rakesh."

Rakesh reclined as much as the cane chair permitted as he listened. "Johnson, you are right, but I came here and stuck it out not just for the job."

"I know that, and that's exactly my point. Have

they not plundered every single minute of your waking hours? When do you even prepare for this goddamn exam?"

"I start at midnight and revise till five in the morning."

"You must be kidding."

"I wish I was."

"When do you sleep?"

"Something like five to eight in the morning with a short nap at lunchtime."

Johnson straightened up in his chair. "I am very happy you are here tonight. I always knew you were smarter than you appear."

Johnson's face was marked with spots and lines, but these were not indicative of age, for he always had them. When he began dental school, he looked like someone in his forties, and his actions supported that. He wasn't the type to climb mango trees, whistle in the corridor, or run in the rain. He seemed to have leaped from childhood to manhood, bypassing boyhood.

Johnson got up and smacked Rakesh. If not for the context, Rakesh might have thought this was an assault because of the sheer force of the blow.

"This is what I said earlier: strength comes from the clarity of one's vision. I know what you are aiming at, but these guys haven't seen genuine people. Show them what constitutes grit. Beat them hollow when the time comes. I am really proud of you. Your working hours now seem to me to be a tribute to your goal. The slush you've splashed through should further energise you."

"That's well said," Rakesh responded. "One the first day, the salary gimmick bothered me. I did feel terribly cheated, but I stayed on although I was bruised.

When they extended my hours, the bother gave way to acceptance because of my dream. Every obstacle I came across was like one more building block. It fuelled me. The insistence that I not spend time studying in the clinic was the best of the lot. That was the turning point. After that it was no longer an exam: It was the sole purpose for my existence in Riyadh. I told myself a million times that if this was what they didn't want me to do, then this was exactly what I would do. I was prepared to pay any price for that. It then became almost impossible for them to get to me emotionally anymore. The Jabber's termination, the allegations of negligence, the investigation, everything was like dogs barking at a train racing by."

Rakesh refilled his glass with the date juice. He gently rinsed his mouth and swallowed as if he were taking medicine. In one motion, Johnson emptied his own glass. His began to smile but stopped and said, "You remind me of Cuba Gooding, Jr. in *Men of Honor*."

"Who is that?"

"Haven't you seen *Men of Honor*? It's a must-see movie."

* * *

"Khalidbhai. What's the news today?" Neerja asked.

"Did you know Dr Tajudeen had a fight with Dr Govardhan?"

Neerja faked surprise.

"How do you know?"

"Ah! Nothing happens in Farooqia without Khalidbhai's knowledge," he said, his face lighting up and his smile exposing his stained, ill-fitting upper denture. "I overheard him shout at Govardhan, 'You keep your hands off my patient!'"

"When was that?"

"This morning. I went into his office, and the argument fizzled out. Govardhan said, 'I want us all to work in a friendly atmosphere.' Though he said so, his tone and his face showed otherwise.

"Khalidbhai, I was looking for you this morning," Neerja said.

"Is that so? How can I be of service to you?"

"Remember last week when you helped me with some grocery shopping and I forgot to pay you?" She handed him ten riyals.

"Ah, this is not correct. I am here to help all of you. You don't have to pay me every time." As he said so, he took the money and put it in his pocket with a smile showing the last teeth in his denture.

"One more thing, Khalidbhai. I was looking for a patient file. I searched reception but couldn't find it. It must be in Rakesh's or Govardhan's clinic. Could you get it for me? No hurry. I just need it by this evening."

"Done. What's the patient's name and number?"

"Anwarkutty, thirty-six years old, file number K1310. And tell me more about the fight when you have time."

For Khalidbhai, Neerja's interest was like a Pulitzer Prize for investigative journalism. His ear-to-ear smile didn't disappear until he disappeared from her sight.

* * *

"Here in the Gulf countries, particularly with such private managements, logic does not work. They see employees as income-generating slaves, I'm sorry to say," Niranjan said. "They never grant anything apart from annual leave in these private establishments. That's their policy, and if you do not like it, you may leave the job. That is it" He laughed loudly.

"So when you meet the manager about your preparatory course, try not to get into an argument. They can be mean, and you know what I'm talking about. They can cook up any false allegation and sack you. I'm not worried about your losing the job but about your losing the chance to sit the exams, and believe me, Govardhan will try his best to achieve that. Here in Saudi, if a sponsor is not happy, he can sack you whenever he wants. Rules, regulations, labour laws, et cetera, et cetera, they exist only on paper. And take it from me; Govardhan has strong ties to the sponsor."

Rakesh listened carefully to Niranjan. He knew of the hundreds of candidates who had sat the exams year after year and of the dismal pass percentage. A preparatory programme just a month before the exams had to give him an invaluable advantage. He knew that, but it was not going to be easy to get away for ten days. The programme was scheduled from 9.00 a.m. to 4.30 p.m. each day with an hour's break for lunch. Somehow this news had made its way throughout the hospital, and Shoshamma had advised Rakesh a few days earlier not to request ten days' leave. Her opinion was that he would not get it, and it would only add further strain to his relationship with management. The mere idea that others were discussing the issue and giving him unsolicited advice annoyed him, although some of their suggestions were helpful.

"An ex-policeman who never went to college and

with no respectable human qualities holding the keys to my career... No, that should not happen," Rakesh said to himself. *There is something wrong with this world*, he thought. Though he projected an image of positivity and optimism, he expressed concerns, stresses, and uncertainties in his private thoughts, although he attempted to overcome them. Rakesh had learnt from his father to derive strength and inspiration from difficult situations. In innumerable encounters, his father proved a simple truth: the power of one's belief is a weapon that never fails.

Rakesh thought back to a football tournament held in the colony where he lived as a schoolkid. Rakesh's father had served in the security department in one of the state's largest factories, and he was mostly addressed as Captain Saab. The football tournament was an annual event, and each department of the factory organised a team. The tournament generated a lot of sound and fury, and for the two weeks of the tournament, everyone speculated about the matches. Most often the youth team walked away with the trophy, but never easily. One year the security team played the youth team. Rakesh's father was not a player, but he actively supported his department's team. The game started at 4.30 p.m., and the schoolkids went to the ground straight from school to cheer on their teams. The youth team were always the favourites. The security team's players were mostly veterans. The pitch was slightly smaller than standard, so teams played seven to a side. By half-time, the security team had swallowed five goals, thanks to the goalkeeper. In the second half, Rakesh's father took over as keeper. With his enthusiasm, energy, and agility, he managed to stop many goals; suddenly the referee stopped the game.

Someone had complained that Captain Saab was in full trousers, which were not allowed in an official match. That was true. Captain Saab had come only to watch and had not dressed to play. He wore his usual casual dress. The referee, an ex-national referee, politely told Rakesh's father to change into shorts. When the crowd heard the news, they swarmed the goal. The youth players wanted him to leave the game, but the security team wanted him to change and continue. Lots of suggestions arose as the crowd on the pitch swelled.

"I have an extra pair of shorts!"

"No, just roll up your trousers and play!"

"I live nearby; I can get another pair of shorts!" Probably the only person in the whole crowd who knew that his father would take none of those suggestions was Rakesh, but he had no clue what his father would do. The noisy, enthusiastic crowd that a while ago was enjoying football was now enjoying a different type of entertainment. Rakesh's father just stood there, as if the events had nothing to do with him. The referee and some of the youth players raised their voices.

"It's getting late!"

"Move out; don't waste our time!"

"Change into shorts!"

Rakesh grew tense, as his father's backing out seemed to be the only choice. Then suddenly, amidst that chaos rose Captain Saab's authoritative voice, silencing all others. He looked at the referee, but he addressed everyone.

"You have two options. First, I play in what I'm wearing now and the match continues. Second, the game ends now. You can decide which you want."

The ground went quiet, and players and fans exchanged surprised looks and whispers. And then the game went on. Though the youth team had more goals on the scoreboard, Rakesh knew his father was the winner. Rakesh went home that day reflecting his father's valour. Talk of this episode was in the air for quite some time. The mere recollection of that simple event now blinded Rakesh to the challenges he faced.

Straight away he dialled the phone on the dining table. "Hello, Moideen? I want your advice regarding the scheduling of my patients' appointments from 12 to 21 April. I will not be able to attend my morning sessions; something very important and unavoidable has come up. Please let me know how best we can sort it without disturbing the bookings."

"Give me some time, and I shall get back to you," Moideen said, and he hung up.

Niranjan was visibly surprised, and Hameed even more, at the casualness with which Rakesh had sorted the problem out. Rakesh knew that it only looked casual.

Moideen rang back in less than ten minutes. "You can put in an extra two hours in your evening shift. Instead of from five to eleven, we shall make it four to midnight. But I am sorry; the accounts department will cut your salary."

"That is fine. Thanks." Rakesh put the phone down.

"This is not possible." Niranjan looked worried when Rakesh told him of the agreement. He continued, "You said your course starts at nine and goes till four-thirty. You think you can continue working till midnight without a break? Don't be stupid."

Rakesh replied with a smile.

* * *

Chapter 14

Rakesh arranged with his taxi driver friend, Devji, to take him to and from the military hospital each day of the ten-day course. Rakesh was excited to be there; it reassured him that he was nearing the goal. There were about thirty-three candidates in the class, most of them Arab, and Rakesh later learnt that for seventeen of them, this was not the first attempt at the exams. The only other Indian was a woman from Bangalore named Shika who worked part-time in a polyclinic in Hoora. She looked striking when she wore the abaya and big sunglasses, but not otherwise. Of the four instructors, two were from Edinburgh, and the other two, including Mr Cartland, who had authored a popular biochemistry book, were from London. The opening session was a brief introduction to the programme and explanation of the different modules they would cover. All that was discussed sat well with Rakesh except the last bit of information: that less than twenty-five per cent of candidates passed. Rakesh knew that many more than these thirty-three candidates would sit the exam, which meant that only two or three from this group would make it.

Asking himself *Will I make it?* became the most automatic thing next to breathing that Rakesh now did. He wondered whether he would be one of the twenty-five per cent. The ecstasy of a possible victory mixed with the agony of a possible defeat unsettled him.

The lectures were not all boring. He absorbed every word as if it provided oxygen instead of knowledge. Compared with his medical school lecturers, Rakesh felt that these were more sincere and committed to the objective of teaching. Humour was an integral part of the lectures. They never shouted or made sarcastic remarks, which Rakesh recalled had been a regular feature of some lectures back home. Shika turned out to be friendly, but she appeared to have no clue about how challenging the exam was. Rakesh wished there were more such candidates so that his chances would be improved. Eating at the cafeteria at the military hospital was an experience for Rakesh. It followed a system that he had seen only in English movies: diners took a tray, picked out their food and drink as they walked along, and finally paid at the till.

He recollected a well-known author's comparison of life to a cafeteria and thought that the recollection was very timely. He said that the tray is your life, and what you fill it with is entirely your choice, but then be prepared to pay the cashier at the end of the line. If you are not prepared to pay, you have to put the food back, or, in other words, shrink your dreams and goals. The author further added that the only part you do not have control over in the cafeteria is the price. If you're willing to pay whatever is demanded, you could pick out whatever you fancy. Rakesh, reaching the cash counter, thought about the price he'd had to pay. The challenges he had to face came in various shapes, some visible and some not, some expected and some not, some dignified and some not. The long hours at the clinic – the eight hours which became ten and then twelve – the lack of a weekly day off, the four hours of sleep, the deduction of his salary for his morning sessions, the allegation of negligence, the distance from home, all of these, personified by the man sitting at the register, were the price he had paid. Rakesh silently told himself, "I shall pay whatever you demand, but I will put what I choose on my tray, and those terms are nonnegotiable."

He had difficulty staying awake during the session after lunch, as it crept into his usual nap time.

An interactive session lasted from four to four-thirty during which each candidate drafted multiple-choice questions, which very much encouraged lateral thinking. But he had to skip that session, as he had to rush back to the hospital for duty. By the end of the second day, he realised that the schedule of the full-day course and late-evening duty was no joke, but then the thought of the cafeteria calmed him.

With each passing day, Devji became more friendly and shared more of his thoughts and experiences with Rakesh. Rakesh enjoyed his company both ways. The mostly bitter stories of his past fuelled Rakesh's determination. Regret seemed to be the common thread through all of the driver's stories.

Rakesh asked him, "If you had to re-live your Saudi life, I mean, if you could go back in time and do it over again, what one thing you would change?"

He started with his usual clap, which no longer

worried Rakesh, followed by an intense silence. He cleared his throat and said, "I would have saved some money in my own account every month. It would take care of me by now. I did not do that. Instead, I sent every penny home." After a pause, he repeated, "Every penny, every penny."

A week into the course, the physical strain was already affecting Rakesh. He could not carry on his usual night studies, as the days were already too long with the new schedule. Reception rescheduled most of the patients who came in in the morning looking for Rakesh for the evening. This meant he saw and treated the same number of patients he would have otherwise, but in half the time and for half the salary.

Shika was not very attentive in class, but she paid a lot of attention to her clothes and perfectly matched her sunglass, bag, and shoes every day. Rakesh learnt that the exam style was different from what he had been used to in medical school. In India, the examiners assessed one's ability to learn; in contrast, the examiners now assessed one's ability to understand. One evening as they drove back to Farooqia, Devji took an unusual turn and looked at Rakesh in anticipation.

With his eyes, Rakesh inquired, "Where are we going?"

"Today you have finished a bit early, so I shall buy you some good tea. It won't take too long," Devji said.

He was right, it did not take too long. A few hundred metres along the improperly metalled road off the highway, they stopped at a small shop. Inside were empty glass shelves.

"Ammava, this is my new doctor friend that I told you about," Devji yelled more than said, his words marked by happiness and a bit of pride. "Two special teas," he ordered.

Rakesh settled down in the comforting warmth of the simple shop. A tea glass landed on the table before him with a thud, as if this was the final flourish to make it special.

"This will make you fresh," said Devji, who seemed to quite enjoy playing host to Rakesh. It was a good tea flavoured with cardamom. Tea, Rakesh felt, was excellent in such small joints. The smaller the restaurant, the tastier the tea. He recollected the long bicycle trips with his friends on Sundays in high school to a nearby village. Rakesh was the only one who had to rent a cycle, but felt like he owned a fighter plane for those two hours. They pedalled a few kilometres along the village road, into the paddy fields, and up to a small village tea shop with a thatched roof made of coconut leaves. The floor was smeared with cow dung, and cinema posters hung from the walls. The man who made tea never wore anything on his upper body. His frothy tea was a reward for the long ride. At times during the rainy season, the roof leaked and rain even trickled into the tea, but that only added to the fun, and now, thinking back, to a sense of loss. *Those were wonderful days*, Rakesh thought. Stress and worries were nonexistent, and life was filled with fun and freedom. The only disturbances were the occasional confrontation with a teacher for not having done homework or facing his annoyed father for having come home late. Besides that, life knew no anxieties.

"Dr Saab, did you not like your tea?" Devji asked, pulling Rakesh back to the present.

"I liked it very much."

They rode in an unusual silence on the way back. Rakesh's mind wandered to his childhood. He realised that he felt not happiness but a peculiar sense of loss: he then felt that the word *nostalgia* was apt. Like myalgia was muscle pain, arthralgia was joint pain, nostalgia too was a sort of pain.

"That man, Shankar Ammavan," said Devji, "lost his brother few months back in a road accident. It was a terrible tragedy. Shankar brought him to Saudi about seven years ago on a driver's visa. The brother was a very honest man; he sent almost his entire salary home every month. The accident was not his fault. A Saudi guy in a four-wheel drive hit him from behind at a red signal. The agony of having lost his brother was nothing compared to the trauma he had to go through to transport his brother's body back to India. He went begging from office to office, from airline to airline. Everything was tangled in a legal and financial web. Finally the Kerala samajam, a social organisation, formed a committee to collect money from friends, and after three weeks of distress, Shankar sent the body home on Saudi Airlines. Our embassy was—" Devji stopped and took a breath to collect himself. "Anyway, what's the point?"

"It seems that you were very close to him."

"Yes. He shared my room for almost a year after he arrived; he was a very loving person. I always told him to keep some money for himself, but he wouldn't listen. Each month after he had sent home nearly his entire salary, you could see the glow on his face.

"Dr Saab, sometimes I wonder, are these people not greater than those soldiers who guard our borders? When a soldier is killed in action, he becomes a hero, and his body is sent home with honours and draped respectfully in the tricolour. What do you say, Saab? Indian expats here in Saudi sacrifice the best part of their lives for the financial security of their families and, indirectly, for the state, but they are never heroes. This country only exploits them. When they die, no one wants their bodies. Dr Saab, do you know why?" Devji sighed and said, "A dead body cannot earn anymore."

"The Army is different; war is different," Rakesh argued.

"Yes, but all those who join the armed forces did so primarily to feed their families and not to defend the borders."

* * *

After dinner, Rakesh watched a video of an old English movie. In the midst of a hectic schedule, people at times sit idle, deriving momentary comfort from detaching from reality. Rakesh was doing just that. When the movie was over, he told Niranjan of the conversation he had had with Devji earlier that day.

"Oh! That is very true," responded Niranjan when Rakesh mentioned the exploitation of non-resident Indians in India. Niranjan knew, for he had already spent five annual vacations over there.

Niranjan continued, "The exploitation starts the moment you arrive in your home town. The customs officers, the porters, the taxi drivers, even your friends, everyone wants something from you. This continues till you get back to the departure lobby at the end of the holiday," said Niranjan.

"What do you mean, even your friends?" inquired Rakesh.

"You have not yet been on your vacation, but soon you will know what I mean. Your friends behave as if part of the Saudi package is to treat them on a regular basis. I enjoyed doing that in the first few years, but not anymore. At first I mistakenly thought that they looked forward to my arrival and to spending time with me. Soon I realised that only the first part was true. No one ever came to see me. Instead, on learning of my arrival, they rang up to fix the party venue and time. Everyone, be they friends or family or colleagues, they all assumed that spending money in my presence was a sin. One guy, who was in my pre-medical school batch and doing quite well in life, made sure to go to the toilet whenever a restaurant bill came to our table. But then, that is the way things are. You just have to get on with it. Even the media are out there to squeeze you. Have you not seen all the ads for money transfer services? These ads keep reminding us how important it is to send money safely without delay to our loved ones. Have you ever seen an ad or news story that even vaguely showed the human value of a non-resident Indian? Never. He is always the giver and never the receiver. All he receives are the tension and eternal insecurity that come with a Gulf jobs. But then, he suffers in silence, for there are no listeners." He stopped. "I don't think I should be talking like this, Rakesh. I remember your analogy of the bird in the cage. But I wonder, which is the cage, our job or our vacation from it?"

"Oh!" Rakesh was impressed by this insight. "That is interesting."

※ ※ ※

On 24 April, with exactly one month to go, Rakesh wondered whether time would permit him another round of revision. He had left revision of biochemistry and community medicine for last. He had a curious envy and a confused respect for those who pursued careers in these fields. He remembered his biochemistry teacher, a middle-aged man with white hair whose speech, lessons, and behaviour exactly matched Rakesh's perceptions of the subject. The preparatory course had helped him immensely to prioritise what the examiners considered important and had augmented his confidence.

"But a UK exam is a UK exam," Abid Hussein, a Jordanian in the course, had said. This was his third attempt at the exam.

Rakesh fell back into the schedule he maintained before the course. Midnight to 5.00 a.m. was prime time for studies, and he studied again from 2.00 to 4.00 p.m. and in gaps between patients. However, the receptionist who had replaced Jabber didn't honour his schedule. He continued to accept patients for Rakesh even after 11.00 p.m. At a time when each minute was valuable, this occasionally ignited his temper. The regularity with which Jaison did this erased Rakesh's belief that he did it out of inefficiency and ignorance. Most days Rakesh had to argue with Jaison as he left for the night, although he never refused to see the patients. But today he said to himself, "Enough of this." He remembered a quotation: "The secret of failure is to try to please everyone."

Two patients sat in the waiting room at 11.45. Rakesh silently walked away. Jaison stopped him in the lobby.

"Doc, you have two more patients."

"Yes," Rakesh said casually. "Have fun sorting it out."

This was a new situation for Jaison. These two patients had already registered and paid their consultation fees, but the doctor walked away. He was momentarily confused, for this was not his fault. He immediately rang up Moideen in anticipation of the patients' annoyance. By now they were at the desk with verbal armour.

Moideen came down to reception. Jaison saw him and whispered to the patients, "Please speak to our manager."

For Moideen this was a sticky situation. If assessed this exclusively from the legal angle, Rakesh was in the right. But the patients, too, were right. Was the receptionist wrong? Technically yes, for he had accepted appointments after Rakesh's shift. *But then, the medical profession does not always work with technical precision*, thought Moideen. This idea was helpful in situations when it worked in management's favour. Also, Jaison served as Govardhan's extension in reception, and that sprayed confusion on every canvas related to Rakesh.

Moideen had learnt one thing – whatever the consequences, take the patient's side. Hussain had driven that lesson into him, and it had helped solidify Moideen's loyalty. But this was a complex situation. It was impossible to get Rakesh back that night. Moideen remembered what Govardhan had said a few days before: "You don't have the authority of a manager."

"Anything I do now," Moideen resolved, "should disprove that opinion." He turned to the patients, lowered his voice, twisted his face into a persuasive smile, and said, "The night duty doctor is here. Do you want to see him? If not, we could consider put your registration and fees towards seeing Dr Rakesh tomorrow. However, if you insist, I can get him to come back now." He was half begging. One of the patients decided to return the next day, but the other was still sitting on the fence although his annoyance was receding.

"Okay, I shall call Dr Rakesh," Moideen said. He dialled the phone.

"Hello, Rakesh Sir, we have two patients who just missed you, and one of them insists on seeing you tonight. His working hours don't permit him to come earlier in the day. I would very much appreciate it if you could come back to the hospital to see him now. I can send the car to fetch you. And, well, how can you be so strict about leaving at a specified time? We are not employees in a factory."

The patient gestured that he was leaving and would not bother anymore. Moideen put the phone down. When the second patient had gone, satisfaction replaced Moideen's irritation. He was impressed with himself. He had asserted his authority over Dr Rakesh in front of Jaison. Only Moideen knew that no one had been on the other end of the phone. He congratulated himself on his management skills in a difficult situation.

Rakesh was just finishing his quick dinner when Tajudeen came in with some videos. Tajudeen often borrowed them from a nearby library and shared them with the residents here.

"What is this, Rakesh? Every day there is a tussle at reception?" Tajudeen asked.

"Same old story. I've told the receptionist a million times not accept a patient after eleven, but it never sinks in to his buffalo brains."

"Rakesh, when telling doesn't work, acting does. And these buffaloes have enough brain to know whom to obey. You should get that straight. Can I tell you something? I think you failed to make your desires clear in the beginning. I remember times when you've seen patients till midnight and even after that."

"Yes, that's right, but that was when I had free time. Now I have every minute, if not every second, tightly packed."

"That's exactly the point. In the last few months I've been here, I've never stayed late, not once. I've lived by that simple policy, and I've enforced my policy since day one. It offended management at first, but then they saw it simply as normal. Management has exploited you, or, more precisely, you permitted them to exploit you, and now to suddenly deviate from the pattern will create turbulence."

"Dr Tajudeen, shall I get you some dinner?" Hameed cut in to the conversation. "Tonight is fried fish and steamed rice cakes."

"Hameedbhai, you make my mouth water," Tajudeen responded, "but I have left my family in the shopping mall. I'll have just the fish."

Hameed left to make up a plate for him, and he turned back to Rakesh. "Now, Rakesh, I tell you this because I understand very well how it feels when people misread one's intentions. People infer what they want to from what you do and largely ignore the thoughts behind them. I have been a good influence on the people who worked for me and have had healthy relationships with all of my colleagues, and all the managers I've served have taken my opinions seriously, but there is one area in my life where I have had absolutely no influence whatsoever, and I'll always carry the burden of this failure with me. That failure has taught me to make my intentions loud and clear from day one."

"Tajudeen, who is it you don't have influence over?" Rakesh asked.

"Burden may not be the apt word, frustration or some sort of incompleteness. Say like a sculptor who did a beautiful figure but then someone came along and made a dent. A dent that can't be repaired because of the materials rigidity; and should not be repaired because of the denter's authority. With time the dent became an integral part of the product, generating an amusingly vague sense of pride to the denter and a sense of incompleteness to the sculptor. In certain moments of solitude or of silent resignation the sculptor gazed at the figure and painfully craved to see the product without the dent. Incompleteness in its finality became part of the completeness. You may be wondering what am I talking about – well my parents. The one place on earth where I have no influence is my own home and on my own parents."

"Is that what you referred to as the dent?"

"Well, the dent is in my personality," Tajudeen explained. "Yes, I was a perfectly obedient son. I earned a reputation as the most obedient son in town. My parents never missed a chance to mention of this to anyone. Many parents envied them, and some of my friends were perpetually annoyed with me, as their parents put them down in comparison to me. From a school kid to a college boy, then into twenties, realisation started trickling in that it was not obedience at all; instead was fear to react; was inability to respond. I became the yes man of my parents. Initially I saw it as an admirable quality that attracted envy, then a habitual pattern of a dutiful son, then a programmed routine that developed roots too deep to be ripped off. The only thing it ripped off was a significant wedge of my individuality. My brothers earned all the progressive freedom through the growing years, but not me. I spoke and acted exactly as my parents wished and insisted, but thought differently. And this contradiction was a suffering. A peculiar suffering for which there are no external symptoms. My parents failed to acknowledge that the transformation from a dependant boy to and independent man had the concomitant development of one's own thinking faculty. On the very few occasions where I expressed against my father's views, the atmosphere at home sunk to a terrible gloom, like the death of someone. These episodes were a painful awakening of the extent of damage I had permitted, by the years of silent submission. So Rakesh, the point is we permit many things in the wrong pretext of being nice. Never attempt to be nice against you inner voice."

Rakesh listened attentively to Tajudeen and showed no expression. Tajudeen was a loud, jovial guy, and it was unusual for him to express such sentimentality verbally or non-verbally.

"Dr Tajudeen, your fish is getting cold," Hameed interrupted.

"I think my kids must be getting impatient," Tajudeen said. He gulped down the fish and said with his mouth full, "You cook fish better than my wife."

* * *

The hospital was usually crowded in the evenings, but

this evening it was even more crowded than usual. The Ministry of Heath had instituted a mandatory health screening for expats prior to issuing a work permit. In addition to the general check-up, the medical examination included blood tests for hepatitis and HIV and a chest X-ray to test for chronic chest infections. Farooqia was one of the few hospitals authorised to perform these tests, and this brought in workers in batches of ten and twenty.

Neerja now had eighteen patients waiting to have blood drawn, so she could not divert her focus to the file which Khalidbhai had left on her long desk. She had already seen that the file was not accompanied by the envelope containing radiographs, which were normally kept with the patient's file for a couple of days, after which they went to their respective storage rooms. Because of this, Anwarkutty's file dropped a bit more oil onto her flame of suspicion.

Neerja drew blood and gave injections with lots of care. Though she was generally quick to deliver treatments, she made a conscious exception to tasks that required needles to make them as painless as possible for patients. She aimed for a complete absence of an "ouch" or a grimace. Her skills were well acknowledged. Some patients even skipped their regular appointments so that Neerja drew their slips.

Any time Neerja held a needle, she thought of Dr B. S. Nair, who had run a dispensary in her home town. Everyone who lived had some dreadful memory of this man. Dr Nair spoke little and smiled even less. He implied that cruelty was an essential quality of a successful doctor. His injections were like stabs. She vividly remembered this man's long-sleeved shirt tucked in to well-ironed loose trousers, which stood out in those days. His dispensary had two rooms: in front was the examination room, and in back was what the kids called Nair's torture chamber. Whatever the complaint, a jab was part of the treatment. The steaming and bubbling steriliser from which he extracted the needle multiplied the terror. As he fixed the needle onto the syringe, he often glanced at the victim over the thick frame of his glasses, a strange look which confirmed the impending danger. The minutes that followed were absolute agony, and the illness for which they had sought treatment was a pleasure in comparison. Once Neerja had to visit Dr Nair after having falling out of a mango tree and injuring her right ankle. She went in with one bandage on her ankle and came out with another on her left arm thanks to Dr Nair's injection.

It was past seven when she finally laid her hands on Anwarkutty's file. Govardhan's handwriting inside resembled leftover noodles on a plate. Somehow she managed to make out two notes, "cough" and "chest X-ray", and that was all she needed. She now had the facts. Anwarkutty had presented in the morning with a cough, and Govardhan had ordered a chest X-ray. Anwarkutty went down to radiation and paid for the test. But the puzzle remained. Had the X-ray been done? The evidence favoured Neerja's suspicion that it had been, though this was still unconfirmed. She felt a victorious excitement building, unsure who or what she had almost defeated. She knew she couldn't share this with any of the nurses, as half of them had jelly for spines, and Shoshamma had eaten away at the self-esteem of the other half. She ran upstairs to Rakesh's office.

Occasionally Rakesh took his lunch break at the

hospital, but he did so less and less frequently. But today he had made an exception, as Neerja insisted that he join her for lunch in the conference room. All she had said for an explanation the previous day was, "The Sherlock Holmes in me is at it again." Rakesh had no clue what that meant. Lunch with Rakesh always had an added attraction –Hameed's delights. Like Neerja's injections, this was very popular. Neerja ate two of the three parathas from Rakesh's tiffin and relished them along with the mixed vegetable curry nicknamed "Hameed bhaji".

Rakesh listened to the story of her investigation. The moment she linked the words *missing* and *radiograph*, he thought of Cyril's daughter and her two missing sets of pictures. Hers were missing not just from the file but from the record room as well. He was now certain of what was going on. For Rakesh this information was a blessing, a shield not just for a defence but a weapon in itself.

"What's your aim?" Rakesh asked her.

"Is it not criminal to expose patients to radiation just for money?"

"Yes, it is, but you need concrete evidence before you make accusations. This could have serious implications if it's confirmed. The hospital could lose its license and can be closed down."

"I don't want that to happen, but this practise should be stopped, and I need your help," Neerja said.

"So that's why you asked me to have lunch with you and instead finished mine." Rakesh smiled and then shared the story of Cyril's episode, which brightened Neerja. Her challenge now, she realised, was to keep a lid on her excitement and investigations. She knew she had to.

"I wish I didn't have exams or I could join you. Right now I think you should get more specific details of those who were duped. Are you aware that doctors get paid ten per cent of the fees for tests?" asked Rakesh.

"So you must be making a good amount."

"Not me. I do not agree with the policy, for it may put pressure on the physician to perform tests when they're not necessary."

"You have a point. At least some tests are done for good reason. Here that's not the case. On top of the fees, these patients were punished for their ignorance with a dose of radiation," Neerja said.

"The person who earns the most through unnecessary lab tests and radiographs is Govardhan."

"That doesn't in any way concern me," Rakesh said.

"But if what we suspect is true, the hospital also saves a good deal on the films," added Rakesh.

"But what if a patient wanted the picture explained to him or wanted a second opinion?"

"That's logical thinking, but they only select uneducated patients, mostly labourers, who fearfully worship doctors. Neerja, I must go – I have lots to catch up on. Good luck to you. Just a remember, don't allow any leaks. Take care of Preetha; don't give her any hints."

Chapter 15

Rakesh was scanning the Arab news just before seeing patients, and an advertisement caught his eye:

All are invited to the opening of a joint Indo-Arab painting exhibition today at 8.00 p.m. in the Indian embassy, Riyadh, by His Excellency Sheikh Mohammed Anwar Rashid, minister for social affairs. Participating artists:

Masood Ali Masood (Jordan)
Ali Manszari (Bahrain)
Fernandez Pinto (India)
Sulaha Gamdhi (Saudi Arabia)

The show will run for ten days and will be open each day from 4.00 to 11.00 p.m.

The name Fernandez Pinto was pleasantly familiar. Rakesh had had a fanciful attraction to painting as a boy, though he had fallen way short of being an artist.

In grade school art class he had drawn the Taj Mahal and gave the drawings to others. He could draw it swiftly under his desk while pretending to pay attention to the teacher. He enjoyed the shading, but that was an extra he did only for his close buddies. If ever anyone said to him, "So, you are an artist," Rakesh corrected them by saying, "No, I just like drawing."

One of his uncles once gave him a drawing book and a set of coloured pencils to keep him happily engaged for his summer holidays, but Rakesh completed the sixty page book, with pictures of horses, the Taj Mahal, and human faces, in less than two days. However, he never pursued any serious activities in art, and his drawing ended with the eggplant incident at school. He still visited art galleries and exhibitions, though. Modern art confused him. The more of abstract art he saw, the more convinced he was that it was all dignified insanity.

Rakesh thought it was strange that if you understood what those scribbles and bizarre images meant, you were put into the category of intellectually isolated. If you didn't understand them, you were considered normal,ordinary , lacking a philosophically fertile mind. The titles of these works appeared to Rakesh like an attempt to come up with anything that was even remotely sensible. Once in a contemporary art show, Rakesh had seen a huge almost empty canvas with linear strokes of different colours in a random pattern. The work was titled *Pride of Shame*. The man who committed this crime, also called as the artist, was at the show only for the camera, and he spoke only to the media. People commented that he had been isolated in the interest of his physical well-being.

To interact with art lovers would have left him with abstract bruises.

Yet another show that he occasionally remembered for its dreadfulness was by a Goan artist who called himself a "neo-partial impressionist". The show was in Bangalore. His creations, Rakesh thought, could have been expensive scarecrows. The hype created by the media brought Rakesh to the crowd to hear the creator describe his work. Rakesh had thought, *If colours had their own judiciary, then this man would be behind bars or at least would have been barred for life from holding a brush.*

The Goan artist, with stubborn enthusiasm, explained to the media, "Art is a reflection of life. Life is complex, and so is art." He said this whilst standing beside a one-metre-square canvas that, if seen on the roadside, would have been ignored as a slush-splashed, weather-beaten election campaign poster. But here it was in the spotlight as the platform for the artist's unique artistic jargon and on sale for $1,700. A reporter was busy capturing sound bites from the artist. Others in the audience didn't have a clue what he was saying.

"In the conglomeration of lives," the artist continued, "in our intricate and inarticulate selfishness, the only distinctively conspicuous streak is the lack of self." He now pointed to one of the lines on the painting. "However, self has two components: selfishness and selflessness. The consistent inner conflict between these, fuelled by one's dominant psycho hemisphere, is what manifests as ego. Fabricating an external manifestation is not a voluntary choice, but it is not involuntary."

"Why do you make it so complicated?" a boy in the crowd, probably in his late teens, shouted out.

The artist turned to him. "You need to think deeply to grasp the unseen architecture of the human mind. Anything precious is deep. What floats on the top and is easy to see is dirt. The precious pearls are deep down in the bottom of the ocean."

Rakesh heard an elderly man next to him whisper, "This painting should be at the bottom of the sea."

The group then followed him to the next work. This was titled *The Sin of Gravity*. On the canvas were smeared, overlapping patches of dark colours, like animals had walked over the canvas when the paint was wet.

The over-enthusiastic reporter asked, "Can you please explain this piece, Sir?"

"This can't be explained, it needs to be experienced. Explanation undervalues it. The experience of each moment is the result of centripetal and centrifugal psychic forces. It's like the work and load on either end of a lever. What matters is the fulcrum, but here the fulcrum is completely smudged, controlled by social and personal parameters. It sounds logical, doesn't it? But the reality is that it is all dictated by our ignorance."

"But how does all that relate to your paintings?" the teenager asked.

"My paintings require one to exercise one's imagination. Let it loose, liberate it, let it take wings and fly."

The elderly man beside Rakesh mumbled, "It'll have wings but no engine and no pilot."

As Rakesh walked out of the hall, he overheard a

couple's conversation: "This should not be called *art*. It needs an *f* attached to the beginning."

All these experiences with modern art gave Rakesh a modern dictum: stay away. After making this decision, he had been dragged to a solo show at Calicut Town Hall by a friend who was the co-sponsor of the event. That was the very first time he realised that abstract art could be attractive. He simply adored the works on display, their indefinable colours indescribably brilliant and their images aesthetically compelling. He spent two hours there. *The artist*, Rakesh thought, *must be a genius both technically and creatively*. The artist was definitely not someone who had had a sudden awakening and in its wake convulsed with a brush against a canvas, defending it with acrobatic verbosity when the product turned out to be a horrifying crime. In this show, the artist had not named each work; instead, he had given the entire show a theme: Why I Am Immensely Blessed. The artist was Fernandez Pinto. Rakesh did not want to miss the new show in Riyadh.

Rakesh had flipped open the calendar when Neerja walked in. She pushed a folded paper into Rakesh's coat pocket and walked out. He waited to open it until after his morning shift. It read: "Seventeen radiographs ordered by Govardhan last week. Two done. Remaining missing. All those missing were done in the morning shift."

* * *

The huge, grand hall with a high ceiling made glamorous by lavish spotlights showcased the works of the four artists. Each had eight or ten paintings displayed in groups. Rakesh easily identified Pinto's works, as he saw similarities with his earlier work. The brilliant colours against the beige background were inviting.

He saw two people talking in the middle of the hall, one was a visitor, and the other seemed to be the artist. Rakesh looked at each work up close. The title of Pinto's show was Synergy of Colours. They were colours in different tones and shapes, and they overlapped to create yet other colours. Vague shapes of contrasting shades added to the pictures' personalities. Some had patches of dark colours which Rakesh didn't care for, but most were soothing to the eye. These were colours that had not come out of the tube but had been created by mixing.

Rakesh moved from picture to picture and then greeted Pinto, who was listening to a group of visitors. Rakesh told him about the show he had seen in Calicut and how much he liked it. They instantly bonded. Rakesh felt happy to see the humility and simplicity of this talented guy.

"Your works are excellent, and they stand out in today's contemporary art," Rakesh said. He requested that Pinto explain his works.

Pinto looked like a normal man. He didn't wear the long, unkempt beard of other artists intended to imply creative genius or the standard long, wrinkled kurta that signified intellectual brilliance. The only hint that he was an artist was a sharpened pencil instead of a pen jutting from his shirt pocket. He was not too tall and wore thin-rimmed glasses on his happy face. He spoke slowly in a deep voice.

"Not many people ask such a question," Pinto said. "Synergy refers to an enhanced effect; that is, two plus two is more than four. Though I have named the show Synergy of Colours, I wish to show human synergy. You must have seen some people bring great happiness to others with their presence, and also the reverse. Let's say you and your colleagues are relaxing when your boss walks in. What emotions does his presence make you feel? It could be happiness, uneasiness, comfort, annoyance, or something else. It all depends on the colour of the boss's personality. Human nature relates to the behaviours of colours, and I have found immense amusement watching both. Through my works, I encourage people to ask themselves, does my presence make others happy? Sometimes the proximity of colours is all that's needed to brighten them; the same goes for human beings. Some personalities can bring out the best in others, and other personalities can bring out the worst. We need to ask ourselves which category we belong to."

Rakesh absorbed Pinto's thoughts with interest.

"Now, colours have another unique feature," Pinto continued. "They behave differently in different situations. This too has a human analogue, and that is the one I love the most."

"I don't follow," Rakesh said.

"You see, people sometimes project qualities which may not be their true nature in certain their interaction. You may also have heard someone say, 'Oh, that man is too hot tempered,' or, 'He uses abusive language,' or, 'He is not a listener.'

"These reactions reflect how the person behaves differently around different people. We change our behaviour when dealing with people in positions of authority, for example, than we do with people who are our peers. Are you with me?" Pinto paused.

Rakesh nodded, so Pinto went on, "A colleague of mine at the university where I worked years ago was so arrogant to subordinates, but he licked the boots of anyone with more authority than he had. I hope you are getting my view. Watching human beings is interesting. I used to get so disappointed when I saw the one person acting in diametrically opposite ways when dealing with different people. Even more problematic was the contradiction between what some said in public and did in private. Ever since I took up painting seriously, I've had a way to vent these frustrations and get some relief. It provides me with a platform for discussions and a way to provoke others to look into themselves. If a beggar in the street tells a lie, it may not impact anyone, but if a person in an important position lies, it affects many people."

This struck a chord with Rakesh, and he listened eagerly.

"The world would be a wonderful place to live if we looked into ourselves at least half as often as we look into the mirror," Pinto continued.

Rakesh smiled in response.

"Looking into oneself is something that everyone does, but most of us do it too late," Pinto explained. "Have you not known or heard of people who were rude or arrogant all their lives, only to change at the very end of their lives? They suddenly try to be compassionate, but no one believes they can be, and the changed person feels regret.

"I shall give you another example. Let's say a heavy smoker is diagnosed with lung cancer. He suddenly wants to change his life. He quits smoking and adopts a healthy lifestyle. But it's too late; the damage has been done. Regret will underscore everything he does from then on. I thought such an example would clarify the point since you're a medical man. This is how human behaviour works. Regret in itself has no benefit. It only enhance our mourning for whatever we've lost. The earlier it sets in, the easier it is to make changes, but we act too late. An alcoholic stops drinking when diagnosed with liver disease, a smoker quits smoking when diagnosed with lung or mouth cancer, an atheist becomes a believer when disaster strikes his family, an arrogant businessman becomes humble when he suffers a heavy loss. We can make positive changes, but most people need to suffer to do so, and then they do so too late. My question is, why wait for an external trigger, be it medical, social, emotional, or financial? All we need to do is to look into ourselves once in a while. In life's journey we interact with thousands of people, family, friends, colleagues, and strangers. The colour of each interaction is painted by our attitudes, be they positive or negative."

"You are not only an artist but also a philosopher," Rakesh remarked.

"Philosophy should not be a separate entity. It is the story of everyday life."

"Pinto, can I ask you something else? When most of the people here in Saudi, I mean Indians, share their thoughts and feelings, I see that they dominantly express regret. Why do you think that is?"

"Interesting," Pinto responded. He was thoughtful for a moment.

"And the degree of regret is directly proportional to the years the person has spent here," Rakesh added.

"Regret is something that all human beings feel in different situations," Pinto said. "They feel it differently in different stages of life. Perhaps their self-esteem has been damaged?"

"How do you define self-esteem?"

"I suppose it is the realisation of one's own worth and then acting in support of that worth."

Rakesh thought about these words as he sat in the cab on the way back. Pinto's definition had two components:one was the realisation of one's own worth and the second was supporting that worth . A person could carry out the second component only if that person made the realisation of the first, and if the second was not carried out, the knowledge of the first did not survive. *Such a simple but apt description*, Rakesh thought.

* * *

Chapter 16

The room had a pleasing ambience. The coffee and the untouched cookies gave it a formal touch. Dr Shewaqee and three others sat opposite Rakesh at an oval table. Rakesh was facing the door to the hallway, and he saw lots of activity out there. In the corner to Rakesh's right was an ornate wooden cabinet with neatly stacked files behind a glass door. Rakesh wondered if those files contained similar documents meant for crucification. There was a folder on the table in front of everyone except Rakesh. Thoughts flashed through his mind like the scenery outside a superfast train: Moideen barging into his office on a busy day; the introduction to Taher's case; the unusual compassion in Moideen's request to treat him; Rakesh's initial reluctance; the involvement of Jaleel, the maxillofacial surgeon; Moideen's enthusiastic co-ordination of Taher's treatment, the discreet fixation of the fracture, the best possible treatment delivered against all financial and legal odds. Rakesh had anchored the proceedings on exclusively moral grounds, and now he would have to defend himself against an accusation of negligence. *There has to be something wrong with the world for such a twist to occur*, he thought. How could he defend himself against people who had luring him into carving a weapon for defence against evil only to use that weapon against him? Why was this happening? Had there been a fundamental shift in values and ethics? Has being fair become unfair? Why was the truth lost in a tangle of lies? Why should the one to prove the truth be at the mountain base with the herculean task of struggling uphill, while those who crafted the deceit were comfortably at the top. Why did those in authority fake ignorance of valuable information? Only questions with no answers popped into Rakesh's mind. He felt no anger but a peculiar mix of contempt and sympathy for the buffoons seated across from him. But he was also aware of his own values which seemed gigantic in comparison to theirs. He recollected what Tajudeen said the previous night: "Stay calm and be firm."

"Good morning, Dr Rakesh," Shewaqee confidently began. "How are you? I'm sorry we had to convene such a meeting, but I hope you fully understand its purpose."

"No, I don't," Rakesh replied.

"I shall explain it, but before that, let me introduce these gentlemen. This is Dr Shashikanth, the consulting surgeon at Al Moaleem Hospital and a member of the Saudi Committee for Medical Ethics." To Rakesh, Shashikanth somehow didn't look like a surgeon or anyone in the medical profession. His pot belly dictated his sitting position. The knot of his tie was at his xiphisternum. His smile showed a villainous superiority. *He should be in politics*, Rakesh thought, *or maybe he already is.*

Dr Shewaqee now turned to the man on his left. "This is Dr Suresh Panicker. You must have heard of him. He's quite popular amongst Indian patients and is an active participant in Indian association activities. Currently he is the treasurer of the Saudi branch of the Indian Medical Organisation." Dr Panicker appeared youngest of all. He wore an oversized coat, but his face was clean and looked happy.

"And this man," Shewaqee chuckled meaninglessly as he pointed to the third man, "he controls all doctors. He is the president of the licensing committee of health specialists in the kingdom, Dr Sulaiman Haqueem Sait. We call him Saitji." Rakesh remembered that this man's name was on his temporary license. His appearance failed to hint at his nationality, but it was clear when he spoke that he was the neighbour across the red sea. People there spoke with an accent, using *sh* sounds in place of *th*. The staff at Farooqia referred to them as "Shank-yous". He didn't appear powerful or harmful, and he didn't seem to have a specific motive for being their except to echo Shewaqee's laughter.

"Let me explain the purpose of this meeting," Shewaqee said. "A patient has complained that he has lost sensation in his lip following your treatment of his jaw fracture. It is understood that you performed the fixation of his mandibular fracture. The patient threatens to file a lawsuit against the hospital for incompetency and negligence to claim compensation. We would like to prevent such a consequence. We understand that it would adversely affect your career and the hospital's image."

"Dr Rakesh, I hope now you understand why we are here," Shashikanth said in a friendly tone.

"I am sorry, but it is still not clear to me." Rakesh said. "Are you here to protect me and my career?"

"In a way, yes," said Dr Shashikanth.

"To protect me against what?"

"Against treatments such as this incompetent one, resulting in this patient's lip anaesthesia."

Staying calm was a challenge, but Rakesh had to. "If you have already concluded that I have been negligent, I prefer not to be a part of this session, for I have no role in that case."

"What are you trying to tell us?" Shewaqee said.

"I assumed that this committee would arrive at a decision based on facts, not based on allegations. Unfortunately, I can't see any intent in that direction," Rakesh replied.

Shashikanth and Panicker exchanged glances as if to confirm a previously held notion. A half nod from Shewaqee took that further, as if to say, "See? I told you."

Shewaqee took the role of a protector and said, "Doc, you shouldn't speak like that. This committee has the power to revoke your license."

"If medical licenses are issued and revoked on a whim, I have only deep sympathy for you, for you lack professional standards."

"Rakesh," Shewaqee continued, "do not prejudge us. We are not working against you."

"Prejudge. Well, you said it. How many of you knew the details of the patient's case and treatment and its complication before this meeting? If not, how many of you bothered to learn about it?"

"We were all given the details of the case," Saitji chipped in with a chuckle.

"May I know what those details are?"

"I don't think that is necessary," Shashikanth said, a bit of annoyance in his voice.

"'I think it is," Rakesh said slowly, calmly, and firmly.

Saitji took on the role of moderator and said, "I think we are taking the discussion in the wrong direction. Let us focus on what to do next and not waste time." He smiled in appreciation of his own statement.

"If news of this case gets out of the hospital," Shashikanth said, "it can only have a negative impact, so let's aim to contain it. We understand that your hospital's management would agree to settle this by making some payment to the victim. The amount can be negotiated later, but first we need you accept responsibility. This will make it easiest for us to help and protect you."

Rakesh looked intently at Shashikanth. "Sir, I understand that you are a member of the Committee for Medical Ethics. Would it not be ironic if the committee itself lacked the ethics they are supposed to maintain? You want to twist a malicious, fabricated story into the truth, and for that you need my help. I can tell you in very simple terms that that will not happen."

"That is arrogance," Shashikanth said.

"If speaking the truth is arrogance, then let it be so," Rakesh replied. "I am puzzled, as none of you are inclined to probe the real issue. Once the truth is established, then the course of action will be smooth."

"Are you challenging the credentials of the committee?" Shewaqee asked.

"Well, I wasn't at the beginning, but now I have my concerns. What if all the information you were given was false?" Rakesh said.

"Okay," Saitji said to calm everyone down. "We would like to know the story from your angle."

"Well, in that case, I need to know the details of the allegation," replied Rakesh.

"There is not much detail except that this patient has been left with a numb lip."

"Is it still numb?" Rakesh asked.

"That is irrelevant," Shashikanth commented.

"I think it is. Suppose feeling has completely returned. Then this whole meeting would be a joke."

"But how do you expect to resolve by itself?" Saitji said, attempting to be intelligent.

"That question raises concerns regarding the committee's credentials," Rakesh said.

That was a clear exposure of his ignorance and an attempt to cover it with further ignorance. Rakesh knew these men had had no association with clinical practise for years. Yet went up the ladder to acquire positions of might. Passage of time only added years to their name, never pulled out a medical text book or a journal, but knew exactly what strings to pull to remain afloat They had responsibilities without abilities, power without knowledge. They were professionals without professionalism. Rakesh recalled what Dr Kamal often said: that today, authority with integrity was like an alcoholic with stability. And here living examples sat right in front of him.

"You are investigating the possible iatrogenic role for the patient's complication," Rakesh argued. "I am surprised that there is no one in the panel who practises the related specialty. I think the patient should also be here. Why was he kept out of this? He would have helped us learn exactly who cooked this whole thing up."

"What do you mean 'cooked up'?" Saitji said.

"Taher had a partial loss of sensation in his right lower lip when I first saw him. This was the result of the fracture of the right angle of the mandible. And I have documented this. I think at least the patient's file should be here. Our manager, Moideen, was fully aware of the details of Taher's case. Yet suddenly he is on a long vacation. All possible sources of reliable information have been eliminated from this hearing. You don't need to be a genius to figure out that there is a vindictive intent behind these proceedings. The moment I received the memo requesting my presence I sensed it, but I expected that this committee would do its rightful job of fact-finding. In all frankness, I must admit that I don't see any purity of purpose here. This case was all fabricated by someone who long ago had every bit of his professional moral code squeezed out of him. I know you all hold positions of authority; however, it is plainly pathetic to see you all dance to the same tune."

"Cut the crap and let's get to the issue at hand," Dr Panicker said. "If you fail to accept responsibility, we may be forced to temporarily withhold your license."

"I am puzzled," Rakesh responded. "Why are you all prepared to bend so low, as if you had no spines, to prove I am guilty? I always perform according to a strict professional code, and I refuse to accept responsibility for this. And if you have some faint idea about the treatment that was performed, you would realise the sickening magnitude of this whole joke."

The men across the table exchanged peculiar glances and mumbled to each other.

Rakesh watched them, not each one but all of them as they were one. Different arms and legs, different tongues and vocal chords, different expressions and countenance but controlled by one brain, a brain that had no freedom: bonded by a grave sense of social values. A brain that feared those who used it fearlessly and then collectively defeated it, not in the name of fear but as act of noble duty. Their verbal choreography was different but the non-verbal agenda was shamefully common. They had respectable and powerful positions in their respective establishments but where consistent in the lack of self-respect. Their unity was that of bandit gang who loved one another when the loot was shared, beyond that it was bitterness. But bitterness never surfaced. When one laughed others joined as if they marched to a single band of music. Rakesh couldn't help wondering why they talked of standards when they had none. Why is it always that such committee comprised of those who were grossly unqualified and gravely disqualified for the job? Wasn't it like a burglar awarded a security guards job??

Rakesh walked out. His thoughts were hazy. He walked the length of the corridor, down the stairs, through the waiting room, and into the crowded streets. He walked briskly and aimlessly. He looked like someone who was already late rushing to a job interview. He was not aware of his pace. Subconsciously, his confusion fuelling his stride; he couldn't recognise what he felt. It was not pain, for pain would have had an identifiable cause. What he felt had a cause, but it was ill defined, denying him a grip, made conspicuous by its absence. He thought further. He was angry at the collective contributions of people who lacked self, who fed on others' thoughts when they were considered acceptable and appeared good to others in society, in their groups, in their committees, in their associations...

He strangely enjoyed his walk, a distancing act from the stink off the committee, where meaningless generalisations and twisted rationalisations drowned the reality. They spoke about humanitarian concerns; about maintenance of ethical standards in patient care; of sustenance of colleague support in teamwork. All of them on the panel were united by one common trait, the disuse of their thinking faculty. Their brains slept, vocal chords worked, they acted to the preconceived approval of an imaginary audience; shared the hollow sense of being guardians of medical ethics. Rakesh wondered, *Why is that the world is full of these actors?*

He took turns at junctions, choosing roads he had never walked down. He derived pleasure from scenery he had never seen before. He passed a ready-made garment show room, and seeing his reflection in the window, he realised that he was still wearing his white doctor's coat. He didn't bother to take it off. The oddness didn't concern him now. At the following intersection, he crossed the street as if he knew where he was going. He stopped at traffic signals as if he was a motor vehicle. He stared at the changing lights, and they amused him. Red, amber, green.

Rakesh thought about his own life. Red lights came from external sources, but green had to come from within, but it wasn't easy to obey it. In the traffic signal, the red and green lights alternated. But in life, green always had to fight the red. Red came in different forms and shapes, voices and vices, some obvious but most not. Sometimes it came from people and sometimes from circumstances. If there was only red, then there would be stagnation. But green alone would result in chaos. The systematic balance of lights regulated the flow of traffic. But in life's journey, the balance was not programmed. The red had to be identified, acknowledged, and then overcome. The green had to be nurtured against storms. Without green, there would be no purpose for living. A few metres away, he saw an ad that told the time. Rakesh was forty-five minutes away from the hospital, and so redirected his strides back there.

He thought of those who crossed the red signal, injuring those who strictly followed the traffic rules. The resulting disability attached anguish to the entire length of their life. The guilty washed the guilt in the legal proceedings and then led their normal life. Did this in some way reflect the world at large; victims never become victors, or do they?

The breeze blew the sweat on his face, and he felt cold. He took a shortcut through the market. He liked the sight of fresh vegetables and fruits in shops and pushcarts. Shopkeepers shouted their prices to woo customers. The competition was open and clean; there was no apparent bitterness amongst competitors. Rakesh felt instantly comforted by the sight. There were more shades of green in the cabbage, okra, and coriander than there were reds in the apples and tomatoes. But in their contrast, the reds enhanced the beauty of the greens.

* * *

Chapter 17

Hospitals and clinics were advertised in newspapers here in Riyadh, a practise unseen at home. Indian-language newspapers always featured eye-catching ads of hospitals and polyclinics. They were big, bold, and colourful. They each gave a brief summary of a doctor's credentials and expertise, and most were overstated. The size and frequency of these ads showed the fierce competition amongst hospitals. Rakesh didn't know that he was pictured in one of these ads until his old classmate Keith saw one and called the number. Dr Keith Pereira was now an assistant professor in the microbiology department at Oman University.

"There are no lazy people, only people without vision", a quotation Rakesh had read long ago, aptly described Keith. During medical school, he had barely scraped by on his exams. He got on the wrong side of every teacher and professor. Students were required to attend eighty per cent of a course's sessions to be allowed to sit the exams. This was always a reach for

Keith, but he managed it each time. No one knew how he managed to pass. Getting back in touch with Keith after six years felt to Rakesh like getting back a kite that had flown away.

Keith often remarked that the curriculum and the teaching faculty in medical school failed to inspire an average student. There were brilliant professors and great physicians on the team, but their knowledge and the wisdom of their experience barely trickled down to even the most dedicated students.

Keith had once joked, "Are our teachers paid exclusively for reprimanding us? Most of them do expertly." Years later, he became a teacher in a medical university in Muscat amongst an internationally qualified multinational faculty. His students selected him best teacher five years in a row, simply proving what he had casually observed as a student. Rakesh, Keith, and two of their friends each believed in their own way that student life was not all about studies. Keith put forth the bare minimum of effort to get by. But his presence was vibrant at every excursion, picnic, and get-together. Any trip without him would have been like Argentina's football team in the eighties without Maradona. Keith made you think that nothing was important except being happy. He had mischievous stamina and youthful energy. After his initial phone call, Keith and Rakesh spoke weekly. Before putting the phone down every time, Keith would ask, "Why don't you call Sayanora Thomas?"

People can only understand what they already know, thought Rakesh. Sayanora had been their batch mate, and she had sparked an interest in Rakesh. The general public had a general opinion of things, and it was useless to argue against their generalisations.

Rakesh had learnt that words sometimes failed to communicate. This always puzzled and slightly annoyed him. For most people, a companionship with someone of the opposite sex meant only one thing, and that fed the rumour mills, and the mills never went out of work.

Once Rakesh had gone to the Indian coffee house with an intern, Roopa, which created such ripples on the campus that they could no longer be seen together casually. Roopa was a tall, hyperactive, bold girl. She had the stride of an army general and the smile of a kindergartener. Rakesh enjoyed her company and her joyful attitude. Within the college's corridors it was acceptable for them to talk, but a visit for a coffee took on other tones. Rakesh felt this perception was the manifestation of a primitive and obsessive mind. But for people of a generation in which interactions between genders were to lead exclusively to matrimony, Rakesh had no argument. Sadly, even Roopa suspected his intentions when she heard the gossip. Rakesh surrendered to the gossip and lost a wonderful friend.

This happened with others too. Interactions between members of the opposite sex were generally restrained, so exceptions became news to those who had been genetically deprived of any skill in making healthy connections. They hid their inadequacies and envy under the brand of social responsibility. For them, women were mere objects and fodder for gossip. An intellectual conversation or a casual relationship was impossible.

Rakesh had stopped reacting to Keith's jokes about Sayanora. Rakesh had liked something in her innocent charm, but the self-imposed watchdogs of social interactions, including Keith, saw what they wanted to. Girls were meant for flirting with or for pursuing romance, even marriage, but no other relationship with them was possible. Rakesh felt this stemmed from confusion and prejudice. When people's values were shallow, so were their thoughts, words, and deeds.

* * *

"Now what?" Neerja asked. She had already fished out evidence to support her conclusion in the mystery of missing radiographs. Neerja wanted to expose it straight away for the pleasure of watching the culprits, but Rakesh felt otherwise. He did not want to lose the upper hand in the scandal. Exposing it now would take away his edge.

"Should we disclose this to Niranjan?" Neerja went on.

"Well, not yet. Niranjan's grudge against Govardhan is intense, so he won't sit on this information for more than a day, and he'll mess it all up in the excitement, so leave it for now," Rakesh said. "What I would suggest is that we gather more evidence. We could go back at least six months."

"Oh, that is a job," Neerja said with a crooked smile, which she often reserved to express disagreement or dislike. The smile revealed her misaligned canine teeth, an abnormality that, for Rakesh, added to her beauty.

"Well, I know it is an effort, but by now you know what to look for."

Neerja nodded and reluctantly smiled. The discussion ended as Judy entered.

❋ ❋ ❋

Rakesh had only four weeks to go before the exams, so he could only chat during dinner. Hameed made sure Rakesh didn't lose much time in whatever way he could, though he missed the post-dinner conversations. Moideen and Govardhan sometimes sat till two in the morning smoking and sipping black tea. Hameed slept only after everyone else went to bed.

"Why is that girl spending more time in reception these days?" Govardhan asked Moideen in a tone of calculated casualness, but his facial expression deceived him.

"Why do you worry about that? She's one of our best nurses," Moideen replied, lighting his fourth cigarette.

"Do you remember what I told you a while ago about some mission she's on?" Govardhan asked.

"Faintly, yes."

"Have you found out what she's up to?"

Moideen sipped his tea and said with amusement, "For your sake, I shall spy on her, but why don't you ask the receptionist to keep an eye on her? But what do you suspect?"

"Well, nothing in particular. I know she's been pulling out old patient files and checking radiographs, and that is not her job. Is she doing some sort of audit?"

"What do you mean, an audit?" Moideen asked sincerely.

"This is what I mean. You are ignorant of many facts, so just follow my intuition," Govardhan responded.

The following day, Neerja sensed that Jaison was

being a bit nosey, so she had to abandon her mission. Her investigations consisted of checking the daily patient data file to find Govardhan's patients, noting their file numbers, and then checking the file for the actual radiograph. It took at least five minutes to complete a check for a single date. After that, checking the radiology records was a lot easier, as the storage room was not busy, although she had no reason to give for being there if someone were to inquire after her. Now the reception check was even more of a challenge.

"Jaison takes lunch break for about twenty minutes. Use that time," Rakesh suggested. It would have been easier for Rakesh to do this bit, but he didn't have time. As the date of the exams approached, the details of this scandal were just as important as his revision.

❖ ❖ ❖

"Are you joining us tomorrow for Purushu's packing party?" Hameed said as he cleared the dining table.

"What party?" Rakesh asked.

"Our driver is going home for his vacation in two days."

"But why should I help him pack?"

"Ah! What a joke! Doc, you should have learnt some of our customs by now. When someone goes home for his annual vacation, all his friends help him pack. It's a sort of celebration. It's fun."

"Are you going, Hameed?"

"What do you mean? I have to be there. Have to arrange the cartons, tape, and string."

"Okay," Rakesh said. "I shall come and see the fun."

The idea of friends packing for someone else didn't appeal to Rakesh at all. But the sense of collective responsibility in a way puzzled him, so he decided to take part. Purushotham, the hospital's driver, was going home after three years. This was probably his third vacation.

The following day in the clinic, when Khalidbhai brought Rakesh black coffee, he asked, "Purushu's packing party is today. Aren't you coming?"

"Sure I am," Rakesh responded.

After a quick dinner, Rakesh went to Purushu's room with Hameed, who carried empty boxes that he had picked up from the nearby supermarket. The room was crowded with stuff scattered all over the place. Packets were on the floor and on the mattress. A half-filled suitcase was lying on the table. Rakesh saw a few familiar faces and many unfamiliar faces, but not Purushu.

"Hello, Doctor, I didn't expect to see you here."

Rakesh looked up to see James, a frequent visitor to the hospital. A veteran expat and the lead character of a tragic family story, as Shoshamma told it, James was everyone's friend.

"Well, I had to know what this was all about since Hameed hyped it up so much."

"Oh, the only thing that lives up to the hype here is the extent of human stupidity. I keep telling these boys not to squander their money on gifts. They don't listen," James said.

"Uncle, why are you such a spoilsport?" commented a guy who was stuffing a milk-powder tin into an already overloaded suitcase.

"See, Doc?" James said. "This is the reaction you get when you share your experience. I used to be like this – going home year after year with bags full of gifts and a heart full of love. It took me too long to realise that the feelings went only one way. Do you know how much Purushu makes? Not more than a thousand riyals, and look at how much he's spent on these purchases. When he comes back, find out what his bank balance is after having been in Saudi for more than seven years. The answer will shock you. It will be a big zero. Lots of us forget why we're here. We get carried away by the carnival at our arrival. The happiness generated by these gifts won't last long. It won't even last as long as the fragrance of some of these perfumes. Purushu doesn't even own a bicycle, forget about a two-wheeler, but you won't believe how he commutes during his vacation."

"This is true," Hameed cut in.

"He hires a four-wheeler and a driver for a month," James said. "See? He earned every penny here through hard work and sacrifice."

"But Uncle, do you want him to scream about his problems at the arrival lobby?" the guy packing the suitcase said.

James ignored him. "More than twice I went home with the plan of settling down there. Both experiences eye-opening. When my so-called friends sensed that I was looking for a job or that I needed help, they become inaccessible. These were the same people who at a hint would report promptly for booze parties year after year before that."

"Uncle, you are jealous of the friends and the fun Purushu has," the other guy said.

"My son, I can revive that kind of friendship and fun with a few tins of Nido, some Tango, and some beer," James said.

Hameed had finished stuffing a massive cardboard box, and he taped the top and tied it up professionally. Rakesh watched other visitors pop in with envelopes and small packages, which he learnt was yet another custom.

"Where is this Purushu? We are already over the weight allowance," another person who had been doing bulk of the packing said.

"Look, Doc," James continued, "ninety-five per cent of the contents of these boxes are gifts bought with borrowed money for family, friends, and neighbours who have no clue about his struggle here. I don't mean he should complain about his problems, but why give the impression that he doesn't have any? Initially he won't expect others to reciprocate. Generosity is the desired hallmark of a Gulf expat, a well-fed delusion. But reality will catch up with him. In human relationships, nothing goes in one direction for too long.and it will hurt him with certainty, the only uncertainty is the time of its onset."

When three cartons and a suitcase had been packed, Purushu walked in.

"I am exhausted," Purushu gasped. "I literally walked through the entire souk for this little bit of stuff."

"It is great that you managed to get it," James said sarcastically.

He ignored James and said, "This is a Mercedes police car with rechargeable batteries. My neighbour's small son wanted it."

"That's enough. No more," said Hameed. "You are already twenty-three kilos overweight."

Chapter 18

In the first thirty or forty minutes of a weekday morning, very few patients walked in unless they had an appointment. Rakesh monopolised that time with revision of self-test manuals. He had a pile of previous year's exams.

The phone broke his concentration.

"Hello, Super Doctor," Moideen said loudly down the line with a laugh. "Today a VIP, Mr Kamath, is coming to see you. You must have heard about him. He owns a lot of businesses here and is shortly opening a supermarket in Cochin. He has a backache and specifically asked for you. I shall bring him in when he comes. Look after him well." In the excitement, he didn't wait for Rakesh's response and hung up.

Rakesh had heard Kamath's name from Hameed and Khalid. They referred to him as an unseen hero. He was unseen because he was too famous to be seen in public, and he was a hero because he had become wealthy by sheer will. They knew nothing more about him, but their imaginations created stories. Once

Rakesh had heard Khalidbhai saying that Kamath had hired a private jet for an urgent meeting when he couldn't get a ticket to Delhi. Rakesh had also heard that he had built a house for someone who had lost his job after losing his leg in a traffic accident in Abu Dhabi. He had also offered this man's son a job in his company. Niranjan often scoffed at such stories. Rakesh never knew how much could be believed, but it was refreshing to hear stories of success and human decency for a change. Khalidbhai had never seen the man but described how handsome he was and said that he wore a silk suit all the time.

When Moideen came at eleven, Rakesh knew who he was accompanying. Moideen's excitement was particularly evident. "This is Mr Kamath, one of our well-wishers," Moideen introduced him.

"Good morning." Kamath extended his hand. Rakesh sensed warmth in his ways and saw a glint in his eyes. He didn't fit Khalidbhai's caricature. He was informally dressed.

"How long have you been here? What about your family?" he asked Rakesh.

Rakesh told him about his wife and child.

"Oh, you must be missing your little one," Kamath said. "What is she called? When is your vacation?"

It unusual for a patient to ask so many questions, but they seemed to come from genuine interest. When Rakesh answered him, he listened too – a rare trait.

Moideen exited more like a dutiful servant than the manager of the hospital.

"I heard about you from your patient Cyril. His daughter was treated here," Kamath said.

"Yes, yes."

"Cyril is my colleague. In fact, he has been insisting that I see you about my back pain."

Rakesh took a detailed history and examined Kamath's back and advised some radiographs.

"I think you should come over for dinner one of these days," Kamath invited him.

"Thanks a lot. Can we set a date after my exams?"

"Oh, yes. Moideen told me about your exams. When are they?"

"The end of May."

"Almost a month away. I don't think we should delay that long. How about this Thursday night?"

"By the time I finish my shift, it's midnight."

"Then how about lunch on Friday?"

"Okay."

"I'll come and pick you up at about, oh, twelve-thirty."

When he left the office, Rakesh felt like he had known this man for years.

* * *

The SUV he drove was the first sign of Kamal's wealth that Rakesh had seen. It was a four-wheel-drive Lexus. Behind the remote-controlled gate they drove through was a big house with an expansive lawn and parking spaces for three vehicles. Inside, the living room was massive. The furniture and the collection of curios had a traditional flavour. Handicrafts and artefacts from around the world were on display, but the room had an aura of simplicity. A bright red Buddha painting looked conspicuously out of place to Rakesh. He loosened his tie and sat down.

"Dr Rakesh, what would you like to drink?"

"Kamath, I'd rather prefer you call me Rakesh."

"Not a problem, Rakesh."

"In the clinic you bombarded me with questions. Now tell me something about yourself. How long you have been here?"

"I came here almost twenty-one years ago."

"But you don't look that old."

"Well, that's because you didn't ask me how old I was when I came to Saudi. I was twenty-one when I landed on this desert soil. I served as a house driver to a wealthy Saudi."

Here comes yet more tales of his self made fortune, thought Rakesh.

Out of the depths of the house walked a woman who could only have been Kamath's wife with glasses of fruit juice. It took Rakesh a few seconds to overcome the guilt of seeing a woman without an abaya. Over the previous eleven months, the structure of the female body had been replaced in his mind with a structureless black object. She had the sort of charm that normally grew with age. As he picked up a glass, she said, "We heard a lot about you from Cynthia."

Rakesh looked confused.

"Cyril's daughter," Kamath explained. "Our families are very close. They visit us quite often."

"How about your kids?"

"My eldest girl, Sanjana, completed her plus two last year and joined Maryland School of Arts. My son has gone out to roast himself in the name of cricket."

The name Sanjana brought back memories of Rakesh's own daughter. That was the name his wife had wanted for her, but it had been vetoed by a strong in-law lobby that favoured Nirupama instead.

From a house driver to here. That must have been quite a journey, thought Rakesh.

"Kamath, it is very inspiring to see that someone from humble beginnings from our state has become so successful. Most often we see and hear stories of pain, failure, and regret. Do you mind sharing your secrets of success?"

Here in front of him was a real-life success story. His story would surely contain more jewels than Rakesh's favourite self-help books.

"Rakesh, there are no secrets. Just keep moving forward, and never limit yourself."

Rakesh observed the casualness with which he uttered such a powerful message. He couldn't help repeating, "Never limit yourself."

"The stories that you just mentioned about pain and regret, most often those come from people who limited themselves. I agree with you that our people here in the Middle East derive a peculiar pleasure from publicising their distress," said Kamath.

"But don't you think that many of these stories are true?" Rakesh asked.

"Yes, I don't dispute that. One can have a very disappointing and even humiliating experience. My point is that you shouldn't let them be final. Move on. When I came here as a driver, I was paid three hundred riyals a month. My boss appeared to be a decent guy. He treated me well, and I sensed that he trusted me more than his own son to drive his family around. Two years on, I bumped into an ad for a driver in a contracting company. The salary was almost double what I was making and had more benefits. I went to my boss and said that I would like to apply to that job, as three hundred riyals was getting me nowhere.

That discussion was an eye-opener. I learnt that most Saudis deep inside share the same idea: exploit the expats. He said that I couldn't change jobs, as that was against Saudi rules. At that time I wasn't aware of such a rule. But I decided that he wouldn't be the one to define my future. As the discussion progressed, I told him that I wanted to quit and go back to India. I had taken up that job as a platform to for better jobs. If I couldn't get a better job, it was useless to stay on. Our discussions degraded into an argument and then into abuse. I refused to drive for him at that moment. He threatened me and even pleaded with me to stay on for a hundred-riyal pay hike. When I declined that, I was deported without being paid the last twenty days' salary. But I managed to come back on a free visa after three months, and I managed to get another driving job part time. I was delivering stock to a supermarket. All the staff at the store were Keralites, so spent my free time there and learnt that a supermarket is a less risky business than others and can turn a good profit. I then wanted to start my own small shop. The challenge was raising the funds. I devised a convincing plan and presented it to my sponsor, a man with inclinations towards business. I asked him for one year's salary as an advance, which he agreed to. All he demanded in return was a small fee for being the sponsor of the shop. That was my first business venture, and I slowly expanded from there."

Mrs Kamath cut in, "Don't bore him with your same old story. Lunch is ready"

"It's not at a bore," Rakesh said. "On the contrary. It's exhilarating."

"The point is," Kamath went on, "if I had yielded to my first employer, I would have been confined in a driver's job. That's what I mean when I say don't limit yourself. Move on."

"But then, some people get trapped in their first job. Don't you think so?" Rakesh asked.

"They need to find a way to free themselves from the trap. If anyone here in Saudi has been in the same job for three or four years or more and is still unhappy, then believe, me it's their own choice to stay stagnant. There is always somewhere to go if you need to move forward. You have to identify where it is and sometimes even create the space for yourself. It's like a fire fighter. In a traffic jam, it creates space for itself with its siren and forges ahead. You have to make noise. Unfortunately, many people only make noise about their pain and misery, which is waste of human energy."

"If it weren't for the exams, I would have loved to spend more time here."

"Your exam is your desire to move on. Good luck."

"Come on, the food is getting cold," Mrs Kamath repeated. Rakesh stole a glance at the clock.

"Don't worry," Kamath said. "I shall get you back by two."

The lunch was a feast. By quarter past two, Rakesh was back at the hospital.

"If you need any help or if I can be of any use, feel free to contact me," Kamath said through the window of the Lexus.

"Thanks a lot," Rakesh said. "And don't ignore your next physio appointment."

* * *

Judy had been called to Govardhan's room a while ago, and she returned with forceful strides and a tearful face. She settled in her corner stool. Rakesh said nothing and gave her the time to compose herself. She dried her eyes with a tissue.

"I would not go anywhere if they forced me. I'm going home," she said, a quaver in her voice. He knew that was an invitation to intervene.

"Go where?"

"To Jeddah. They want me to go tonight."

"Why is that?" Rakesh was surprised. He knew that such a transfer would affect him more than anyone else, and that was the real goal. Rakesh's clinic was a smoothly running machine oiled by her presence. Her absence would disrupt the system, not just professionally but personally. Management had chosen a time when it would hurt him hardest, just a few days before the exams. His focus and time would have now to be diverted to training a new assistant when every second was precious. That was sharp move, the latest in the dirty games of those with official power. Rakesh was the victim; Judy was only the tool. He knew he couldn't interfere in the plan because it had the stain of official priority. He couldn't mention the delays and inefficiency it would cause the clinic, for they engineered that to happen. Rakesh couldn't bring up the difficulty it would cause his exam prep, for that was purely personal, and they wanted to disrupt that too. This seed had to have sprouted from Govardhan's brain. He would have forced Moideen to nurture it.

Judy burst into another bout of sobs. She had come from Jeddah to take this position when Rakesh had arrived. She was strongly attached to her work and excelled as an assistant. She also had stronger reasons to be around Rakesh that couldn't be named, and that explained the sobs.

"What will they do if I refuse to go? They can't drag me. They may punish me, but the worst they can do is sack me. I'd prefer that."

"You don't have to think so radically. Talk to Moideen and request time to think about it."

"I don't need time to decide. I am not going anywhere."

Rakesh saw her determination and the clarity of her decision through her tears.

Judy excelled in her duties, and everyone in the hospital thought so. She was never restricted by the boundaries of her job description, and she contributed anywhere and everywhere. *Something is wrong*, Rakesh thought.

Why was it that the sincere ones always got the beating?Is sensitivity another component of the psyche that formulates sincerity.These two can only coexist. For a moment he wondered if Shoshamma was the one to have got this transfer to Jeddah. How would she have reacted ? Maybe she would have packed up with a smile. She was attached only to her monthly pay cheque and felt nothing for her colleagues. Her pleasure derived entirely from what she could buy with her salary. Her work held no pleasure; it was only a means to an end. But for Judy enjoyed interacting with others. Relocation for Judy meant severing all of the relationships she had built here. For Shoshamma, there was nothing to cut off. Rakesh remembered something he had read: "The more human you are, the more you suffer."

"When do they want you to leave?" Rakesh asked.

"Tonight. Govardhan wants me to be ready by eleven. The flight is at one in the morning. I just walked out of his office."

"I would think it would be appropriate for you to meet with Moideen after a while. Express yourself calmly and firmly. Walking out of Govardhan's office has left the issue suspended, and that will not work in your favour."

Judy didn't reply, but her silence indicated her agreement.

The phone rang, and Rakesh answered. Shoshamma was on the other end.

"Doc, can I speak to Judy? This is very important."

"Important for whom?" Rakesh asked.

"Oh, so you're aware of what's happened. I shall come to your office."

Shoshamma took up such tasks with a satisfying sense of duty. She acted as though she were a part of the management team, or, more precisely, that's how she desired her colleagues saw her. She put up a facade of authority and compassion. The authority was necessary and natural; The compassion was faked. Rakesh and Judy greeted her with silence as she walked in.

"Why are you so upset? Jeddah is a much better place than here," Shoshamma said.

"Then why don't you take my place?" Judy shouted.

"This is your problem, you yell at those who try to help you."

"What help are you here to provide? Just conveying what those nasty minds decided?" Judy snapped.

"Try to understand, the orthopaedic assistant in

Jeddah had to take emergency leave, so they need an immediate replacement. And you are the only one with adequate experience. Moreover, you are already familiar with the system in Jeddah. Once Dana is back, you can return."

"What a wonderful story. I'm still not going."

Shoshamma was steadily losing her patience, as her steadily rising voice showed. "You have no choice. No one here has. We work as we are demanded. The monthly salary should be our only aim. And that's going to be same in Jeddah as it is Riyadh. So calm down and be sensible. Govardhan wants you to be ready by eleven. I think Purushu has gone to get your ticket."

"I am not going."

Shoshamma looked at Rakesh. She knew which side he supported, but he remained silent. She was failing to get Judy to make the transfer smoothly. She appealed to Rakesh with a glance to help her make his assistant understand the futility of her will.

"She has to go," she said to Rakesh. "Whether she accepts that happily or painfully is her choice to make."

"Are you concerned about her happiness?" Rakesh said.

"Why do you always take that side? Why don't you think from the management's angle?"

"I could ask you the same thing."

"I think talking is pointless."

"I agree."

"Okay, I am going. I have things to do. I shall report to Govardhan that you will be ready by the end of the evening shift."

"Did she say that to you?" Rakesh demanded of Shoshamma.

"What am I supposed to report?"

"Report exactly what she said."

"She can't say that."

"No, I think she can. Abraham Lincoln had abolished something years ago. Do you want your colleague to revive the practise?"

Frustrated, Shoshamma started to leave. At the door she sighed and shot Rakesh a smile that said, "Let's see what happens."

The clinical work dragged on. Patient complaints, history taking, examinations, investigations, treatment, advice, follow ups, relevant doubts, irrelevant queries. The process had to take place but enthusiasm was out of place. The synchronised energy with which Judy and Rakesh preformed their routine duties lost the energy. It was like an express train in full fury that had to slow down along the length of a defective rail. Both derived momentary comfort in the awareness that they shared the awareness of their worry. Judys sudden absence would derail Rakesh's intricate time management. Their bond of understanding had attained a level where verbal communication wasn't needed anymore. As if it were four hands that took orders from the same brain. And now all that would be crushed, not as a by-product of a decision but as the main desired product. Like the naughty whims of boys who purposefully stamped and killed ants. Simply because they had the unquestionable ability and the sadistic joy to do so. The same boys who would nervously scream at the sight of a spider on the bathroom wall. It was the courage of the cowards, the strength of the weak. The fog of anguish hung in the office. He knew that nurses and assistants in the past were never consulted; even doctors were not offered much say in many matters. Decisions were unilateral. Evidence doesn't show much to predict relief for Judy, but her vehemence encouraged Rakesh to think otherwise.

Back at the nurses' station, Shoshamma was fuming. "Who does she think she is? A princess? If she thinks so highly of herself, why is she here? Can't she sit at home and give orders?" Judy's response to her orders had made her furious. The others nurses gave her the attention she sought.

"How dare she refuse orders?" Shoshamma continued. "Does she need a reminder that she is the employee and not the employer?"

"Who are you talking about?" Richa asked.

"Who else? That stupid girl Judy. Anyway, she deserves it. She thinks she's superior to the rest of us, and now look at what's happened."

"What has happened?" Neerja chipped in.

"Judy has been kicked to Jeddah. She's been ordered to report there tomorrow for the morning shift." The word 'kicked' reflected what she liked to feel.

Judy had never been a member of Shoshamma's coterie, timid, submissive and spineless nurses.The ones who retained the luxury to think,choose and express were her opponents.

"Who made that decision?" Neerja inquired.

"Govardhan."

"I think we should pack him off to Jeddah," Neerja said casually. The other nurses' jaw dropped.

"There should be a limit to your jokes." Shoshamma raised her voice in Govardhan's defence. "Neerja, you are making very arrogant statements that won't serve you well."

"Why don't you say that to Govardhan? He's the one making stupid decisions."

The other nurses tried to suppress a giggle.

"You all can have fun here," Shoshamma said. "Tomorrow this could happen to you as well."

"Not to me," Neerja said. "I choose where I work; that man doesn't."

The other nurses knew that Neerja would have a say in such matters, for she had made that known from day one, but that Judy would have to yield.

"So what is the plan, Madam Shoshamma?" Neerja asked.

"She will have to leave tonight. I went to convince her about that, and she turned violent. She refuses to go. That poor girl doesn't realise that that's not her choice."

"If she doesn't want to go, why force her?" Neerja's questions were always simple, and that often confused others. "You're close to Govardhan. Why don't you tell him that she prefers to continue on here."

"And you want me to get on his bad side."

"Let me talk to Judy," said Neerja. She got up to leave, but Shoshamma stopped her.

"Look, you should stay in your place. You are an overenthusiastic girl with no knowledge of the system here. They brought us here to work for them. And so they reserve the right to make these decisions."

"Why do you say they brought us here? We decided to take up this job. Is it not so?"

"Either way, we are here to make a living. As long as they provide it, we should obey them."

"This is not a matter of disobedience, but of choice."

"It's exactly as I said; you have no knowledge of the system. Aren't you aware that many have lost their jobs and even their end-of-service benefits for being overly smart? Do you want to be added to that list? Don't you remember what happened to Jabber? No one's seen him since he was disobedient."

"Let me see her anyway."

"I do not want you spoiling the plan," an annoyed Shoshamma added as Neerja walked out.

"Oh, you are so keen to see her off," Neerja called over her shoulder.

Shoshamma retorted, "You should be the one to be packed off to Jeddah."

"I'll go only if I want to." Neerja laughed, annoying Shoshamma further and entertaining the others.

Most everyone enjoyed Neerja's comments. She often said what they thought but were too afraid to utter. They envied her fearlessness but didn't think this quality a beneficial one for them to possess. Shoshamma had successfully managed to eliminate any dissent over the years.

Six years of unfailing commitment, skilful assistance, pleasant and polite, no signs of stress or annoyance when the work load heaps up, enthusiastic to help others, good aptitude for learning; these would be the wordings if someone wrote a professional reference letter for Judy, but then the cruel reality is that she stands in agony, a reward for all the above and the proximity to Rakesh.

At about six-thirty, Neerja came into Rakesh's

office. Judy looked exhausted but worked in occasional spurts of energy, the energy that uttered repeatedly that she would not go. She was like a trapped cat hissing at an attacker.

"Cheer up, Judy," Neerja said. "We'll find a way out."

These words gave Judy a wisp of hope. Neerja never made hollow statements, Judy knew.

"I'll tell you what," Neerja continued. "Go meet Moideen right now. He's in his office; I just saw him go in. He must be fully aware of the whole issue. Don't request permission to stay here. Instead flatly say that you will not transfer to Jeddah. If you want, I can accompany you."

"That may not be appropriate," Judy replied.

"Who cares what's appropriate now? Just do what you need to do."

Rakesh cut in, "Moideen will give a lengthy explanation to justify the move, but stand firm."

"At the end of the day, he's just the same as Govardhan," said Judy, who was steadily regaining her composure.

"But Moideen is marginally better than Govardhan, particularly when he's alone," Rakesh said.

Judy who was like a collapsing building a while ago, now stood still; the collapse froze as if held by the strength of the one last pillar .

"And Judy," added Neerja, "if Moideen insists on the transfer, take out the trump card: threaten to resign. And stick to it, come what may."

❖ ❖ ❖

Johnson was pleasantly surprised when Rakesh called to ask if he could go to his place that night.

"Oh, of course. I'll be at your hospital in fifteen minutes," Johnson said, and he put the phone down.

The May air was unusually heavy with humidity. The noise of the engine and FM radio made conversation a challenge. Rakesh was unsure what he felt as he rode along. Was it relief that Judy would stay back or triumph that the manager had yielded to the firmness of a subordinate? Why should Govardhan, who seemed to have risen from the burial ground of human values, hold the key to happiness for those who held such high values? If someone like Judy could be pained by the same managers she served with devotion, what purpose did her devotion have? His thoughts wandered violently and randomly like molecules in hot water, bouncing around the confines of his head.

As they approached Johnson's villa, Rakesh observed the security guard's salute. It showed reverence more than rigidity, the human touch of loyalty. It was a wordless display of gratitude. As soon as Johnson cut the engine, Rakesh jumped out. He seemed to be in a rush to relax. Johnson didn't probe him for the cause of his uneasiness.

The fact that Rakesh had chosen to spend few hours at his place only a few days prior to the exam conveyed a lot.

Johnson provided him with a comfortable place to sit, a drink to sip, and a pair of ears to listen. Rakesh was in no mood for slow sipping and gulped his drink down. This time Johnson had made a new juice out of potatoes and grapes.

The taste was odd, but soothing. They both sat in silence, the increasing length of which didn't appear uncomfortable. A silence that fit precisely into a prefabricated slot.

The fabrication that came from years of knowing one another – not just words and deeds but the beliefs and principles on which their professional and personal life grew. "When I started my career," Rakesh started to speak his mind. "I thought that ethics was one quality that would form the foundation of every human endeavour. That those who based their decision on ethics and their actions on values would always be the winners, and that those without these in a confrontation would be the losers.

And that one who upholds integrity would automatically attract respect and that those without it would eventually follow him by delayed bruised realisation.

A name build on truth and dignity can't be tarnished by those who do not possess it, and that it would only tarnish the tarnishers.

And that intelligence would be a trait that can exist independently without fear and that its expression would be welcome in the circle of literates. And that performance of one's duties with commitment and sincerity would win the applause of the management.

And that would provide a foot stool onto the ladder of success; and those devoid of these would sediment at the bottom of the ladder.

And that consistent hard work would wipe of all challenging up rises like a wave that erases the writings on the shore.

And that logical thinking and performance would always outmanoeuvre its illogical counterpart. And that twisting of facts and framing of lies would all be burnt in the heat and glow of truth. But then ...I started getting to realise…. that's not how our system functions. There are no universal codes of ethics. It is the ease and choice of those who hold power, position and wealth.

The possession of any of those in abundance makes ethics and values appear as an optional fragment of ornamental fabric, which can be conveniently discarded. And for those for whom this not an option, each strand of this fabric has a meaning – the code of meaningful existence. But then in a conflict doesn't this fabric get torn apart?

Isn't it objectively very fragile? And then those who treasure it walk around half nude covered with the ripped and tattered bits of that fabric, deriving comfort and strength only from thought.

Can the vigour derived from the intangible assets counter the consistent denial of tangible gains? Who wins? Who loses…?"

Johnson didn't move. His face implied that he was waiting to hear more. His didn't express acceptance or of denial but amusement.

"Your observations are all true, and I completely agree with everything except…"

"Except what?"

"Except that that's not the way to view life."

"How else would you? This is the true order of our times."

"Rakesh," Johnson said, sitting up. "Visualise a highway at a busy hour. Everyone is going along at a different speed in different lanes, but the common aim is to move forward. There's a fast lane for ambitious people, but it's not always open. It opens up in windows that last only seconds or minutes. The assertive drivers speed ahead. This is how you need to view life." Johnson paused to let that sink in.

"When you're involved in a purposeful pursuit," he continued, "you need to be assertive to get into the fast lane and aggressive to stay there. Like you said, not everyone's a saint. They apply every trick they can to get past others. Some of them pack the rules in the boot, and some never learnt them."

"Others assume a driving license is an excuse to circumvent civilised norms. But do the rest of us not still move forward? Do we pull over?"

"Resentment and irritation swarm all around us. Idiots overtake on the wrong side, drive on the hard shoulder, change lanes without indicating. This is the chaos of life. I used to let these people bother me, but not anymore."

"Now I regard them as stray dogs on the street. All I have for them is sympathy. They are not my competitors but creatures that need to be cautiously acknowledged because they are insane."

"We co-exist with them but we don't compete with them. Like on that motorways, we come across vulgar display of misplaced heroism, dangerous acts of shrewdness, and over-smart attempts to overtake. The key is to watch them carefully, sympathise with them, and then move on."

"Johnson, you are right, except..."

"Except what?"

"Except moving on may not always be possible. Their actions can slow you down, stop you, or even throw you off the motorway."

"If they slow you down, accelerate again; if they stop you, start again; if you are thrown off, get back on again. Simple truth, persist or perish. Frustration will be generated in abundance. Frustration if hinders your path, that's because you compete with them. Never do that; only compete with yourself."

"Now, Rakesh, what happened to that guy with the jaw fracture? Jaleel was telling me about it."

"I still don't know who crafted the allegations of negligence. He hasn't returned for a follow-up."

"He must have completed his treatment elsewhere."

"He was always just a pawn."

* * *

Chapter 19

"Hi, Rakesh."

Without looking up, he knew who that was. The only other person who addressed him without the prefix. "Hi, Kamath, come in. What brings you here?"

"I just completed the torture you prescribed – the last session of physio. That guy is really tough. My back pain was mild compared to what his savage hands did to me."

"You will slowly get better. How is your new shop gearing up?"

"We have the usual challenges, but it's moving ahead."

"Kamath, suppose your second sponsor had refused to support your first business venture?" Rakesh had an enormous appetite for stories of success, and he was curious to know more.

"I would have left him."

"And then what would you have done?"

"Do you remember that last time we met, you

229

mentioned that most people tell stories of pain and regret? Such stories are told by those whose lives hang on the question, 'and do what?' I am not sure what I would have done, but I was certain that I wouldn't permit anyone to block my path. They may have made it longer and more difficult, but not..." He trailed off as though searching for the right words.

"Let me explain it this way. It's like someone waiting for cab. Let's say he's waited for almost thirty minutes. He's seen lots of cabs pass by, but none of them have been empty. What should he do? Well, he has three choices. First, he can continue to stand there till he runs out of energy or patience. Some people call this persistence, but persistence without common sense is stupidity. It drains you. His second option is to give up and go home. These first two choices are what most people choose. Both have merit, especially to people with appetites for surrender. They can spice up the story and serve it at social gatherings. Then it's no longer surrender but a self-awarded medal for enduring such hardship, and is on constant display.

"The third option is to go somewhere else. He could walk a bit further up the street or go to the next street over or the nearest junction. He'll find many empty cabs this way, but it requires much more than just desire ."

"But, Kamath, suppose he found no empty cabs even in the new location?" Rakesh asked.

"He'll find them depending on how passionate is he about getting to his destination."

"You mean to say that most people don't have enough passion?" Rakesh prompted.

"Some may fall into that category, but most people feel they are incapable of reaching the destination.

They make strong decisions about their weaknesses but never take responsibility for those decisions. Instead, they blame the street, or the time, or the cab drivers, or the weather, whatever suits them."

Khalidbhai entered with coffee, and Rakesh saw an opportunity to play a little joke.

"Khalidbhai, do you know this gentleman?" Rakesh asked him.

Khalid looked confused.

"Ah, you should be able to recognise him. He's the man who always wore a silk suit."

Khalid instantly smiled and made an embarrassed apology. He bowed, and then bowed deeper to express his respect.

"Hello, Khalidbhai," Kamath greeted him. Khalid's smiled so broadly that he exposed the space behind his last tooth. For Khalid, people like Kamath were fairy-tale heroes. They weren't seen and spoken to.

"How long have you worked here?" Kamath asked him.

"With this management, almost nine years," Khalid answered.

"Do you like it here?"

Khalid looked unsure. He smiled again and escaped.

"Rakesh, look at this guy. He has been here for nine years, serving tea. Don't you think it was his own choice to stick to this low-paying job? Maybe in the first couple of years he didn't have an option but over time he decided that this is it. People like that project an image of sacrifice. Sacrificing for their families, sacrifice their time, money, and effort and the rest of their lives. But in the absolute privacy of their unbiased thought, they very well knew that they have limited themselves by ignoring their own talents, discarding their own goals, and disowning their own intelligence." He took a breath. "I think I have taken too much of your time and should leave."

"No, not at all," Rakesh said. "Why is it that most expats, especially those in low-income groups, lack the zeal for life? I mean, why do they always look like they're suppressing grief?"

"You seem to be especially concerned for our people here," Kamath responded.

"It surprises me that two out of every three patients I see are of this sort. Back home there is always an enthusiastic greed for a gulf job.But after they serve here for a few years, most of them don't act as though they've achieved anything. This is baffling to me," Rakesh explained.

"I agree with you. To understand that, you need to understand the cause of it. In our society, when a person obtains a Gulf job, he instantly fills the role of a saviour or it is forced upon him. He is glorified as the one with the magic wand to settle family debts, to pay for his sister's marriage, to pay for his brother's education, to take care of his parents' health, to repair an old house, to construct a new house, on and on, the list never ends. By the time he has completed all the formalities and boarded the flight, he has also been burdened with unrealistic expectations. Every single person who lands here brings with him or her a completely wrong or at least an inflated idea of what can be accomplished in the Middle East.. They were made to believe that money is easy, quick and abundant in the gulf countries. This is an unavoidable product wrongly delivered by those who walked earlier; their extravagant life style during vacation mostly from borrowed money; lavish distribution of gifts – mostly ill indicated ones; construction of huge homes – mostly beyond their means; availing bank loans mostly beyond their repay ability. It is like the euphoria from intoxication, Unreal, enjoyable and temporary. For the beneficiaries and viewers the show was good. Those with a casual dream to reach the Gulf who saw the show will then have an intense desire. Those who already have an intense desire get impatient. But when expats get back to Saudi after vacation, the euphoria subsides, the intoxication wears off, and they painfully realise the financial losses. Time heals most of the wounds but financial wounds can only be repaired by financial dressings. Year after year they suffer more injuries and their attempts to repair fail. The alternating cycle of losses and attempts to catch up continues."

Rakesh stopped him here. "But how were you able to wriggle out of this mess?"

"All you need to do is look in the mirror once in a while and ask yourself, 'Who decides my happiness?' I had a friend who often said, 'Keep the key to your happiness in your own pocket.' Unfortunately here, people make umpteen duplicates and is distributed. Eventually they even give away the master key."

❖ ❖ ❖

Govardhan never arrived for his evening shift before four-fifteen. At four o'clock, Neerja decided to use the next fifteen minutes to fish out the file of Deepak, a patient who saw Govardhan two days before and had paid for three radiographs. His case would add to her evidence.

She sneaked into Govardhan's office. By now she knew exactly where to look for the files. Files for that day's cases were on the desk, and those for the previous two to three days were normally stacked in the desk's bottom drawer. Neerja knelt down and quickly searched through the nearly fifty files there. She found Deepak's file and noted that he had complained of frequent headaches. Only one radiograph was in the folder. She then heard the door slowly creak open.

"What the hell are you doing stealing from my office?" Govardhan yelled. He had come in unusually early. He was trembling with anger. She stayed in the same position, half kneeling and half squatting, and looked up at Govardhan awestruck, as if examining a tall building from its base.

"Didn't you hear me? How dare you fiddle with my stuff? You thief!"

Govardhan's eyes ran over her body, taking in the visual treat of Neerja's body in a position that stressed the outline of her curves. She sensed a change in his thoughts. She said nothing. Govardhan bent down and, with one swift move, snatched Deepak's file from her.

"Why are you tampering with my notes?"

Neerja stood up without a word, as she wasn't sure what direction was best to take. Rakesh had warned her never to spill the beans unless the time was right. She thought it was still early. She was sure she'd be sacked.

Govardhan's eyes went wide when he identified the file. He said in an unnaturally loud voice, "Explain yourself right now or prepare to pack off tomorrow."

"Neither of those will happen," she whispered loudly. She walked out.

Neerja went straight to Rakesh's office and told him of the unexpected encounter.

Govardhan immediately picked up the phone and dialled Moideen. When he answered, Govardhan said with impatient fury, "Do I as the chief, have the power to terminate an employee with immediate effect?"

"Yes, of course, with strong and valid reason," Moideen said.

"Cut the crap about reason. I am firing Neerja right away. Make arrangements for her return. She should be on a flight tomorrow."

"But—"

"No buts. I am serious." Govardhan hung up.

Neerja was uneasy after the confrontation. She unloaded her burden onto Rakesh.

"Rakesh, I'm not concerned about being sacked, but I don't want to go as a loser."

"No, that won't happen," Rakesh said. "I'll take care of that."

"I don't want you to apologise on my behalf or anything like that."

"Come on, Neerja, you still haven't learnt how I do things. Just listen to me. Write up all your findings now, and keep them handy. Don't forget to include the dates payments were made for the radiographs and the patient's contact number whenever possible. Then carry on your duties as normal, and leave the rest to me."

As Neerja left, he wondered why he had to deal with more and more distractions when he had so little time to do so. The exams were three days away, and now this issue had to be sorted out. He knew it was his problem more than hers.

A confused Moideen came into Govardhan's office.

"You can't fire someone without proper reason," Moideen explained.

Govardhan was still furious. "I caught her red-handed, stealing from my desk. Isn't that reason enough?"

"Why do you say she was stealing? She was probably taking out files or radiographs."

"Yes, that's right, radiographs. Did I not warn you about the possible complications if someone were to expose our radiation protection shortcomings?"

"Yes, you did, but we have fulfilled most of the criteria required by the ministry. That's how we were able to renew our license this year. So what's the worry? What's more, everyone, including the authorities, know that complete adherence to these regulations isn't practical. But I don't understand why that should concern you more than the radiology head. And what has that to do with Neerja?"

"There you are – there are lots of technical medical things which a policeman will never understand. Don't compare me to that radiology head of yours. I've been here right from day one building this institution day and night. The reputation this hospital has now is largely due to my sweat. All the other staff joined to earn a living in a properly run establishment. For them, this is just a job, but for me, this is my baby, and so anything that happens will hurt me more than anyone."

What Govardhan said was irrefutable, but Moideen also sensed that he was covering up for something else, but what that was completely evaded Moideen. In a similar situation a few years before, Abbey, the hospital driver, had been sacked on the spot. Govardhan never liked waiting for transport after he finished his clinic duties, and he expected the ambulance to be waiting for him. Management respected his wishes and saw to it that the ambulance was ready most of the time. However, one day, Abbey made Govardhan wait in the lobby with the nursing staff for almost twenty minutes.

When he finally walked into the lobby, Govardhan yelled at him, "Where have you been sleeping, you bastard?"

Abbey wasn't apologetic. He replied with almost the same volume, "Somewhere other than where you bastards sleep!" That was his last day on duty. Abbey was Moideen's friend's son, but no apology or persuasive argument from Moideen succeeded in reverting Govardhan's decision. He knew that Govardhan would have his way in this situation too, and Neerja would suffer the same fate.

"I will not interfere," Moideen said. "You can issue a memo and go ahead. But I'm not comfortable with the decision and shall stay away."

Each such event further strengthened Rakesh's resolve to pass the exams, although it stole a good amount of valuable time from his studies. He sat in the solitude of Niranjan's room at a little past two in the morning. A Nat King Cole album played quietly on the stereo. The serenity of the small hours used to calm him, but lately they had become a time for ruminating helplessly on the gross irrationality of the world. Why was someone who had never harmed anyone being harmed? Why was someone who had never abused anyone being abused? Why was power always in the hands of those without values? Why was it so hard for people with integrity to rise up? Why were shrewdness and cunning the hallmarks of success? It was as though they had replaced truth and sincerity as ideal qualities. Could those who were completely truthful ever achieve their goals? Rakesh knew that he would never get answers to these questions. This web of confusion multiplied the challenge in the pursuit of one's dreams, but it also augmented the sweetness of accomplishing those dreams. He spent the remaining time until sunrise reviewing anatomy, the only topic that boosted his confidence.

* * *

Rakesh lay flat on the floor the day before the first exam. He had the multiple-choice questions in the morning and essays in the afternoon. This was the end of all the challenges he had faced in the last fifty weeks he had been here.

"Will I make it?" That question had hung over him, sometimes so heavily that it made even breathing difficult. Two weeks earlier, he had moved to Niranjan's room, as he was on his vacation. Sharing a room with Govardhan had become increasingly difficult as their relationship soured. Niranjan did not have an attached bathroom, and the mattress sagged in the middle like a country boat, but Rakesh liked the privacy and the freedom it afforded him. He slept on the floor with just with a pillow and nursery rhymes to keep him company. He played the nursery rhymes quietly on the stereo. Hearing them in the background had become a necessity for Rakesh to concentrate on his studies, and that puzzled him. Judy had given him this collection for his daughter. He wasn't sure if their appeal came from the simple words or the innocent melody or the reminder that life was beautiful in early childhood.

He stared up at the ceiling. He felt blank, dull, and confined. He longed for the days when he had slept on the terrace of the medical school hostel with ten to fifteen other students. They arranged their cheap bedding haphazardly like a camp and looked up. The endlessness of the starry sky gave him a sense of eternal freedom, of delight, of comfort, and of many emotions. Confinement wasn't one of them. He thought now of the shooting stars that vanished even before he could think of a wish, of the occasional plane in the distance that was nothing but a tiny amusement, of the drizzles that sent the other students running inside with their bedding. Rakesh wasn't deterred by a drizzle; the drops on his face brought him closer to nature.

He thought of the next day's exam. It was scheduled to begin at nine o'clock, but because it was the first day, candidates had been requested to report thirty minutes early, and he had arranged this with Devji. Rakesh had set three alarm clocks: two near him and one he gave to Hameed. He had decided against mental revision; that would only shake his confidence. He tried to turn his thoughts away from the exams to the arrival lobby of Calicut airport, where he would be in two weeks' time. He suddenly couldn't bear to wait. Fifty weeks had been manageable, but the next two were impossible. He closed his eyes and imagined kissing his little girl. She had changed a bit, he saw from recent photos. He imagined hugging his wife so hard, as if the pressure had to be directly propotional to the time they had been apart.

He could not help recalling the departure lobby from almost a year back. That scene had flashed on his mental screen a thousand times every single day. The scenes at the departure and arrival lobbies were exactly the same, but the emotions were different – pain at parting and pleasure at meeting. The second one couldn't happen without the first. Rakesh clearly remembered some of his fellow passengers waving to their dear ones before check-in, after check-in, before immigration, after immigration, before security checks, after security checks – not even caring if anyone could still see them, continuing till they boarded . To know exactly what they felt, one had to be in their shoes. They had left behind everything dear to them and taken up a job so far away, unsure of the facilities, unsure of the management's credibility, unsure about the salary, unsure when they would return, unsure of a million facts but driven on by dreams.For how many were those dreams misplaced? Rakesh thought of James, Devji, and the others about whom Shoshamma had told stories. He did not know when his thoughts were overcome by a deep sleep until he was jolted out of bed by a sequence of two alarms and a knock at the door from Hameed.

"This is my day."

* * *

It was a routine day at the hospital. Rakesh walked though reception like he normally did, and Jaison greeted him as he normally did. A crowd of patients swelled around the desk in every pattern except a queue. Khalidbhai loitered in the lobby with a mop, his key to enter any office at any time he chose. If anyone watched him for two minutes, they'd see that cleaning wasn't his priority. But the hospital was clean, thanks to his fear for the security of his job.

Occasionally Rakesh peeked into the lab to say hi on the way to his office. Each person stamped even this simple greeting with his or her personality. Nurse Richa's hi was just audible to the person it was intended for, and she accompanied it with a submissive and mischievous smile. She and the other nurses, except Neerja, never initiated a greeting. Neerja was loud, bold, warm, and welcoming. When she entered a room, she turned every head in the vicinity and stayed longer than necessary. When greeted, she made the greeter feel important and expressed joy when she reciprocated. Her vibrancy nullified despair and dullness and was a clear sign of the buoyancy of life. Shoshamma wasn't there in the morning shift, but if she were, she would have responded with a hello that showed off her authority. Then there were those who responded with a feeble gesture, implying that the greeting was an unavoidable, unenjoyable social requirement. They knew only how to survive.

The routine was abruptly interrupted when Judy handed Rakesh a tiny bit of paper. On it had been scribbled, "This is Kevin. Call me at 276653091." Rakesh was delighted.

Judy had recovered from the previous day's disturbances. Like other Filipinos Rakesh had met, Judy was resilient.

"Who gave you this?" Rakesh asked.

"He said his name was Kevin John."

"You mean Kevin came here?"

"'Yes. Why is that hard to believe?'"

"When was he here?"

"Maybe fifteen minutes ago. He said he had to rush off to work."

"Oh my goodness. Kevin is in town."

Judy stood up and stared at Rakesh. Such an expression of excitement was quite unusual for him. He read the slip again, looked up, and said in Judy's direction, "Kevin, you're in town."

Judy knew Rakesh's excitement was mounting. "Who is this Kevin?" she asked.

"He is… how do I explain it? We were best friends beginning in second grade. After college he went into the computer software business, but we stayed in touch. But three years ago he just vanished. And now suddenly he's left this bit of paper. Was the man who left this short, fair, and a bit obese?" he asked. He had no doubt this was old Kevin. All he had to do was dial the number on that paper, but he purposefully waited to enhance the anticipation.

In the routine of his life in Riyadh, Rakesh had little time to think of old friends. His mind wandered to his first attempt at smoking, his first taste of alcohol, and the umpteen other mischievous deeds he had shared with Kevin. Secrets were safer with Kevin than a bank locker. Rakesh first met Kevin the year Rakesh's family moved to Calicut for his father's job. He remembered meeting Kevin at the paper mill high school. Time failed to obscure the details of memories close to the heart. And if they started to get foggy, like the windscreen of a car, all that was needed to clear them was to switch on the heater. The heat from that slip of paper cleared the mist from every single event in their relationship in Rakesh's mind.

Kevin was a fair boy with a mischievous smile and a gleam in his eye. He had abundant energy. In second grade, he was too shy to look at girls. He easily slid into the slot of best friend in Rakesh's life. He could never control his giggle. Rakesh had the habit of whispering jokes in class so that teachers only saw Kevin's failed attempt to control his laughter. Kevin never told on Rakesh, even if he was caned. More than once he was sent out of the class for giggling and had to stand at the door. The telepathic communication continued, and he kept giggling there too. If enjoying jokes could be someone's passion, it was his.

Kevin's father was rarely seen but very much talked about. His father was highly committed to his job and the lack of it towards his family. Very few educated fathers did not know which grades his kids were in, but Mr John was one of them. When Kevin's marks on exams dropped, Mr John turned into a monster. For him, parenting meant flogging. The physical scars healed, but not the emotional ones. Kevin often spoke of his dad's cruelty. The only contact he had with his father was the end of a cane, leather belt, or other instrument that tore his skin.

When Kevin started working and his father retired, a sense of duty partly replaced his hatred for his father. He sent money home religiously and with such zeal that he earned the nickname "Volleyball Player", for he smashed money into his father's account faster that it came into his salary account. The effortlessness and regularity with which the money came swelled his dads ego. He belonged to the cult that believed that the eldest son was nothing but his parents' orderly and his wife the husband's maid. Their services were welcome, their ideas were not. Their money was welcome, their feelings were not.

Kevin was the eldest of six kids, two boys and four girls. After he graduated with a degree in maths, he took up computer science, which got him a job in the Middle East and the painful medal of a Gulfee. It was like a wedding ring on a finger that gradually grew fat. At first it glittered as a symbol of joy, but over time it tightened painfully on his finger. The more he attempted to remove it, the more pain it caused him, and the only option for ending the pain was to cut the ring off. And so he learnt to live with the pain like so many expats.

His sisters' weddings came in regular intervals that squeezed out his finances like toothpaste from a tube. Kevin's own marriage and the birth of his two kids were events that just passed by like irrelevant milestones on the roadside. His duties didn't permit him to celebrate any of these. The toothpaste tube was now rolled up and crumpled. Yet he continued to spike money home, but the vigour with which he had done this had been replaced by a vague sense of regret.

Kevin's parents' forgot his wedding anniversary, but his sisters they sent gifts. His parents ignored his wife's birthday, but for their sons-in-laws expensive presents were couriered, partly financed by Kevin.

Though Rakesh and Kevin drifted apart physically, they were constantly in touch. They met during all of Kevin's annual vacations. Kevin let slip his feelings about the downward path of his life in their conversations. Rakesh had witnessed his gradual transformation from fulfilling his duties with pleasure to fulfilling them with pain. And then came the confusion: who should come first, his parents or his own family? On the balancing act, which was financially inclined to his parents and emotionally to his family he often lost his balance. Parents saw him as a useless son. Wife saw him as a spineless husband. Only two people knew what song played in the innermost privacy of his mind: himself and Rakesh.

"Hey, what are you thinking?" Judy said, pulling him from his reverie. "Give him a call." Rakesh picked up the phone.

* * *

Neerja held the memo, read it a few times, folded it and tossed it away then picked it up and unfolded it again. She was looking at it, but her mind was wandering. The only words that she saw were "hereby terminated with immediate effect".

Those were the only words that spoke of action, and their strength came from a criminal's mind. Khalidbhai had hand delivered the memo in a sealed envelope which at least on the surface guaranteed confidentiality.

She told herself, "I shall not vanish like Jabber." She took it to Rakesh's office and let him read it. Neerja's enthusiasm was rekindled on observing Rakesh show no emotion —it was as if this were a normal memo he would read any day. This gave her hope. He looked up, and Neerja saw a calm smile on his face. Their silence continued, but Neerja knew they shared a private thought. Rakesh never said that he would protect her, but she knew he would.

"What are you thinking?" Neerja finally broke the silence.

"What are *you* thinking?" replied Rakesh with a peculiar smile that did not in any way fit the situation.

"Rakesh, I wanted to work in a hospital where I could be free to be efficient. I am fed up with this atmosphere of partial slavery. I am sick of my words and actions being critically scrutinised by authorities who have no skills to be role models, only the power to punish. I wanted to see someone at the top who would earn my respect. But I will not leave silently."

"Hmm. I like that: free to be efficient. Okay, now listen. Do you have your write-up of the data of the missing radiographs with you?"

"Yes." She pulled it out of her pocket and handed it to Rakesh.

"Good. It is well tabulated. Now just come with me. You don't have to say anything; simply follow me."

Rakesh walked out. Neerja followed. She felt like a schoolgirl following her guardian to the principal's office. In the grace of Rakesh's protection, her anger at the memo evaporated. A few minutes before this was her problem. But now it was theirs. At Govardhan's office, Rakesh stopped at the sign outside, as there was a patient inside. When the patient came out, Rakesh stepped in.

"Hello, Doc. What brings you to my humble place?" Govardhan's jovial expression drained from his face when Neerja stepped in.

"Can you please wait outside?" Rakesh asked Govardhan's assistant. She appeared confused, but Rakesh's firm and low tone could prompt only one response: obedience. He closed the door and bolted it.

Govardhan couldn't stop him. Govardhan seemed to have difficulty finding words.

"Now sit down and have a glass of water," Rakesh instructed.

"What are you up to?" Govardhan said, partly regaining his composure.

"Shut up and listen to me first. After that you may speak if you please." Rakesh took the memo from Neerja's hand and continued.

"Only we three and maybe Moideen know about this memo. This shall not be followed. You will act as if it was never issued. She isn't leaving. This is not a request. I am sure you have difficulty taking orders from me, but don't worry, I can help you with that too."

He took out Neerja's write-up from his coat pocket and read it out:

"Dr Govardhan, the chief medical officer of this hospital, in the last six months advised one hundred and seventy-four radiographs. However, only thirteen of them are on record. Radiographs of the remaining one hundred and sixty-one are missing, but there is evidence to suggest that all of the patients for which these were ordered paid for them and were exposed to radiation. In some cases, a single patient was exposed two or even three times."

Now Rakesh looked up from the paper to Govardhan. Neerja gaze followed. Govardhan looked like a rowdy felled in a street fight. He appeared to be debating whether to fight back or invite sympathy from lookers-on by taking more blows in his helpless state. He didn't take his eyes off Rakesh; he didn't look at Neerja even for a second.

Rakesh placed the memo in his desk and continued,

"You may now do as you please: either send this back to Neerja or throw it in the trash bin. I know you are an intelligent man with rudimentary brain tissue in some wrong places. And one more point that might help you: I have photocopied all of the patient files mentioned in this write-up and the evidence of their payment."

He motioned for Neerja to unbolt the door. As they walked out, Rakesh stopped, turned back, and said, "For her, it's only a job, but for you…" He trailed off. He shot Govardhan a menacing look. Govardhan was scared at the unsaid.

Chapter 20

Devji dropped Rakesh at the military hospital for the last time so he could collect his results. Devji parked the car and walked to the lobby with him. Rakesh took the stairs to the receptionist's office. Most of the other candidates were already impatiently hovering around the desk.

"Silence, please. You will have to wait another fifteen minutes," the receptionist said. That was the longest fifteen minutes of Rakesh's life. He made two trips to the loo.

At three-fifteen, two men walked in. One was Dr Ahmed Jabber, a friendly guy who was closely involved in the conduct of the exam. The other man, an obese guy, was a stranger, and he held a bunch of envelopes. The results. Rakesh's heartbeat increased almost beyond physiological limits. The candidates' heartbeats would have done well in a rock band. The receptionist called out candidates' names, and the obese man handed them their envelopes. Rakesh took his and left it unopened as if by not looking inside, he could change an unpleasant result. He just held it. Screams and sobs erupted around him. Rakesh still did not open his – something held him back.

His mind flashed to his days as a medical intern, where the seed of his dream to earn a Western degree were sown. The impossibility of the task made his desire intense. The job in Riyadh was a tunnel to that dream. Now, having travelled all the way through its twists and turns and over its obstacles, some easy to tackle, others, those that were manmade, agonisingly difficult, he stood with his exam results in his hand not as someone who was sure to be successful but as someone who had done everything possible to become successful. If the exam were a war, Rakesh had oiled, loaded, and fired every single gun in his arsenal. He prolonged the uncertainty, fearing what he would find on the small piece of paper in the envelope. It could change the course of his life. He visualised himself as the bird in the cage standing at the opened door. Would the door shut on him, or would he fly away to freedom?

Dr Jabber had a twinkle in his eye, and he gave Rakesh a nod, signalling him to go ahead. Rakesh tore the envelope open. He read the letter, and before he could comprehend what it said, Dr Jabber grabbed his hand and shook it. Rakesh wasn't sure if this was meant to comfort him or congratulate him. He looked at the letter again, but the tears that flooded his eyes magnified and distorted the words. "We are pleased to inform that you have been successful..." Rakesh hugged Dr Jabber as tears rolled down his cheeks. He had no words.

He ran downstairs and dragged Devji by his sleeves to the car. He directed Devji to the nearest public phone booth. Before Devji had fully stopped the car, Rakesh dashed to the phone.

"I do not have many coins," he shouted behind him.

Rakesh's wife was in the prayer room when he called. She said she had been there for almost an hour, as she now did so regularly.

"I have made it with your prayers," was all Rakesh managed to say. Emotions silenced them both. By now, Devji had squeezed into the cubicle and had brought all the coins he could gather. He fed a coin into the machine every fifteen seconds, confusion spreading on his face as the non-verbal international telephonic conversation continued. On both ends of the wire were people for whom words meant nothing in this context.

When they returned to the car, Devji asked, "What next?"

"I don't know. I do not want to think or plan."

When Rakesh entered the reception lobby, Tajudeen threw open his arms. "When is the celebration?"

"How did you know the results?" Rakesh asked. The news had still not completely sunk in for him.

"Oh, we all knew the results a long time ago." Tajudeen chuckled.

Rakesh then went up the stairs two at a time. He felt light. No one was in his office, so he went looking for Judy. He found her in the pathologist's office. Through the crowd, his look conveyed the results, and she dashed towards him and shook his hand for a great length of time. A man shaking hands with a woman, and that too in public was an unusual sight in Saudi. Around them, jaws dropped and eyes popped. But in that moment, all was drowned out but one single fact:

the war had been won. Judy's eyes shined as she fought back tears. Were those tears of joy or of anticipated pain? Rakesh did not know.

"I always knew you would win. I told a you a thousand times." Judy's voice cracked. Rakesh for a moment wished that everyone were like her: committed to the success of someone they valued. He realised that Neerja was absent. She was not normally someone who had to be searched out. Rakesh was curious, especially because this was so soon after the episode with Govardhan. He and Judy went back to his office. In his euphoria, he whispered endless thanksgiving prayers. The books scattered on his desk were a reminder of the pains he had gone through for this reward. He recollected Govardhan's words about not revising during clinical hours and Moideen's echo: "You have been hired to work for the hospital and not to sit for exams."

At five o'clock sharp, in walked Neerja, giggling loudly, along with the new driver. She had brought a big cake. She gently punched Rakesh on the chin and asked, "When do we go to the Hyatt?" She laughed. "Today's celebration is one me."

He was touched by this act of affection. "But why did you do this?"

"Because your results are not entirely yours to celebrate. This victory owes to persistence, and I feel in some way that I've won too. But why should I justify it? It's my day today."

Out of the corner of his eye, Rakesh sensed Judy's unease.

Neerja then asked the driver to distribute cake to all the staff members except Govardhan.

"That isn't fair," Rakesh said.

"You are stupid at times," Neerja said. "Do you really think I would ignore him? No. I want to give him a piece personally so that I can look into his eyes and see the frustration, embarrassment, and envy. I want to see every bit of it myself. I may even shove a huge piece into his mouth."

Rakesh took out the results again and read through it. It mustn't have taken more than a few minutes to print it. He thought of all the effort that had led to that result. Once upon a time, a feeble streak of desire escalated into irresistible ambition. The Riyadh job was his ticket. Getting here had been like swimming against the tide. He thought of the waves of discouragement that crashed down on him, of the welcoming warmth of those who faked enjoyment in their jobs among the burnt smell of their dead dreams, of the mental dexterity that he had had to employ to slip away from their tempting grip, of the heavy chains disguised as professional ethics weighing him down, of the irony of someone who never went to college holding the key to his academic future, of the frustrating battle against the committee chaired by people for whom the law was whatever was convenient, rules were whatever was most comfortable, ethics were whatever they fancied. He thought of the threat of losing his job constantly hanging over his head, suspended by misplaced firmness and misused authority. He thought of how he never took his eyes off the ever elusive goal. Rakesh deeply sighed. Now what he had worked for was in his hand, and it was real. The sensory mechanism of his fingertips can feel the results; the visual mechanism of his eye can read the results.

❖ ❖ ❖

"This is the first time one of our docs have cleared a UK exam," Moideen said on the phone when Rakesh invited him to a party. "I am proud of you."

Rakesh could only smile at the hypocrisy. Wasn't this the same Moideen who, a few months before, had expressed displeasure at his plan to sit the exam, at his preparations, even at the sight of his medical books in the office? And now this.

"Yes, we should celebrate. You should throw a big party." Moideen laughed.

"What I have planned is a small party for all the staff this evening. I need the conference hall. Could we do it from four to five o'clock?"

"The conference hall is all yours. As for the time, I think four to four-thirty would be perfect, but Doc, why don't you have it tomorrow? Then Hussain can attend."

"Okay," Rakesh replied, "but I have some other commitments tomorrow, and I need to—" He stopped himself.

"Well, it's up to you. But Hussain should share in your celebration."

"Maybe later," concluded Rakesh. A get-together in the hospital had never happened before. The heavy fog of management policy had prevented the staff from thinking in that direction. The distribution of sweets to mark birthdays and anniversaries were the rudimentary reminders of celebrations. So when Khalidbhai spread the news of the party, the disbelief he was met with was only natural. Everyone knew about it before Rakesh started making invitations.

"I shall try to come," Govardhan said. Rakesh knew that the words "shall try" meant "shall not" in this case. Govardhan often made excuses on the pretext of being busy with patients whenever an event did not hold his interest. His authority was an inflated balloon. In his chamber it was safe, but in a gathering it was always punctured.

"You should have waited for Hussain. He probably would have considered a pay hike," Shoshamma told him in response to the invitation.

Tajudeen said, "Don't settle for a small party. You need to take us out for dinner. Anyway, who is this special guest I heard is coming?"

"Why are you in such a hurry? Can't you wait for Dr Niranjan to return from his vacation?" Nurse Richa said.

Neerja enjoyed listening the conversation in the nurses' station.

"Sometimes he acts smart," Shoshamma said. "Why should he waste money on a party? At the least, he should have done it tomorrow."

"What's wrong with holding it today?" the lab technician said feebly.

"Oh, don't you know Hussain is visiting us tomorrow?" Shoshamma replied.

"What is your problem?" Richa said to Shoshamma.

"I have no problem. But when you share your success with Hussain, he might be encouraged to give you a salary rise. What's the point in having an advance qualifications if there's no increase in pay? I told Dr Rakesh about this, but as usual, he had a mind of his own."

"Maybe he's not interested in a salary hike, or even continuing here at all," Richa said.

Shoshamma laughed. "What a joke. Who wouldn't

be interested? Give him a few hundred riyals more and he wouldn't leave the premises."

Neerja came in. Her silence supplemented Shoshamma's interest to talk.

"But who is this guest Khalidbhai said would be coming?" Richa asked.

"He refused to reveal that. He said it's a surprise," Shoshamma responded.

"Maybe his wife has joined him!" Richa speculated.

"Oh! That may make someone a bit unhappy," Shoshamma said.

"And who would that be?" Neerja's usual frankness caused Shoshamma to change the topic.

"Why should we bother with guessing? We will all be at there at four."

For the rest of the day, as the staff greeted each other in the lobby, in the corridor, in reception, they said, "See you at four!" Some added, "Do you know who the surprise guest is?" When they left for lunch, they said, "Don't forget the party."

As Rakesh was getting ready to leave, Neerja appeared in his office. She asked, "Are you sure Moideen doesn't know who the guest is?"

"I've given him no hint. I told him it's a good friend of mine whose presence would mean a lot to me."

Neerja suppressed a giggle like an excited young girl who just told a secret.

When four o'clock came, the staff came to the conference room in two batches as the ambulance dropped them off. Because this was within the boundaries of evening duty, the women had to forego the pleasure of party preparation, though they lightly reapplied their lipstick and blush. Moideen greeted the staff, particularly the doctors, with more excitement than was necessary as they came in. Rakesh wondered whether he was overreacting to hide his guilt. Dr Shewaqee hugged Rakesh.

Shoshamma drew a small audience as she displayed her new gold necklace. Her fondness for gold was well known. Khalidbhai said that she ate only once a day to save money for gold and that on her annual vacations, she could put an elephant decorated for a temple festival to shame. Niranjan's absence kept her from being the target of direct attack.

Tajudeen's voice rose above the other voices. "Let's eat!" The table had been richly spread.

"We should congratulate Rakesh," Shewaqee said, initiated applause that found only few reluctant followers.

"Where is Govardhan?" Moideen said quietly.

"He is performing open-heart surgery," replied Tajudeen in the same tone. The partygoers settled into a semicircle of chairs.

"We have only fifteen more minutes. Where is he?" Neerja discreetly asked Rakesh.

"He is already in my office. I shall get him after I submit my paper."

"You better be quick."

"Dr Rakesh!" Moideen called from across the room. The room went silent. "You said that you had invited a special guest, someone very important. Where is he?"

"He should be here any moment," Rakesh said. "Before he arrives, I have an announcement to make." He moved to where everyone could see him. He took a deep breath, smiled, and said, "Thank you all for coming to this get-together on such short notice. I wish to thank every staff member who has supported my exam preparations, particularly Judy. I wonder whether I would have made it without her. I would also like to thank the management for giving me the opportunity to work here and make all of this possible for me. However, I would like to inform you all that I have decided to resign. I am here by submitting my resignation."

He handed his letter over to Dr Shewaqee. The silence seemed to deepen, and the guests exchanged puzzled looks. Before anyone could muster a response, Rakesh continued, "I have invited a friend of mine to this gathering today. He has been in the Middle East for a few years during which he has pursued a programme in business management, and he completed his course in hospital management. He has now taken over as assistant manager of Al Baraha Hospital. He has been a source of inspiration to me. I am sure you will all love meeting him."

He winked at Neerja, who opened the door. Everyone looked over in surprise and disbelief. Rakesh welcomed Jabber in.

❖ ❖ ❖

Hussain's visit was normally a feast for Govardhan and Moideen. They ate in the best restaurants. But this visit was different because of time constraints. Hussain was stopping over on way to the Philippines to recruit new staff.

Rakesh's resignation became the main topic in reception, in the corridors, in the offices, and in the clinics. People talked openly, as he had submitted his resignation openly. For an employee to discontinue at a job was normally the arrogant choice of an employer, not the conscious act of an employee. This made the management trio of owner, director, and manger uneasy. For Govardhan, the uneasiness was only an act well performed to hide his joy.

"I think we should persuade him to stay," Govardhan lied.

Hussain saw such resignations as an employee's tactic for seeking a pay rise. He felt that he had total control of the sail and could go in whichever direction he chose. But Moideen's concern was genuine. He knew Rakesh had no hidden agenda, and he knew his absence would leave a dent in the staff that would take a while to hammer out.

"How much does he want?" Hussain asked Moideen.

"We haven't discussed that."

"What is the average monthly collection from his cost centre?"

"Without investigations and prescriptions, about forty thousand riyals."

"Offer him an extra five hundred and see what he does. If he pushes, settle for a thousand," Hussain said patly.

Govardhan prayed that the negotiations would fail.

"It is worth giving him a raise of fifteen hundred?" Moideen asked. "He receives lots of ortho cases that are being referred from other centres."

"Not more than thousand," Govardhan quickly intervened. "Any more would set a bad precedent."

"Yeah ya." Hussain liked to agree with Govardhan. Financial equation was the only equation known to him. 'If you have to choose between money and man, choose the first; the second will follow." This was a motto he was taught by one of his uncles who was more like a father to him. Sayeed Ali was a timber merchant. He earned lots of wealth and had lots of men around. As a boy Hussain had seen this man wield power, money and men. His decisions were the rules not just in the timber yard, but also in the village. As a boy what Hussain failed to note, was the glue that held the men around him was conspicuous by the absence of respect. For Ali the men were only means to get his business going. For the men it was merely a mode for survival. The bare minimum of mutual needs kept the fragile strand of relation scarcely alive. And so for Hussain too, entrepreneurship was an engine driven by the exclusive aim of accumulating wealth. Significance of logic and value for sentiments were not meant to be fuels of that engine. And for him it performed well. But for those whose carriages were pulled by this engine, the joy of movement wasn't there; instead the dispassionate relief of movement.

"Tonight, I think you should talk to him," Moideen told Hussain. He had always thought Hussain was a better negotiator.

✻ ✻ ✻

"Hello, Rakesh," Hussain greeted him that evening as he and Moideen sat down. "I'm disappointed that our second meeting has to happen under these circumstances. Why are you leaving us? You have got on so well in the system and have a good patient base."

"This is purely a personal decision," replied Rakesh.

"Well, is there anything we could do to change your mind?"

"Thanks for your concern, but I am planning to continue my studies in the UK."

"But that may not happen straight away. Am I not right?" Hussain said, watching Rakesh carefully. "Why don't you stay for one more year? You could use that time to find a suitable placement in England. And that would give us adequate time to find a replacement."

"Mr Hussain, I agree that I may not get a placement within the next few months, but frankly speaking, I wouldn't want to continue on anyway."

"Can you tell me why?"

"It's is too late to go into my reasons. I do not want to upset you whilst I am leaving," Rakesh said. This was a calculated statement that he intended to increase Hussain's inquisitiveness.

"As the owner of the hospital, I need to know."

Rakesh took this chance to open up. Inefficient, unfair, and corrupt management: this was the dish they had served him. He had silently accepted it, even thought it made him nauseous, like someone who gulped down a distasteful diet drink. He had held back his resentment, for he believed that silence safeguarded his dream. But now he had earned his freedom to express himself, to expose others' misdeeds, and even explore what else he was capable of.

"I do not believe that you ever wanted to know how the staff felt about their work," Rakesh said.

"How could you say that? All employees and particularly doctors are important. Their welfare is my concern," Hussain countered.

That was a meaningful statement stated without meaning, Rakesh thought. "Most of your employees are under constant threat of losing their jobs. Their fear keeps them pulling on mechanically. Your people fed this fear into their psyches. Your people, who know nothing about management, think fear is the best motivator. But it takes away people's passion for the profession, the energy for the work, the compassion for patients, and the joy in interactions. Is this what you want in your employees? I faced a lot of rubbish at this hospital, but I refused to react."

"That's the mistake you all make. You should have reported it."

"Whom do I report it to? To the same guys who devised the stressful situations? Or to you, the invisible owner? What do you do when the security guards become robbers? And the policemen become looters? How do you seek protection from the protectors?"

Hussain glanced at Moideen to either acknowledge shared knowledge or share surprise at where this was going.

"People in power," Rakesh continued, "should be powerful not through the position they hold but by the values they hold. Those in positions of authority should earn their employees' respect by the fairness of their deeds, not demand it through force. I had to swallow quite a bit of injustice, but I stuck on, for I had to. But today I am free to leave. Most of my colleagues here also have their reasons for sticking on, but believe me, the pleasure of working here is definitely not one of them."

The pink glow was steadily draining from Hussain's face. His image as a caring boss was taking a beating – a slow beating that he had invited.

"I think you are wrong," he said. "We receive so many CVs almost every week from general practitioners, specialists, and nurses who are keen to join our team."

"I don't dispute that," Rakesh said. "They have no clue what they would be getting into. But I am sure that you too must be aware that every single Indian who accepts a job here makes a lot of sacrifices, financially, socially, and emotionally. The lower the person's class, the bigger the sacrifices. A work place like ours is a trap. Workers can't escape once they accept a job; for there is much at stake. Have you managers not exploited them without shame?"

The word *shame* took away the veil of diplomacy in the dialogue.

"You mean most people are unhappy here?" Hussain asked.

"It's worse than that."

"I think you are making biased judgements based on personal experience."

Rakesh laughed. "Give everyone the liberty to apply for jobs elsewhere, and then you will realise that I am right."

"But that is not possible, as they would need a No objection certificate."

"Yes, they will need NOC. They will request it, and you will deny it. And they will stay here not because they want to but because they have to. NOC is a weapon many managers use to enhance their power without integrity. It's like a leash.

"Employees should feel happy to be associated with their workplaces. Does that exist here? A job here is monotonous and mechanical; work is performed with exacting discipline born of fear. Work has to be done with dignity, liberty, and quality to be uplifting. When dignity and liberty are denied, quality suffers, no matter how hard you push for it. Each individual brings to his or her job valuable personal qualities, and it's essential for management to encourage and nurture those qualities. Applause or a pat on the shoulder for excellent work is a valuable tonic. Instead, employees are rewarded with abuse and punishment."

"I think you are exaggerating," Moideen put in.

Rakesh ignored Moideen and continued, "When people are happy, they tend to be more productive and effective. When you fall sick, would you rather be treated by a doctor who serves with conscious clarity based on purity of purpose or by someone who has lost clarity because of the polluted principles of the establishment? Would you prefer to be nursed by a happy, vibrant person who takes pride and pleasure in what she does or by someone who carries the burden of having to cling to the job?"

Moideen impatiently interrupted, "Doc, I think you are painting a very dark picture which is not true."

That comment ignited Rakesh. He went on, "Is it not true that Jabber did a fantastic job? Is it not true that his brilliance made you feel insecure? Is it not true that you used your authority to eliminate him? Is it not true that you disappeared for two weeks after sacking him to hide your guilt? Is it not true that you were instructed to be in inaccessible protecting others who shared the guilt?"

A sudden wave of astonishment engulfed. Not because of the contents of what Rakesh said, but because it was said. A common knowledge that normally found voice only in whispers behind the mainstream.

Moideen knew that defending the management would provoke Rakesh further and further embarrass him and Hussain. But silence would be taken as acceptance of guilt. He responded with a deep sigh that implied the futility of words.

"Why did you not update me on this?" Hussain said, attempting to portray himself as a commander in chief betrayed by an incompetent lieutenant. The sudden dismissal of his smile, the flatness in his expression, and the firmness of his posture all failed to support that. Hussain never had looked important, and his speech only highlighted how unimportant he was. The only element of his appearance that hinted at authority was his oversized, expensive jacket, and he appeared to be hiding in it. Rakesh responded before Moideen could.

"I am sure Moideen must have updated you, but with what information?"

"That is true," Tajudhin chipped in and said. "If you truly cared about it, you should have paid us a visit every month or appointed Rakesh the chief medical officer."

All three men laughed. Moideen's face was still red with embarrassment, but the humour was a welcome relief. He laughed loudest and longest, as if to ease his anxiety at hearing the truth. Tajudhin often packed his opinions into humour. Moideen now lit a cigarette and watched the curls of smoke from the end.

"All my staff should be happy," said Hussain to no one in particular. Rakesh had heard this statement before; Moideen had echoed it multiple times. It was an attempt at magnanimity. A year of experience had proved to Rakesh that it was unsupported even by a fragile pillar of action. The statement resembled some of the expats' houses in north Kerala: it had a colourful exterior but a dull and vacant interior. To a passer-by, it epitomised financial success, but to a close observer, the reality was markedly different.

"Look, Hussain," Rakesh said. "In any establishment, be it a hospital, a hotel, a garage, long-term success depends on the joyous energy of the workforce. Big, flashy signboards, a lavishly decorated lobby, and unlimited handshakes will not create it. These gimmicks may work for a while, but the success they generate won't last. An organisation needs the vitalising nutrients that a happy bunch of employees pump through it. They are the organisation's heart. Management, like the brain, should regulate it but not suppress it. A hospital with a weak heart can survive, but it will not be the place where the public looks for care and comfort. People will stop going for treatment except for the common cold or other simple ailments that would subside even without medical care. Only those uneducated patients who still believe that just seeing a doctor will cure them will continue to visit. The consultation fees they pay may look like charity, and to keep the financial boat from sinking, doctors then must order investigations: the unnecessary blood tests and radiographs. Then, over time, the muscle fibres of the heart weaken as any enthusiastic employees leave and are replaced by those who have given up or whose values tally with those of the sick management. Generating money becomes the establishment's only purpose, and receiving a pay cheque that of its staff's. Signing in and signing out for a shift defines the boundaries of a meaningless day. But if that's what you want, you are on the right track.

"I think most of our nurses here are doing a great job," Rakesh continued. "No one ever shows appreciation for what they silently do. Instead, any minor lapse is highlighted. I have heard the CMO and even you, Moideen, yell and scream at the nurses many times."

"Dr Rakesh, at times that does happen, but it is in the best interest of the hospital," Moideen said.

"How about if one of them shouted back at you, also in the best interest of the institution? Rakesh asked , and a knock at the door silenced the conversation. The door creaked open, and Neerja stepped in. It was her day off. She was the only employee in the entire hospital who had refused overtime. She wasn't in her uniform or in the abaya. The only other time she had been seen like this was at Tajudeen's get-together. She wore fawn-coloured corduroys and a slightly darker half-sleeved shirt that hung graciously on her torso. She held herself with a casual pride and carried a folder. Hussains's irritation at the intrusion disappeared when presented with the visual feast of the intruder. She paused after two steps.

"Hi, Neerja," Rakesh greeted her. The others said nothing.

"I'm sorry to interrupt your meeting," she said, coming closer to the desk.

"Hello, Nina," Hussain said.

"It's not Nina, Sir. It's Neerja."

"Oh, whatever."

"No, not whatever. My name is Neerja," she emphasised.

"Okay, Madam. How we can help you."

"This is the best opportunity I'll have to speak to you all, and particularly to Mr Hussain here. I won't take too long." She took out a piece of paper from the folder and said, "I would like to be relieved from my duties the same day Dr Rakesh's contract ends. This is my letter of resignation." She placed it on the desk in front of Hussain. Surprise marked their faces, even Rakesh's. She had mentioned her desire to leave quite a few times, but Rakesh had never thought that she would actually do it.

His resignation the previous day had tipped the scales, and her desire became resolve.

"Is this a joint venture?" Moideen said, lightening the scene.

Rakesh fixed his gaze on her.

"This is a matter that requires discussion," commented Moideen.

"Yes, Sir, that's true, but that doesn't happen in this hospital. Notifications are typically given without discussion."

"Look, Rakesh has not decided to leave. We have not agreed on that," Hussain said, squinting at Rakesh. "You can't leave just like that. Don't you know that you are supposed to give at least one month's notice?"

"That's true, and that should go both ways, but that doesn't happen here."

"This is not how our system functions. I need to know if there have been any problems we could help you with," Hussain said, trying the caring employer role.

Rakesh kept quiet. Moideen searched his face, but Rakesh hid his emotions.

"I did not," started Neerja, "come into the medical profession because of a passion for it; it was just a way to make a living. But having been in it for few years now, I've realised the faith patients place in their doctors and the respect they have for their diagnosis and opinions and the reliability of their investigations. However, I have observed that there has been a vicious breach of this trust in our hospital. This is a regular process caused by greed."

"What do you mean?" Moideen asked, appearing shocked.

"I owe Rakesh an apology. The observations which I place before you now are the result of our joint effort. He did not want this to come out until after he had left, but I feel they have to be brought out now. I don't want a different story to tarnish him and protect the real culprits. Too many patients are being cheated with investigations that are not indicated and—"

Tajudhin cut her off. "Neerja, this happens in every hospital all over the world, not just here."

Hussain was quick to intervene to prevent further mud-slinging. "I think we can have this discussion in my office after dinner."

"There is nothing much to talk about. The details of our findings are here." Neerja placed the file and resignation letter on the desk. Moideen didn't know she was quitting at the same time as Rakesh, but he didn't ask about it.

The ease and charm with which she sidelined Moideen's suggestion was evident.

"Apart from these investigations, what complaints do you have?" Hussain asked. "I was told you were one of the best nurses on staff. So let's hear how we can—"

"I do not think my concerns should be addressed here and now."

Neerja caught Rakesh's eye, and they exchanged a look of mutual admiration.

"Leave hospital issues aside. Let me know if you have any personal problems," Hussain said.

She smiled, exposing her crooked tooth. "After a few years, when I look back, I do not want to regret having served longer in an establishment like this."

"What do you mean, an establishment like this?" Moideen asked, almost shouting.

Employees who spoke frankly were instantly tamed by the management with the whip of a threat to sack them. Now there was no point in taming her, as she was resigning.

"I am a person for whom fun has to be an integral part of my job. I tried my best but it doesn't happen here. Most of my colleagues are always under the fearful cloud of losing their job. This I am sure is not their own creation but a design ingrained into their psyche and that has been very effective. For many here, they are the only hope for their families back home. And hence they not only perform with dedication but also perform from a point of weakness. And that has been conveniently exploited, both the dedication and the weakness. The joyful charm of living for many has been transformed into a constant look of distress. Happiness of having obtained a gulf job soon gets replaced with the fear of its sustenance."

As Neerja became more emphatic, the attentive silence of the others in the room became palpable. "Within this web, I still found happiness in Rakesh's presence. He knew how to blend joy into his job. For him, values were not a matter of convenience. His office was a place where I could find relief. It was the only place where I could laugh openly and speak frankly."

Rakesh watched Neerja like someone sitting on the front row of a play; watching with detached amusement; amusement with admiration and joy; joy with respect and love This was not the kind of love that caused sleepless nights or painful longing but the kind that re-ignited his sense of individuality, reinforced his self-esteem, and reminded him that integrity was not a choice. His mind flashed back to Roopa, the woman with whom he had once gone to a coffee house during medical school. Gossip had ended their relationship, the price he had to pay for living amongst people who knew nothing of this kind of love between the sexes.

"And so I have decided to leave," Neerja concluded.

After a long moment, Hussain said, "Okay, you may go. We shall discuss this further and inform you of what we have decided." She walked out with a glance that receded over everyone except Rakesh.

Hussain, annoyed, shouted, "Where is Govardhan hiding?"

Chapter 21

Rakesh enjoyed every minute of his last week at Farooqia. He was no longer bound to a tight schedule, so he could sit chatting after lunch. "Hameed, what are you doing this evening?" he asked.

"What a question. I am doing my normal work, cooking. What else would I be doing?"

"I want you to come with me at four o'clock this afternoon. I need to buy myself new clothes. I want your help."

"My help? Ha!"

"I like your shirts, so stop laughing and make yourself available."

"Doc, I didn't pick those out. Anyway, I am free in the evening. That's when I normally sleep, but I can make an exception. But select clothes for you?" He smiled in a way that expressed innocence, embarrassment, and joy.

"Don't come in that dhoti. Put on trousers. We may go to Raymond's."

"Raymond's?"

A Raymond's showroom had opened close to their residence a few months back. The store advertised in most of the leading newspapers. This chain's exclusive showrooms were limited to big cities in India, and for someone like Hameed from a small village, the idea of shopping in such a store was confined to the imagination. After the store opened, Rakesh had once overhead Hameed telling Khalidbhai, "Raymond's suits are the most expensive in the world. Only film stars can afford them." Khalidbhai commented that there were no movie stars in Riyadh, and Hameed said that here, top businesspeople shopped there.

"So you are planning to go on your vacation in style," Hameed said excitedly.

The last few years had steadily increased Hameed's central circumference and to squeeze into his only one fading pants was a job. The buttons and every single stitch were stretched in obedience to a man who expected his clothes to grow with him. An obedience that strangulated many body parts in un-rhythmic movements of his stride. But if he had to bend down, this obedience was sure to snap. However, at four o'clock, he was waiting and smiling like a kid who spotted an ice cream vendor at a fair.

He and Rakesh walked along the streets that were slowly waking up after the long lunch break. Raymond's stood out in its neighbourhood. The decorative lights were reflected in the mirrors and glass doors. Hameed followed Rakesh with wide eyes. One of the salesmen had been a patient of Rakesh's, and he greeted them when they walked in and displayed the latest in men's fashions. The salesman spoke to Rakesh, and Rakesh looked to Hameed for opinions.

"That one, the one with grey check, is great. It'll look good on you," suggested Hameed once he was finally at ease. Rakesh bought the shirt and the matching trousers. As he settled the bill, Hameed peeked at the amount.

"Oh my God! Two hundred and eighty riyals!" Hameed exclaimed when they left the store. "That's almost three thousand rupees for a single outfit. No wonder there are no customers here."

"Now, I want this to be tailored before I go."

"I knew it. You are preparing to look stylish at the Calicut airport. I know all these tricks." Hameed giggled.

"Take me to that tailor friend of yours, the one who visits us."

"Oh, Nadir Shah. He is excellent. I'm not sure if he is around. He might be on vacation. Anyway, his shop is close by. Doc, clothes are too expensive here. You could get the same stuff in India for a lot less. But then, if you want to shine right at the airport, what can I say?" Rakesh was the only doctors to whom Hameed spoke freely and with whom he could take the liberty of teasing.

Nadir Shah was busy at his sewing machine when they entered, and he jumped up with respect when he saw Rakesh.

"Salaam alaikum. What brings you to my small world?"

"I need to have some alterations made, and Hameed says you're the best in town."

"I would have come to your villa. You need not have bothered with coming here."

"That's okay."

Nadir Shah approached Rakesh with the measuring tape.

"It's not for me," Rakesh said, "but for Hameed."

Nadir Shah paused in surprise. Hameed laughed loudly with his hand covering his mouth. "Why do you make such jokes?"

"It's no joke. It's for you." Rakesh's tone was firm.

"Why do I need such costly clothes? They are not meant for people like me. Where would I wear them?" Hameed said, baffled.

"We shall sort that out later. Now let Nadir take your measurements."

Still surprised, Hameed stood still with Nadir Shah measured him and jotted down the measurements. When he reached up to measure Hameed's shoulders, Hameed's eyes were tearful.

Nadir Shah whispered, "Hameed, you are a lucky guy." Hameed could no longer hold back the tears.

On the way back to the villa, Hameed was mostly silent. Most of Hameed's shirts were hand-me-downs from doctors. He was too moved to talk. He couldn't even command his vocal cords to articulate a thank-you. But for Rakesh, his silence said more than a thousand thank-yous or a hundred handshakes could.

❊ ❊ ❊

The sunrays peered in through the slit between the curtains. Today was an end and a beginning: it was Rakesh's last day in Riyadh. He was impatient to reunite with his family late that evening, excited at having fulfilled his dream, pained at leaving behind beautiful human beings. These emotions fought for a place in his thoughts. He had packed two days before with Hameed's insistent assistance. Rakesh had denied others the usual festivity of the packing party, as he was not very much into shopping. Moreover, he was not leaving for a vacation. He was leaving for good. His flight was at one that afternoon. The driver was to drop him off at eleven, and a management representative would hand over his passport only after he had arrived at the airport and completed the check in formalities. Rakesh went to the hospital to take care of some last-minute formalities.

"You should not have invited Jabber to your party. That was arrogant. Why do you want to irritate Govardhan and Moideen all the time?" Shoshamma commented as soon as he entered the nurses' station.

"No more confrontations," Rakesh responded. "I just came to say goodbye."

"Did they settle all your money?" Shoshamma was nosey.

"No, I am going to see the accountant now."

"I hope they pay you in full."

He then went off to meet with other staff. Though wasn't keen to do it, he was obligated to meet with Govardhan as well.

"Okay, Rakesh, good luck," Govardhan said, happy at his exit.

"I am grateful to you for all your nasty deeds. They made me stronger," Rakesh said.

"What do you mean?"

"I met Suhail a few days ago."

Govardhan's false smile had been replaced by look of terror. He was helpless now that he had been exposed. Suhail had helped Govardhan twist Taher's case into a complaint of negligence, but the two had fallen out. Govardhan's embarrassed silence continued as Rakesh walked out.

The accountant's office was a place employees visited only on the first of every month, and the accountant distributed cheques more like giving alms than paying a well-earned salary. The accountant's personality defied categorisation. No one knew if he was cruel or kind.

"Yes, Dr Rakesh, come in," the accountant said when Rakesh knocked. "I think you are a bit late. It's already ten-thirty. Please sign here."

Rakesh uncapped his pen, and he was surprised by the figure he saw in the ledger.

"Oh, yes," the accountant said. "I have been advised to cut twenty days from your leave salary. You gave only ten days' notice."

Rakesh suppressed his annoyance and signed. He wondered how Shoshamma had known what management had done.

Back at reception, Judy was holding back tears. Rakesh shook hands with everyone in the lobby. Judy held his for a moment longer than was expected, and with cracking voice, said, "Call me whenever you can." She handed him a gift. This was the day Rakesh had waited for with all-consuming desire. This was the day Judy had dreaded.

* * *

The area outside of departures was bubbling with chaos. Vehicles stopped and unloaded people and luggage. He recalled something Niranjan had once said: "Indian expats have an inherent fancy for huge boxes." Rakesh saw them all over the place – inside gaping car boots, on van tops, and in piles on trolleys. Passengers queuing to check in for other destinations had trolley bags and big bags, suitcases and attaché cases, but no boxes. That type of luggage seemed to be an Indian preference. He knew that part of the reason for this lay in what James had said. The Indian expat rarely sobered up from the euphoria of giving gifts, and his life resembled one of those boxes: fully packed, compact and heavy, proud and sturdy, valuable and special, welcoming and wanting. With the passage of years and a string of experiences his life erodes like an overused and discarded box. Dull and boring, bruised and torn, hollow and empty, unwelcome and unwanted.

The officer in the immigration cubicle wasn't a happy man. Bitterness was what Rakesh read on his silent face. He quickly flipped through Rakesh's passport and stamped it. That act seemed violent – he stamped with enough strength to shatter a pile of seven tiles in a karate demonstration.

After the security check, Rakesh walked away from the crowd along a deserted corridor in the massive airport building. The duty-free shop was not inviting, but he picked out some chocolates. Through his impatience, he saw the hand of the large clock move in slow motion. He settled into a reclining chair, for he had another hour to go. He then opened Judy's gift. It was a CD, *The Complete Collection of Orangegate.*

Through a glass partition that separated his gate from the arrivals walkway, he saw a sudden rush of passengers. He watched them as they sped along the corridor with heavy bags and probably heavier responsibilities. How many of them, he wondered, would fall into the trap of believing that an expat's life is not for him to enjoy, that their mission was to selflessly serve others' needs and greed? How many of them would realise their error and get out of that trap? But then, what was the point if they realised this when their faces were wrinkled and their hair grey? His stream of thought was suddenly and pleasantly broken by the sight of a tall woman amongst the arriving crowd. She had the same elegant stride, the same mischievous smile, and the same earthy skin tone.........'do not inflate your life jacket....'

* * *

"Passengers, your attention please..." Rakesh recalled hearing the same announcement almost a year before. How different he felt now. A sense of nervous excitement dominated his first trip, and now he felt definite happiness. Then, he was uncertain of what was in store; now he was certain. Then, he had the hope of an ambition; now, the happiness of its accomplishment. Then, he felt the pain of distancing from his family; now, the joy of reuniting. As the aircraft began losing height, he saw the greenery out the window and then the wavy white line that danced along the shore as if to rejoice his homecoming. The sea was blue and green, the same indefinable colour that he had seen a year before as the aircraft ascended. Today, that colour induced in him a very well-defined emotion –pure joy. The greenery became increasingly clear. Then small houses and buildings sprouted from it. Things that looked like insects moved along the thin curved lines.

As the picture of his homeland became clearer, the relief of belonging crept in.

The initial thud on the runway was followed by a roar as the aeroplane decelerated. The landing was smooth. A friend who travelled a lot had once told him that in European countries, the passengers and crew applauded the pilot if the landing was smooth. But here no one took notice. They were focused on one thought – get out and meet the family.

The air hostess requested that passengers keep their seat belts fastened, and the clatter of unbuckling immediately followed, as if its Malayalam translation instructed them to do so. The next request that came over the PA was, "Please be seated till the aircraft has come to a complete halt and the seat-belt sign has been switched off." Four hours of patience snapped, most passengers got up and opened the overhead compartments. The air hostess yelled over the commotion for them to sit down. The passengers ignored her, as if to say, "This is my country. I'll do what I choose. I had enough in Saudi." Thank God the windows could not be opened or some passengers would have squeezed out through them.

In the long queue at immigration, the chaos was amplified. Three flights had landed at roughly the same time, and the ensuing show was worth watching. At baggage claim, no one knew which luggage carousel served which flight. Passengers asked other passengers, who replied with intelligent guesses. Then they asked porters, who gave intuitional guesses. And last they asked the airport staff, who gave informational guesses. What finally prevailed was absolute ignorance. Trolleys packed every inch of the space. Movement became a luxury. Circumstances had a way of calming passengers down, Rakesh realised. After a long wait, out came a chain of cartons and massive, irregularly shaped parcels. Each was boldly marked with a name, the proud declaration of one's material achievement.

Then came customs, the officers in white calm, smiling, and inquisitive. The attributes of their job permitted them to taste a few drops of expats' sweat. If an expat on vacation was a sponge, then the wringing out started here.

And finally, when Rakesh wheeled out past security, he saw an ocean of people. Some had probably stationed themselves there even before the flight in Riyadh was boarded. Amongst the people were fathers who hadn't seen their sons for two or more years, kids who scanned the security exit for their dads, and spouses whose eyes scanned the human wall. Hugs, kisses, and tears blocked every possible passage.

Rakesh spotted his brother, his wife, and his little angel. Anakitha had became chubby in the last year. She clung to her mum and refused to go to Rakesh. Like a tributary, they branched off from the expanding crowd, driven out. There was too much to say, so they said nothing. There was too much to express, so their bodies were rigid. The only movement apart from the wheels of the car was the trickle of tears from Vineetha's eyes. For her, the waiting had ended. In the last three hundred and sixty-five days, the only happy event each day was the realisation that the pain was less by one more day. Rakesh put his arm around her, and the trickle turned to a flood. Anakitha pushed Rakesh's arm away. How could a stranger put his arm around her mum?

Chapter 22

"Gadi number che theen char aatt, thiruvanathapuram Jane vale Mangalore express thodi si dher per platform number ekh se javana hogi."

The announcement silenced the tea and coffee vendors. Rakesh and his family had just settled into the second air-conditioned coach on a short trip to Trivandrum. His five-year-old boy, Akaash, kept shifting between the upper and lower berth, enjoying the inability to make a choice. Anakitha sat in her own isolated world with a book. As if to further enhance the isolation, her ears were sealed with earphone. Vineetha relaxed on a corner seat and stretched her legs across to Rakesh's berth. The visit to her home in Trivandrum always gave her a distinctive glow. The excitement of anticipation replaced her weariness from balancing her job and home life. Rakesh always saw that even the plan to go to Trivandrum spread a joyful smile across her face that completely hid every other emotion and remained with steady intensity till the end of the trip.

She was eldest of five kids in every sense. Her ideas were their agenda. Her suggestions were their rules. Her choices were their fashion. Her vision was their future. But in the matrimonial world, all that changed. To her in-laws, her ideas were absurd, her language impolite, her manners unpolished, her thoughts mean, her words harsh, and her style obsolete. Vineetha and Rakesh, two confused people, had spent day and night trying to figure out the origin of this perception. They couldn't. They secretly and sincerely hoped that Anakitha's birth would tidy up things. Giving his parents their first grandchild, she thought, would win their acceptance. And the birth of Akaash rekindled her fading hope of being a link in the family chain, but it was once again in vain. It took almost twelve years of bewildered disappointment and persistent endurance before she finally accepted a simple truth: that parents and in-laws are two entirely different entities. The few overlapping qualities were but sparks of social drama.

"Do you know the date today?" Vineetha said as the train slowly moved on.

"How could I ever forget that?" Rakesh responded.

On this day ten years before, he had been on the Air India flight bound for Riyadh. He carried with him one suitcase, a bit of excitement, and the seed of a dream. The seed, he had been told, will not grow if planted in rocky soil. But if that was all he had, why should he throw the seed away? That seed meant his existence.

When the seed sprouted, they said it will die if not watered regularly. Should he abandon it if he didn't have enough water? No, for that tiny green life was his own life.

When it became a small plant, they said it will wither away if not fertilised properly. Should he give it up if there was not enough to nourish it? No, for the plant's growth was his own.

As it grew, they said it will wilt under the scorching heat of the sun. Should he leave it to destiny or stretch a protective rag over it? When it became a tree, they said it will not bear fruit for it is not a tropical plant. Should he quit? No, for he had watered it with his sweat, fertilised it with his grit, protected it with his guts, and watched it with his heart. It had to bear fruits, a natural consequence of providence bypassing every possible law to honour the unseen power of ones dream .

"Hey, Rakesh, I asked you a question. You are lost in distant thought."

Oh yes, it was distant. "You reminded me of my Riyadh days and the years in the UK. I was thinking of the surgical training, the diploma ceremony...

"Even after all these years, my memories of Riyadh are still fresh. They bring up a complex mixture of agony and ecstasy. I always felt that I went there with a tiny flame that I had to protect all year to light up a lamp that would illuminate our life at the end. But the winds from all sides were strong and threatened to blow out the flame at every turn."

"Daddy, I'm hungry. Let's eat now," Akaash said from the upper berth. He wasn't hungry, that was certain. But he was impatient to indulge in the aloo paratha Rakesh's mother had cooked and packed for them.

For Rakesh, train journeys were always fun, and

the thousands and thousands of miles he had travelled failed to diminish his enjoyment. To feel the wind in his face was not just a childhood pleasure, but travelling in the air-conditioned coach took that simple pleasure away. He owned a bicycle quite late in life, but the few years of usage reduced it to an equipment of mere utility. Same applied to the bajaj scooter, and later to the maruti car. Initially it was excitement in anticipation, then the pride of ownership, then the pleasure of travelling and then with time it tapered to the bare purpose of mobility. Few trips on air did the same to flights. But the rail retained the charm.

It curved through the plantations, cut through mountains, flew over rivers, pierced through boulders as if nothing could stop its entry. The visual treat of limitless expanse of nature's beauty became an inseparable part of train journey. The gift of constantly changing scenes: greenery to brownery, lush green paddy fields to bright yellow sunflower farms, silent backwaters that gently massaged the land to the violent ones that rippled into the sea, the setting sun that brightened the horizon with nameless colours, the buildings that swiftly passed behind, the distant valleys that slowly accompanied, the lone fisherman on his country boat who didn't hear the rattling train that sped over him, the adjoining residence who always stared in nascent admiration, the school kids who cheerfully waved, the crossing gates where traffic stopped behind in respect, the sudden bustle at platforms, the luxury of buying a bite across the window, of meeting a friend amidst the floating crowd, the amusement never ends.

Vineetha brought Akaash down and gave him his food pack. The aloo paratha was the same as it had always been. In the last ten years, depression and recession had taken turns in different parts of the globe. Two more wars had been fought and two more Olympics had been held. The concept of communication had changed. Cell phones change from a rich person's luxury to every person's necessity. Men had begun wearing junky ornaments, and women competed by piercing many more body parts. Everything changed. But not his mother's aloo paratha. When Akaash opened the banana-leaf wrapper, Rakesh smelled the same aroma he had smelled twenty-five years before. The rhythm with which Akaash chewed confirmed to his delight that this dish would never change.

A person's sense of belonging in one's own country was matchless. The beauty of his own country reassured Rakesh and restored that sense as he looked out. The huts and houses, mostly small, came and went. Occasionally they passed a house proud in its size, colour, and or ornamentation. Rakesh's thoughts wandered. Were members of these households somewhere in the Middle East? If they were, did their families truly know what jobs they did and how many hours they worked? What their living conditions were? What food they ate? Were they comfortable dispatching the monthly remittance? It was if all of the answers to these questions were packed inside a box, and opening it, or even seeing it, was a sin. All that was allowed was the receipt of the monthly remittance. Thousands and thousands of families relied on that monthly remittance. Initially it was like IV fluid for a dehydrated patient. The lifeline continued, but later for a normally hydrated patient and then for a well hydrated and then sometimes over hydrated ones. It was no more a lifeline. The regularity with which it came made it appear a normal phenomenon. Anything regular has to be considered normal. Normalcy was only at the receiving ends. The giving end masked the discomfort; the receiving end masked the comfort, the occasional expressions were but the reverse.

The accompanying sky turned orange from blue and then to red and slowly darkness forced out every shade. Rakesh stepped out of the AC compartment. The sudden rattling was deafening. But then it gradually mellowed with familiarity. This in a way he felt symbolised the life of an Indian labour expat in the Middle East. The initial hardships were mostly never initial – they blend into an inseparable part. They slowly got trained to be unaware of the awareness, or were led to think that was heroic. The heat and fury of the engine coupled with a dutiful obedience of metal laboured the movement of the train. Those in the confinement of the AC, like many families here, were shut out of reality by the closed door and the tinted window

The air in Rakesh's face was strong and refreshing. The lakes and rivers were no longer shining, as sun had gone but the moon hadn't come up. The green and brown of the coconut farms had turned to green and black. In the distance, out of the darkness, he saw a spot of light approaching. It swiftly revealed itself as the flickering illumination of a celebration. He briefly heard a song. It was oppana, popular dance music performed on the eve of a marriage in the Muslim community. Was the girl getting married to a Gulf guy during his short vacation? Had the time pressure forced a quick decision? Had the girl's parents really bother to find out what he did for a living over there? Did they have a clue about his financial situation, or were they carried away by the perfumes and the gifts? Did they know if he was allowed family status at his workplace? Or, like many, did they simply want to latch on to a gulf guy with a ticket called marriage? Rakesh couldn't help thinking of such questions. He knew that only time would answer them. They would find out whether this ticket would grant them entrance to a new world of happiness or whether it would take away the existing ones. Rakesh thought of Devji and James and the thousands they represented. The likes of Kamath were much rarer.

Rakesh whispered into the gush of air, "Love yourself and move on."

* * *

figure and a central minister, found time to go through this and provide me a review

This book would not have reached your hands without the efficient support of Author house publishing company, who I must say did a wonderful job and I am greatly indebted to all the staff particularly Gian Brown my publishing consultant. She made sure that the entire process was not only professional but also enjoyable by her charm.

A note about my parents is purposefully placed last, for foundation is always at the bottom. All the strides I made in this world derived its nourishment from that foundation which was built by two wonderful human beings. My father left me last year, and so this book will have a birth defect, for it shall never be read by him.

encouraging comments and thoughtful suggestions, she was not helping me, instead was contributing to our dream. For an established author, such support and encouragements are probably obvious tags. But to believe and support a first time author like me has to have an unusual ingredient; the same ingredient that made our matrimonial sizzler consistently delightful!

My son Nihal, also known as 'daddy's hero', just turned a teenager this year. He too had his share of contribution, mainly in criticizing the titles, a venture in which he had my daughter very much on his side. Very rarely do they both share a common agenda, this was one. Every title I so thoughtfully came up was instantly made to look silly by their logic. The initial title of "curry leaves", they said would be mistaken as a cookery book; then the "Aroma of sweat", they said would find its way to fitness book shelf. And so it went on, an exercise I thoroughly enjoyed until this 'algebra of hope' was reluctantly approved by the pediatric committee.

I also extend my sincere gratitude to my small circle of friends and colleagues who reviewed the synopsis and some chapters and provided valuable feedback. Among them was one who said "this is all very ordinary and boring stuff". Nothing fuelled my desire to see this in print more than these words. I am indebted to him as well.

I am also very much grateful to the Gwalior rayon's school group, the members of which appreciated some of my write ups that provided the much needed reassuring energy.

I am greatly indebted to Shashi Tharoor, who in spite of his time pressure both as a leading literary

"This is a tale which has been waiting to be told. The story of the Indian diaspora in the Arab world is mostly of misguided aspirations. It's also about determination, sacrifice and achievement.

Ranjit has brought together a cast of convincing characters into amilieu that will be familiar to any expatriate. Amidst the frustration and despair that so often characterize the expatriate's existence, there is also the uplifting story of determination, of fighting for what you believe is right, and of self-belief. And that is what this story too, is all about."

Dr. Venu V.
Joint Secretary, Ministry of Culture,
Government of India

between need and greed. At work, an expat's employer squeezes every bit of his sweat, blurring the line between use and abuse. Indians have been going to the Middle East in search of financial success for the last three or four decades. For many that journey did not find fulfillment. As years are added to their colorless life, regret replaces hope. Against this backdrop, one man struggles to achieve his dreams in 'Algebra of Hope'.

I wanted to write. But the contradictory mixture of intensely wanting to write with the uncertainty of the ability to do so, like a faulty concrete mix failed to harden enough to generate the kind of strength needed. But the passage of time coupled with some imaginative inspiration straightened the curve of hesitancy. However I owe a lot to my friend Bobby who constantly encouraged me. He was my class fellow at the dental school and presently a professor at Kuwait University. In all the regular telephonic conversations we had, there were always shreds of enthusiastic support, which immensely helped me.

There wasn't any one as much as my daughter who was so closely associated with the writing of this book. My handwritten script which often challenged left over noodles in appearance had a very short expiry period. Within that short time Nikitha regularly fed it into the computer with her amazing typing speed. Her role was not confined to typing alone. As a voracious reader with a writing flair, she made a lot of criticisms, some of which were taken on board.

How can I thank someone who over the last twenty years became a part of my existence? My hopes and happiness, pain and disappointments became hers too. When Lekshmi (Leiju) proof read this a few times, with

Author's note

I am a native of the Indian state of Kerala and a Maxillofacial surgeon by profession. I have lived in the Middle East countries, in Saudi Arabia, UAE, Qatar, and Bahrain, for almost twelve years. This has given me ample opportunities to see and feel the pulse of the Indian expat community and that has influenced me to write this book. Though this story is entirely fictitious, it is a deep reflection about Indians in Gulf countries. All the characters and events here are my own creations, though personalities with similar attributes may well be seen all around, which is but only a natural coincidence.

Pleasure cannot exist without pain, and pain has a unique way of enhancing pleasure. But when someone's pleasure has to arise from another's consistent pain, there has to be something fundamentally wrong. This is the norm for hundreds of thousands of expatriate Indians living in the Gulf countries. Their families and societies back home derive financial pleasure from an expat's struggle, the regularity of which blurs the line